"Hello, Angel."

The smooth richness of his voice over the phone caressed her skin like a silk feather. "Tell me, Mr. Black. Do you make it a habit of stealing women's cell phones?"

"Actually, this was my first time." His amusement belied his words.

"I'm not sure if I believe you."

He laughed and its electricity stunned her.

"Why did you take my phone?"

"To see you again, of course."

Angel shook her head. "So how do I go about retrieving my stolen property?"

"I guess we have to meet somewhere, maybe for lunch. Or dinner."

"Or for a cup of coffee?"

"No. You had your chance for that. I want a bigger commitment from you."

Angel laughed and suppressed the butterflies in her stomach. "Wow. Commitment. That's not a word you hear often from a man."

"I'm not your ordinary man."

An instant heat simmered in her feminine core. *This* man was dangerous to her peace of mind as well as her traitorous body . . .

D1559979

ADRIANNE BYRD

If You Dare

HarperTorch
An Imprint of HarperCollins*Publishers*

This is a work of fiction. Names, characters, places, and incidents are products of the author's imagination or are used fictitiously and are not to be construed as real. Any resemblance to actual events, locales, organizations, or persons, living or dead, is entirely coincidental.

HARPERTORCH
An Imprint of HarperCollins*Publishers*
10 East 53rd Street
New York, New York 10022-5299

Copyright © 2004 by Adrianne Byrd
ISBN: 0-06-056537-3

First HarperTorch paperback printing: August 2004

HarperCollins®, HarperTorch™, and ❦™ are trademarks of Harper-Collins Publishers Inc.

Printed in the United States of America

Visit HarperTorch on the World Wide Web at www.harpercollins.com

10 9 8 7 6 5 4 3 2 1

To Shirley Harrison and Bridget Anderson.
You girls are the best.
And to Deirdre Knight.
I knight thee Lady Dragonslayer.

Prologue

Paris

Lieutenant Louis Broche arrived at the Musée d'Orsay angry. First of all, he was supposed to be on vacation. Second, it was three-thirty in the morning.

He was fifty-nine, and with retirement dangling like a carrot above a starved rabbit, his enthusiasm for the job had gone the way of his golden locks, cheery disposition, and lean profile. The job had also cost him his marriage, his children, and even Bowzer—the best damn guard dog in all of France. Truth be told, he missed Bowzer the most.

For the first few years of his career, he was a good cop. Then over time he liked to think he became a smart businessman. Sure, he'd roughed up a few people and maybe even took a few francs to look the other way. None of this made him a bad person—not necessarily.

He emerged from his car while the strobe of police lights pierced his brain like daggers. Before he was able to shut his car door, the young, bright-eyed François Choay scrambled toward him to blurt out the news.

"Le Fantôme struck again."

No further explanation was needed. Louis looked up at the imposing museum with a mixture of dread and anticipation.

"Black," he whispered in the early morning air. From the corner of his eyes, he saw François smile. A wave of caution swept over Broche. "How can you be so sure? It's been over a year since his last job."

François's smile faltered. "We can't be, but it's him. There's enough evidence that points to him anyway."

Louis frowned. "What sort of evidence?"

"The fact that there *isn't* any." The young man's face ballooned into another smile. "Nothing, nada, zip. No forced entry, no hiccup in the alarm system. And we're talking about a top-of-the-line system. Monsieur Guillium, the executive director, is spitting fire as we speak. Can't say that I blame him."

"What was taken?"

"Cézanne."

Louis automatically reached inside the lining

of his trench coat and removed a pack of cigarettes. *Black*. The name echoed hauntingly in his head and exposed old feelings of angst and lost opportunity. His mouth salivated before his thin lips settled around the butt of his cigarette.

It wasn't over. He was going to get another shot. He would do what the Swedes and the Americans had failed to do: capture the world's most ingenious art thief—Damien Black, a.k.a. Le Fantôme.

CHAPTER

1

United States
One year later . . .

All heads turned toward the sleek silver pro-file of a shiny new Lamborghini Murcié-lago as it whipped up to the valet of Lafonte's restaurant.

A couple of teenage boys pushed each other out of the way in their desire to be the one to park the car.

When the driver's door slid upward, a six-foot-four African-American gentleman dressed in black, casual Armani emerged.

"Yo, man. You can get Janet Jackson with that car. For real!" The young boy with the name Todd engraved on a bronze name tag rushed over to him.

The man gently lowered the rim of his dark Oakley shades so his onyx gaze locked on the gushing teenager, and a small smile curled at the side of his mouth. "Be careful with my lady," he said, and then tossed him the keys.

"You can count on me," Todd reassured him.

Turning, the gentleman slid his hands into the pockets of his linen suit and entered through the restaurant's glass doors.

He immediately liked the low lighting and intimate ambience of the place. He caught a dozen covetous gazes from women linked on the arms of impeccably dressed men.

The hostess, a petite ebony beauty, greeted him with a magnanimous smile. "Good evening, thank you for choosing to dine with us at Lafonte's. Do you have a reservation?"

"I'm afraid I don't. I'm here to see Sean Lafonte. He's expecting me."

Still smiling, she reached for the phone on the podium. "May I have your name?"

"Black. Damien Black."

Seconds later, Sean Lafonte straightened his tall frame, showcasing a Valentino white suit as he gestured for his visitor to enter. "Damien Black, it's good to see you again."

"How long has it been—five, six years?"

"Something like that." Damien walked to the desk and accepted the extended hand being offered. "You still look good."

"Such a smooth liar." Sean patted the small

bulge of his belly. "Now you, on the other hand, look as though you were born in a gym."

"You know me. I've always believed in taking care of the mind, body, and spirit."

"Spirit?" Sean laughed and gestured toward the vacant chair across from his desk. "You're an interesting bag of contradictions, my friend. You're the only spiritual thief I know."

Damien curved the corners of his lips, not quite smiling.

"Now, now. I was just teasing you. What's a little humor between friends?"

"Is that what we are—friends?" Damien asked with perhaps more sarcasm than he intended.

Sean's false cheerfulness died with his smile. "Perhaps I overstated myself. Associates, then—does that work for you?"

Damien's smile warmed. "At least it resembles the truth." He glanced at his surroundings. "I see the restaurant business is doing well for you."

"People have to eat."

"True. How many locations now?"

Sean eased back into his chair. "If all goes well, the third Lafonte's will be opening out in Alpharetta."

"I take it this *job* will be financing the restaurant?"

"Not entirely, but something like that. Are you up for it?"

"Depends on how much we're talking about."

"Two fifty."

"Two hundred and fifty thousand dollars? What's this—minimum wage or something?"

Sean laughed and grew serious. "Five hundred."

Damien stood. "It was nice seeing you again. Call me when you want to talk business." He turned and headed toward the door, but didn't get far.

"Wait," Sean said.

Damien faced him again, with his brows arched high over his eyes.

"Throw out a figure."

"I deal in percentages. Fifty-fifty."

Sean shot from his chair. "What? That's outrageous."

"I did a little research, and I know how much the Degas collection will go for on the black market. It's a fair deal."

Damien watched Sean's expression harden. Sean could easily tell him to go to hell, but both knew Damien was the best man for the job.

"I'll have to run some numbers." Sean eased back into his chair. "How can I reach you again?"

"Don't worry." Damien winked and turned back toward the door. "I'll be in touch."

CHAPTER

2

"I thought we were retired," Jerome Mc-Cleary's grainy voice crackled through the cell phone. "Why are we risking everything to work for Sean Lafonte again?"

Damien glided his silver Porsche Boxer S into a city parking lot. "We've worked with him once. He was fair."

"Then consider ourselves lucky. The man has a reputation. Word has it that he runs his business like a true godfather. People have been known to disappear, if you catch my drift. I wouldn't mess with him. Not that I'm punk or anything. Personally, I prefer to work with Marshall. She's reliable."

Damien laughed at his friend's ramblings. "Don't chicken out on me. I need you."

"Yeah, yeah. You still haven't told me why.

We don't need this aggravation. For the past year, I've enjoyed not having to constantly look over my shoulder for the feds."

"Fine. If you want out just say the word."

Silence filled the phone line, and a smile expanded across Damien's lips. "Look, I haven't accepted the job yet. I'm still weighing my options. I know we agreed to retire at thirty-five. But what can I say? I miss the job. I miss the thrill of the chase."

"Hey, I miss certain aspects of the game, too. But remember what your father always said: 'Leave on top.' Pearls of wisdom, I'd say."

Damien sighed. "Consider me warned about Lafonte."

"Just promise me you'll seriously think everything over before you do this."

A silence stretched over the line. "I promise." He ended the call and exited the car.

With one cursory glance at his surroundings, he counted eight patrons, three parking lot attendants, and one mutt marking his territory against an expensive Pirelli tire.

However, Damien focused on the Atlanta High Museum of Art building half a block up the road. As he strode forward, he locked its every detail into his steel-trap memory for future use.

When he entered the white majestic building, he purchased one ticket from the box office, and then blended with the growing crowd.

His gaze drifted over various contemporary paintings without the slightest interest. However, he noticed the positions of the security guards and counted the cameras suspended from the ceiling.

A short blond woman leaned in his direction. "It's breathtaking, isn't it?" she asked.

He shifted his attention to the painting he'd stopped in front of and frowned. "It sure is." Was this what they called art nowadays? The splash of vibrant color and indistinguishable shapes felt like a slap to his intelligence.

"I absolutely adore Clifton Day's work," the young lady continued to praise. "He's so ahead of his time. Are you a fan?" She lifted her sparkling blue eyes up at him.

Damien smiled. "I guess you can say that."

The woman's eyes lit with interest—his cue to move on. "Excuse me, won't you?" He bowed and then walked in the opposite direction before she had a chance to respond.

"Pardon me," he said, approaching the nearest security guard. "Could you direct me to the men's room?"

The attractive older woman smiled before pointing to a side hallway. "Straight down—last door on your left."

"Thank you." He smiled and watched a rush of burgundy stain her mocha complexion.

He turned and followed her directions. As he walked, he counted more cameras—all digitals.

The images, of course, were being recorded elsewhere.

Entering the empty restroom, Damien performed a quick assessment of the ceiling's push-up paneling. There was no sense in risking a quick glance to see if the beams underneath would support his weight. Experience told him they wouldn't.

"This job is definitely going to be a challenge," he whispered under his breath. A slow smile curled his lips. He loved challenges.

He strode back to the main exhibition room with his mind scrolling through the list of men he would need if he accepted this job. Men he trusted with his life. Needless to say, it was a short list.

A thunderclap drew his attention to the tall glass windows. The sky had turned an ominous gray while lightning streaked and blinding sheets of rain pelted the city.

Damien exhaled. It looked as though he would be stuck until the rain let up. He turned his attention to the glass door and caught sight of a figure racing toward it. He pitied anyone caught in such a downpour.

The museum's doors swung open, and the drenched figure rushed inside. The strong wind caught the door and slammed it back on its hinges. When the person jumped at the unexpected sound, her wet hair splayed about her shoulders like a fan.

The sodden flower intrigued Damien.

He guessed her height to be five-foot-six, but he was unable to get an idea of the figure hidden beneath the many folds of black clothing.

"I got it, ma'am," the female security guard said, rushing to close the door.

"Thank you," the wet woman said with dramatic gratitude. She placed a tote bag at her feet and shook the rain from her body onto the mat in front of the door. "That storm came out of nowhere," she complained.

"April showers are no joke in Atlanta." The guard chuckled.

"So I see. I'll be more prepared in the future."

She glanced in Damien's general direction and bewitched him with her chocolate eyes, dimpled cheeks, and full lips.

"Where's the ladies' room?" she asked.

Damien moved from the hall's entrance a fraction before the security guard pointed in its direction and murmured instructions.

"Thank you," the mysterious woman said again, and moved toward the hallway.

Damien averted his gaze, but was well aware of the woman's every move.

Her heels clicked against the stone-tiled floor. Their sound bounced and echoed throughout the otherwise quiet room.

He cut his gaze to view her from the corners of his eyes and met her eyes just as a heel scraped instead of clicked.

A cry of alarm escaped the woman as her arms flailed out and her body pitched backward.

Damien's keen reflexes responded. "I got you," he announced, and caught her well before she hit the floor.

Clutching his arm, she closed her eyes and expelled a sigh of relief. "Oh, thank goodness," she gasped and adjusted her tote bag back on her shoulder.

"Are you all right?" he asked, waiting for her to steady herself. The scent of strawberries clung to her and filled his head.

"Sure, I'm—" She jerked and landed back into his arms.

He laughed and immediately regretted it when embarrassment colored her face. "I'm sorry."

"No need to apologize. I'm the klutz," she said, trying once again to support her own weight. She looked down at her feet. "Damn. I broke my heel."

Damien followed her gaze. She now stood on one high heel and one flat shoe. Again, he laughed.

"I better go and see if I can fix this." She bent down and snatched the broken heel from the floor. "Thanks again. I'm free to break my neck another day."

"That would be a shame."

Another rush of color crept along her cheeks, further amusing him at her uneasiness with flattery. Her smile, sweet and kind, fluttered his heart. "You have a beautiful smile," he added.

Her gaze deserted his. "Thank you."

Though Damien was content to stand there and gaze at her for the rest of the day, she appeared uncomfortable with their silence and extreme closeness.

"I better get going."

"Mind if I asked the name of the lovely woman whose neck I just saved?" He watched a flicker of hesitation cross her features.

Finally a slow smile caressed her lips. "Only after I receive the name of my gallant knight."

"Damien Black," he responded, lifting her hand to his lips and fully enjoying their comic book introduction.

Her brows sprang high above her eyes. "Black," she repeated with amusement highlighting her gaze. "Sounds mysterious."

"Do you like mysteries?"

"Some say a little too much."

"Then you sound like my kind of woman."

Though she laughed at the comment, caution slowly seeped into every inch of her body. "Instinct tells me that wasn't the first time you've used that line."

The rebuttal surprised Damien. Mainly because just moments ago the intriguing beauty possessed a boundless amount of innocence, but now her demeanor hinted at something more.

"It seems you have me at a disadvantage."

"Oh. Where are my manners?" She stretched out her hand. "I'm Angel."

He studied her. "This may sound corny, but your name suits you."

She nodded. "You're right. It does sound corny." Still smiling, she glanced down, and horror filled her features. "I've got to get cleaned up," she said, and then glanced back up at him. "It was nice to meet you."

With a surge of regret and clueless about how to get her to stay, Damien released his grip on her arm. However, his gaze trailed after her.

She was quite a sight—seesawing from one high heel to one low. When she finally disappeared into the restroom, Damien came out of the strange trance he'd fallen into.

He turned from the hall's entryway to see the female security guard smiling at him.

"I know that look," she said, with a wink.

Damien forced a smile.

"She's new here," she went on to add. "Starts next month, I believe. I mean, in case you wanted to know." She winked again. "Yeah, I definitely know that look."

CHAPTER

3

Frustration settled on Sean Lafonte's shoulders as he leaned back in his office chair and listened to an angry Tevin Merrick vent through the telephone. At the first break in the man's ranting, Sean tried to appease the one person he feared. "I don't have the money right now, but I'm working on it."

Sean jerked the phone from his ear to dodge the resulting stream of expletives. This was what he got for having such a weakness for gambling. How wealthy he could've been had he just ignored the call of craps, blackjack, and most importantly, the poker table.

He placed the phone back against his ear. "Give me twenty-four hours and I'll have your money." He listened. "I know I've been late a few times, but don't I always come through?"

The line went dead.

"Damn." Sean slammed the phone down.

He really needed to get out of this crazy cycle. He was a smart, self-made man, the owner of two successful restaurants and a popular night-club in the heart of Buckhead. By all accounts he should be sitting on top of the world. However, with monthly trips to Las Vegas, a man can lose a fortune with one toss of the dice.

The knock at the door rescued him from his thickening cloud of depression. "Come in."

Lea Reynolds, one of his best waitresses and part-time playmate, poked her smiling face through the door. "You're going to kill me."

He lifted an amused brow. "I am?"

She nodded and slid into the office. "Angel called yesterday, and I forgot to tell you."

"Yesterday?"

Lea sucked in her bottom lip while she nod-ded timidly. "She called in the middle of our eight o'clock rush last night. She said she couldn't reach you on your cell."

"What was the message?" He struggled to keep annoyance out of his voice.

"That she'd arrived in town safe and sound."

Sean's hand shot to the phone. "What? She's not supposed to be here until next week." He thumbed through his Rolodex for Angel's new home number and dialed.

"That's all she said." Lea shrugged, settling

her hands against her hips while a soft and inviting smile curved her lips.

Waiting for the call to go through, Sean took in Lea's provocative appearance. He especially liked the way her black lacy bustier accentuated her best assets and how the short skirt paid homage to the runner-ups.

Lea winked. "See anything you like?"

He exhaled and dragged his attention away from the leggy waitress. "She's not there," he said and hung up. "Maybe I should run over."

Lea rolled her eyes and turned back toward the door.

"By the way," he said, stopping her before she reached her destination. "How did things go last night?"

She smiled. "You mean with Mr. Merrick?"

"Yeah." He leaned back and studied her. "Were you nice to him?"

Her long legs erased the distance to his desk. "You know me. I'm *always* nice."

Unable to dispute that fact, Sean laughed. "Any juicy details?"

Leaning back against a corner of the desk, Lea rolled her eyes. "Heavens, no," she said in a disappointing whine. "Sweet guy though."

Sean cocked his head. "He's a ruthless businessman. I should know—he just took a chunk out of my backside."

She tilted toward him, her breasts drawing

his complete attention. "Some say the same about you, and I think you're nothing but a big pussycat."

"Is that right?" His hand snaked out behind her head and jerked her forward.

Their mouths parted beneath a rough kiss while Sean's free hand cruelly pinched a firm breast. His excitement heightened at the sound of her submissive whimper. As he focused on the task at hand, all thoughts of Angel's whereabouts disappeared.

Angel entered the museum's restroom and slumped back against the door. She released the air imprisoned in her lungs and waited a few seconds for the dizziness to lift. "Damien Black." Her lips curled wickedly upward.

Her heartbeat accelerated at the vivid memory. He had to have been made of solid muscle, judging by what she felt during the short entanglement in his arms. His creamy complexion reminded her of the richest milk chocolate, and his eyes were the color of black licorice.

Someone pushed against the door, and Angel propelled forward.

"Oh, I'm sorry."

Angel turned toward the friendly voice. "Don't be. My fault."

The young girl smiled back, entered the restroom, and then disappeared into a stall.

Angel limped over to the long counter of

sinks to clean up. One look at her reflection, and a scream of horror lodged in her throat. This was what she looked like out there?

She touched her hair and fought back a wave of nausea. No wonder there had been amusement in his voice. She looked like a drowned rat.

After digging through her tote bag and purse, she retrieved a brush and performed a small miracle on her hair. Her shoes were another matter. She could walk around the way they were, break the other heel, or go barefoot.

She broke the other heel.

Afterward she grabbed the rest of her things, satisfied that she was ready to rejoin the human race.

While the rain continued, Damien took his time perusing the rest of the museum. However, all thoughts of business disappeared the moment Angel entered the room.

It was a strange reaction, he acknowledged, but his gaze continued to follow her every move.

She was young, he guessed—perhaps twenty-three or twenty-four years old. Since he was cruising past his mid-thirties, she was just below his preferred dating age. Damien frowned at the direction of his thoughts—but damn if he could help it.

She smiled politely to those she passed and gazed with great fascination at the collection of paintings. Was she an artist?

As she moved around the room, he took notice of her awkward stride, and then looked at her shoes. *Interesting solution.*

The rain long forgotten, Damien spent the next hour following the intriguing woman. In that time, he discovered she spoke Spanish like a native, was kind to children, and had a smile that squeezed his heart.

Angel glanced at her watch, and then out the glass windows, relieved there wasn't a dark cloud in sight. In all, she was quite impressed with the museum and couldn't wait until next month when she took over as the new art director.

Heading toward the door, she smiled at the security guard who had helped her earlier. But as soon as she waltzed out of the building, she was jerked back by the strap of her purse caught on the door.

"Whoa," a familiar voice called out from behind her.

Once again her bottom never hit the ground, but half the contents of her bag did.

Angel laughed and regained her footing before she turned toward her rescuer. A sweet ripple of pleasure intoxicated her at seeing Damien again. "I swear I *do* know how to walk." She laughed.

"I'll have to take your word on that," he said, joining in on her laughter. "Otherwise, three near spills in an hour is highly questionable."

"Good point." She knelt and crammed her things back into her tote bag—the first being the pink and white wrapped tampons.

He knelt down and helped her.

"That's okay. I got it," she insisted.

"It's not a problem," he informed her with amusement.

Seconds later, their laughter faded into awkward bursts of short chuckles as they stood and faced each other.

"Well, thanks again," Angel said, deciding it was probably a good idea to stop staring.

"You're welcome."

She smiled and turned away while praying that her weak knees wouldn't cause another tumble.

"Wait."

Angel glanced back at him and pretended that her heart hadn't lodged painfully in her throat.

"Do you like coffee?"

"Love it."

"Then I shouldn't have any trouble talking you into joining me for a cup at the cafe down the street."

She hesitated.

"I promise I'm not an axe murderer," he added with a soft laugh.

"I don't imagine that axe murderers do a whole lot of advertising."

Despite being thrown a curveball, Damien

laughed good-naturedly as he realized his charm wasn't producing its normal magic. As a result his interest heightened at the challenge.

Her full lips parted again and continued to have a strange effect on him.

"Look, I'm sorry, but I'm actually supposed to be meeting with someone." She glanced at her watch either for emphasis or for dramatization. "In fact, I'm late."

He nodded in understanding and made sure that his disappointment didn't surface in his expression. "What a shame."

She looked as if she wanted to say something else, but then changed her mind before turning and walking away without so much as a goodbye.

CHAPTER

4

Damien's thoughts tangled between work and the extraordinary woman he'd met at the museum. It was true he'd always been intrigued by women: their smell, their shapes, and especially how they felt in his arms; there was something uniquely different about this Angel.

Angel.

Hell, she never even offered him a last name. Maybe she was already taken. He frowned. There were no rings on her fingers. Of course, that didn't mean anything.

His eyes lowered to the silver cell phone on his desk in front of him while he contemplated his first move.

"Sir?"

Damien glanced up to the door of his study,

annoyed at how his butler, Nigel, moved about the house with muted footsteps. "Yes, what is it?"

"Mr. McCleary is here to see you," he informed in succinct Queen's English.

"Show him in," Damien instructed, glad for the reprieve from his new obsession.

Seconds later, Nigel escorted Jerome through the heavy oak doors.

"One of these days, I'm going to get you to call me by my first name," Jerome said, with a lingering gaze on the butler.

"Yes, sir. Can I get you anything?"

He shrugged. "The usual."

"One Red Bull coming up," Nigel said sourly before looking toward his employer. "Anything for you, sir?"

"I'll fix myself something later at the bar. Thank you."

Nigel gave the faintest incline of his head, and then disappeared from the study.

Jerome's laughter quickly filled the room. "I just love that guy." He lowered a black leather duffel bag to the floor. "Maybe I should import one from England, too. I feel like I'm missing out in life."

Damien laughed, unable to see his friend import anything other than the stereotypical French maid fantasy to dote on him hand and foot. "Nigel is the best."

"So you keep telling me. Maybe I should borrow him for a weekend."

"One doesn't loan out his butler." Damien shook his head. "That's like a man loaning out his wife. It's personal."

Jerome's eyebrows sprang high into his forehead. "Is there something going on between you two that you want to share with me?"

"No." Damien rolled his eyes as he leaned back against the leather padding of his chair.

"Now, you know you can tell me. We do go way back—"

"Your beer, sir."

Jerome jumped at the unexpected announcement, and then again when he turned to find Nigel within inches of him. "Why do you always do that?"

"Do what, sir?"

Jerome shook his head and snatched his beer bottle from the man's small serving tray. "Never mind. Thank you, good buddy."

Nigel's irritation remained visible for all to see in his brightening color. "If there is nothing else?"

"We're good," Damien said, and watched as Nigel left the study. "I don't know why you insist on getting under his skin."

Jerome took a swig of his beer and lowered himself into the chair opposite Damien's desk. "And I don't see why you don't buy that man some shoes that squeak. His sneaking up on people isn't natural."

"That suggestion just might make the Christmas list this year."

"Good. I'll chip in a couple of bucks."

Damien smiled and stood. "Look, I called you over for a favor."

"No news flash there." He leaned back and took another swig. "What is it this time? I'm sure it's something I'm not going to like."

"But it's nothing you can't handle."

"Oh," Jerome perked up. "You're actually going to stroke my ego. Must be a big favor. What is it?"

"I need for you to get some information on a woman."

Angel waltzed through the door of her empty townhouse with her mind still occupied with the handsome stranger she'd met earlier. Not since her deceased fiancé, Gary, had a man intrigued her in such a way.

Damien was taller than Gary, and his chiseled form reminded her of LL Cool J. Then there were those eyes. Where on earth did that man get such dark, penetrating eyes?

Anyway, she'd handled herself well. Though if she'd stayed in his company much longer, her instincts told her that her very soul was at risk. A sly smile ghosted around her lips. She couldn't imagine too many women resisting Black's charms. In fact, she was willing to bet money on it.

Shedding her coat, she opened the empty

closet door off the foyer and quickly put away her things.

"It's about time you made it home."

Angel jumped at the intrusive voice and then spun around to see Sean leaning against the stair rail. "What are you doing here?"

"Well, for the last hour, I've been waiting for you." A wide grin monopolized his face as he moved toward her.

She closed the closet and then went still when he pressed a kiss against her cheek.

"Don't you ever return messages?" he inquired.

She stepped out of his embrace and then bent down to remove her shoes.

"What happened to those?"

"Long story," she said with a dismissive wave of her hand. "It's just the last time I buy cheap shoes."

"Oh, I see," he said, but his expression said otherwise. "So how come you're not answering your phone?"

"I wasn't home."

"I mean your cell phone. I called you." He followed her as she strode out of the foyer and into the wide empty space of her new living room.

"I must have turned it off at the museum." She stopped and put her hands on her hips. "This is going to be a great room."

"Yeah. Just as soon as you buy furniture."

She turned at his sarcastic tone. "I *have* furniture. It'll be delivered on Monday."

He shrugged. "I'll have to come back and see it then." He flashed her a smile. "Have you eaten dinner yet?"

"An hour ago. I met with Tonya this afternoon."

"Tonya?" He rolled the name through in his mental Rolodex. "She's a cousin, right?"

"That's Tina. I met Tonya when I was in college." She left the room and walked into the kitchen.

Sean followed with a frown. "College? Talk about being vague. Which one?"

"The fourth one. University of Georgia. She was dating one of my professors at the time."

"Oh, the one-semester jaunt."

"Two."

Sean shook his head. "I'll never understand why you went to so many colleges."

She shrugged. "Trying to get away from your prying eyes."

"Ouch."

Angel jerked open the refrigerator. "You want something to drink?"

"What's the strongest thing you have?"

"Orange juice."

He cringed. "Nothing unhealthy?"

"Sorry." She shrugged and removed a bottle of water. "Maybe you should stop drinking."

Rolling his eyes, he crossed his arms and leaned against the breakfast bar. "You've been in Atlanta for one day and you're already conspiring to change me."

Angel groaned. "That would require some serious undertaking, don't you think?" Slowly, she moved toward him with a considering smile. "But since we're going to be living closer together, maybe that's not such a bad idea."

Sean's hands shot up in surrender. "Hey, no woman will *ever* change me."

Her face crunched with amusement. "Throwing out a challenge?"

Sean's laughter echoed throughout the house. "I know better than to throw out a challenge to you." His arms opened, and she slid into his embrace only to lay her head against his shoulder.

"I'll take that as a compliment," she said.

Another wave of laughter rumbled through his chest. "I just bet you will." He brushed a kiss against her forehead. "Can I talk you into coming by Lafonte's tonight? I want to show everyone that I do have something beautiful and pure in my life."

"Beautiful and pure?" She pushed away from him. "You don't think you're kind of raising the bar a bit high?"

"Not at all."

There was no sense in arguing. Sean had made up his mind to view her through rose-colored glasses.

"Maybe some other time. The last thing I feel like doing is parading in front of your friends and coworkers like some prized trophy."

Sean shrugged and moved away from the counter. "Fine. But you'll have to do it sooner or later."

"Then I choose later."

"All right, then I'll call you later to check up on you. Answer your phone, and if you leave the house turn on your cell phone. I'd hate to send some of my boys out to look for you."

"Your boys or your thugs?" she asked, annoyed.

"What difference does it make?"

Angel's spine stiffened. "I hate it when you do that."

Sean cracked a small smile. "Save me the 'I feel like a piece of property' speech. I just want to make sure nothing happens to someone I love. There's no harm in that."

She stared disbelievingly at him.

"Indulge me," he added playfully.

Their gazes warred with each other during the thickening silence before Angel allowed a smile to curl her lips.

"Fine." She removed the silver phone from her hip and held it up. "If I go out, I'll make sure I turn it on." She glanced at the phone and frowned.

"That's all I ask." Sean caught her expression. "What is it?"

Angel erased her confusion and smiled away

his concern. "Oh, nothing. I'm sure I'm not going anywhere tonight."

Sean nodded. "Good. That leaves me with one less thing to worry about." He turned when she linked her arms through his and guided him toward the door. "But I will call you."

"I'll be here." She presented a cheek as he leaned in and kissed her.

When he withdrew, their gazes met again.

"In case I didn't tell you before, I'm really glad you moved back from France," Sean said, with a genuine smile.

"So am I," she said, and meant it.

Sean nodded and walked away.

Angel held on to her smile as she closed the door, but when her gaze lowered to the silver phone in her hand, her confusion returned in full force.

"You stole her cell phone?" Jerome asked incredulously. "You're now reducing yourself to petty thievery?" He eased into a wrought-iron bar chair and waited while Damien selected a bottle of wine.

Damien winked as he opened the Chardonnay. "There is a method to my madness, my friend."

Jerome looked doubtful. "You know, most men ask a woman for her phone number."

"Ah, but I do things differently." Damien poured his drink as his lips held on to his wide smile. "Besides, she was being difficult."

"You mean she wasn't interested."

"Oh, she *was* interested," he stressed to a disbelieving Jerome. "I could tell that much by her eyes, and a woman's eyes never lie."

"You keep telling me that, but I know it's not true, because I have five alimony payments to make every month. Which brings me back to the Lafonte job. Is there any chance I can still talk you out of this?"

Damien eyed his friend. "What has you so nervous? Lafonte was a good customer for us."

Jerome took a long swig of his beer.

"Is there something you're not telling me?" Damien crossed his arms and tried to read his friend. "If you know something, tell me now."

"Word has it that your man has quite a gambling problem."

Unsure where his friend was going with this, Damien remained silent and waited for Jerome to continue.

"So much so, I'm wondering how he's coming up with the cash for a job like this."

"I'm sure he has a buyer."

"Then let's deal with the buyer directly."

Damien laughed. "A little unscrupulous, don't you think?"

"We're thieves."

"Ah." Damien held up his finger. "But we're honest thieves."

"I'm sure that only makes sense in that well-organized brain of yours, because it's not going to make a damn bit of difference to my parole officer."

"You're still on parole?"

"Three months and fourteen days to go—and this job better not screw it up for me."

Another smile broke across Damien's lips. "You should have known better than to beat up on your ex-wife's boyfriend."

"She was still married to me at the time." Jerome slammed his beer down onto the bar's counter. "How could you forget that?"

"Whoa, whoa." Damien held up his hands in mock surrender. "I didn't mean to get you started."

Jerome clamped his mouth shut and huffed out a stream of frustration.

As always, Damien felt sorry for his friend's tattered love life. "You know what your problem is?"

"No, but I'm sure you're about to tell me."

"You never hold anything back. It's always all or nothing with you."

Jerome snorted. "Why would I take advice from a man who's never been in a relationship that lasted more than a weekend?"

"Because I'm a man without five ex-wives and a parole officer."

Jerome rolled his eyes. "I still say you need to experience true love before you can give advice on it."

It could never be said that Damien didn't

know when to stop beating a dead horse. "Then let's toast."

The men raised their drinks.

A bemused smile lingered on Damien's face. "To the day I experience true love."

Jerome tapped his beer bottle against Damien's wineglass. "Now that's the day I'm looking forward to."

CHAPTER
5

While Angel soaked in a tub of strawberry-scented bubbles, she continued to contemplate the mysterious cell phone. The day's events played in her mind in slow motion, and she now recalled the slight brush against her hip during her last fall outside the museum. This was definitely a different approach to getting a woman's phone number.

Her suspicion and curiosity raged a war, and she could feel herself being sucked into Damien's intrigue. "I just bet there's nothing but women's names and numbers in this thing." She lifted the silver cell phone from the ledge of the tub and tried to access the address book, but of course it was locked. She laughed as she eased further into the tub. "Should I or should I not call?" she debated.

The minute she'd asked herself the question a barrage of excuses and reasons told her no—with Sean being first and foremost.

Beneath Sean's tough-man persona, only she knew there beat the kind heart of a vulnerable man. Whenever she thought about the extremes he went to trying to hide his imperfections, she couldn't help but love him all the more. Didn't everyone hide behind masks?

Her gaze fell to the phone again, and she wondered what lay hidden beneath Mr. Black's carefully constructed mask.

"I must be crazy." She laughed and lowered the phone back onto the tub's ledge while she continued to battle temptation. Was she supposed to call him, or was she supposed to wait for his call?

If she had his phone, it stood to reason that he had hers.

She leaned her head back against the tub's inflatable pillow and stared up at the ceiling. "You said you loved mysteries," she whispered.

When the lids of her eyes grew heavy, she was transported back to a pair of strong arms that sent electrical shockwaves through her body. She remembered vividly the intensity of his onyx stare and how incredibly female she felt.

No doubt she wasn't the first woman he'd affected that way.

"Angel," he had said in a voice with an unbelievable combination of power and seduction. No doubt the man was able to sweet-talk his way into many bedrooms—to the point that this was probably a *game* to him.

Her eyes fluttered open, and for the first time she was irritated by Mr. Black's assumptions.

Laughing, Jerome dropped his weight onto Damien's black leather sofa. "Frankly, if I was her, I wouldn't call."

Damien lifted his gaze from the silver phone. "She'll call."

"Nah. You're coming across as too cocky," Jerome said as he nursed his second beer. "What you should have done was slipped her a business card or something."

"A business card?"

"Yeah. That way you still come across as cool but without the psychopath slash criminal aura, you know?"

"*You're* giving me advice?" Damien laughed.

Jerome ignored the sarcasm. "I never had problems meeting women—just meeting the *right* women."

Damien rolled his eyes, purposely choosing not to travel down the same worn road. "Well, there's definitely something different about Angel. I can't put my finger on it—maybe a kindred spirit."

"That's highly unlikely."

Damien flashed him an annoyed glare.

Jerome's hands shot up in surrender. "Just an opinion." He chuckled and lowered his hands. "But you have to admit the probability of you finding a mirror image is low—and a bit scary."

Drawing in a deep breath, Damien realized his friend was right. But Angel's beautiful face seared a place in the forefront of his mind. Maybe he'd only imagined a commonality between them. Now he suspected it was the woman's wholesomeness and innocence that attracted him. Did he long for something he could never recapture?

Jerome studied his friend. "You've got it bad. Maybe I don't have too long to wait for this true love thing to happen."

Damien shook his head. "I'm just intrigued. Just as I have been with countless other women." He had no idea why the lie tumbled easily from his lips, but he was relieved when his friend didn't call him on it.

"So, how long are you staying in town this time?"

"The same as always." He swirled his wineglass and watched absently as the liquid sloshed around. "Until the job is done."

Humor faded from Jerome's stare. "And what are you planning to do about Broche?"

"I'll worry about him if he shows up." At Jerome's silence, Damien sighed. "Don't tell me he's here."

"Fine. I won't tell you." Jerome shook his

head. "But that man has nothing on Captain Ahab." He met Damien's gaze. "He's on you like white on rice. So watch your step."

"I thought he retired."

"Hell, I thought *we* retired."

The beginnings of a migraine pulsed around Damien's temples, which was normal whenever they discussed Broche. "Put a man on him."

Jerome smiled. "Already done."

"Good." Damien stopped playing with his drink and drained the remaining contents in a single gulp. "I want to know where that man is at all times."

"Hey, the way I see it, protecting you means protecting my own butt." He chuckled. "Besides, I fear the day he does catch you. Pretty boys don't do so well in the clink."

Irritation forced a vein to twitch along Damien's temple. "How long will it take for you to get information on Angel?"

"Well, as soon as you supply me with a last name. No time at all."

"I thought you were the magic man. Can't you dig that information up?"

"I could." Jerome nodded. "But that would require more work on my part, and since this is a *favor* and not something I'm getting paid for, I see no reason to tax myself."

"So it's like that now?" Damien's amusement returned. "Our friendship has a price tag on it?"

"Did you forget about the five alimony payments I mentioned earlier?" Jerome stood from the sofa. "Of course I don't want to wear out my welcome, either, so maybe it's time I hit the road."

"Don't let the door hit you on your way out."

Jerome's smile broadened. "I'll make sure I watch out for that." He reached the study's door before he stopped and tossed a curious glance back at Damien. "Are you going to contact Rock while you're in town?"

Damien had expected the question, but he hadn't decided on an answer.

"You two need to talk. We've all gone through too much together to allow petty things to come between us," Jerome said with the same severity as the first time he'd delivered the speech to Black months before.

Meanwhile, Damien had a devil of a time trying to ignore the painful swell in his chest as he thought of his old friend. Somehow the rift between them didn't seem so petty.

"He blames me for his brother's death."

"He's just hurting. Talk to him."

Damien didn't respond.

"I've never seen two people more stubborn in all my life," Jerome said, shaking his head as he jerked open the study's door. "Never in all my life," he mumbled again and disappeared.

Damien lowered his empty wineglass to the bar's countertop while guilt and regret cloaked his shoulders. Then his gaze shifted to the silver cell phone. What was keeping his little Angel from calling?

Angel paced the empty space of her bedroom while her eyes darted excessively to the phone she'd placed in the center of her pallet. "I'm not calling," she vowed as her long strides shortened into angry quick steps. However, the desire to call continued to dog her.

The man's approach was definitely different, however, unorthodox.

Her feelings and thoughts continued to contradict and confuse her, but one fact remained true: She *wanted* to call.

Her house phone rang, and Angel emitted a startled gasp as she jerked toward its shrill sound. Placing a hand over her heart, she laughed at herself, and then went to answer it. "Hello."

"So you're still up." Sean's voice filtered through the line.

Angel exhaled and smiled. "Is this check-in or roll call?"

"There's no crime in checking in on my best girl, is there?"

An instant smile curled her lips whenever he referred to her as his best girl. "One of these days I'm going to fall off your precious pedestal."

He laughed. "I highly doubt that."

She shrugged as her gaze returned to the cell phone. "I hope you're right."

Damien stood staring out at the city skyline through his bedroom's floor-to-ceiling window. In one hand, he carried another glass of his favorite wine, and in the other, he held Angel's cell phone. At this point either one of two things had happened: She hadn't discovered the switch or she'd decided not to call.

Patience is a virtue.

It was one of the many lessons he tried to practice. However, there was something different about tonight. He couldn't explain the anxiety coursing through his veins, and he definitely couldn't explain why he enjoyed the feeling.

"Angel," he whispered as if the simple act would make the phone ring. When it didn't happen, a small laugh escaped him. With his soul as black as his name, surely the powers that be knew better than to send him an angel.

But wouldn't it be nice if they had?

Pacing while wearing only the pants of his black silk pajamas, Damien sipped from his glass and contemplated making the first move. When he couldn't come to a conclusion, he closed his eyes and recalled the bewitching color of her eyes and the captivating curve of her lips.

Damn, he wanted to call.

This suave maneuver of his didn't leave many options for a plan B. Of course, there was the conflict of interest he'd yet to analyze. She was, in fact, employed at the place he might rob. Shouldn't he practice some ethics in his bizarre lifestyle?

He laughed at the thought. "I'm cracking up." Turning from the window, he walked over to the handsome mahogany nightstand and withdrew his tried-and-true black book. It made no sense for him to retire to an empty bed, especially when he had access to the most beautiful women the city had to offer.

When he opened the book, something slipped from the pages and fell to the floor. He bent down, but before he picked it up, he knew what it was. As his hand grasped the old and folded photograph, his body tensed.

He stood, only to sit on the edge of his bed as four smiling faces stared back at him in the picture. Four young boys with their arms draped across one another's shoulders looked, if only for that moment, as though they didn't have a care in the world. A chubby Jerome with thick Coca-Cola bottle glasses thrust a thumbs-up signal to the camera, while a thin and lanky Peter struggled to balance his weight on one good foot as the other wore a dirty, over-autographed cast. The next boy stood a full foot taller and looked a deceiving five years older than the rest. It was no wonder they'd nicknamed him

Rock. He was the biggest boy at the adoption home but possessed the kindest soul.

Finally, Damien's gaze moved to the last boy in the photograph, and he marveled at how different he looked. Being the smallest, Damien remembered vividly how ecstatic he'd felt when he'd been accepted into the small, close-knit group.

With a heavy heart, he refolded the picture and returned it to the safe haven of his address book. Those childhood days felt like another lifetime. And as usual whenever he stumbled across the photograph, he wished that he could go back to those times.

The loud shrill of the cell phone interrupted his stroll down memory lane and even made his heart skip a few beats.

He picked up the phone and read his own phone number on the screen's caller ID. A broad smile spread across his face as he answered the call.

"Hello, Angel."

CHAPTER
6

"Is this Damien Black?" Angel inquired.

"That's correct."

The smooth richness of his voice caressed her skin like a silk feather. "Tell me, Mr. Black. Do you make a habit of stealing women's cell phones?"

"Actually, this was my first time. I hope I didn't come off too cocky." His amusement belied his words.

"I'm not sure if I believe you."

He laughed, and its electricity stunned her.

Angel shook her head. "So how do I go about retrieving my stolen property?"

"I don't know. I guess we have to meet somewhere, maybe for lunch—or dinner."

"Or for a cup of coffee?"

"No. You had your chance for that. I want a bigger commitment from you."

Angel laughed and suppressed the butterflies in her stomach. "Wow. Commitment. That's not a word you hear often from a man."

"I'm not your ordinary man."

An instant heat simmered in her feminine core. *This man* was dangerous to her peace of mind as well as her traitorous body.

"Well, I'm not sure if I can *commit* to more than a cup of coffee," she made herself say.

"Try."

Stumped, Angel's brain scrambled for a response.

"I even know a perfect restaurant out in Buckhead that you might like," he continued. "I've never eaten there, but I stopped by the other day and was quite impressed."

"Please don't tell me it's Lafonte's." She laughed.

"You've been there?"

She nearly choked. "A few times."

"You didn't like it?"

"I wouldn't say that." She rolled her eyes.

"Humph. And here I was trying to make an impression."

"You've already done that," she assured.

"Good or bad?"

"The jury is still out." She smiled during another lapse of silence. "Why did you take my phone?"

"To see you again, of course." Damien listened acutely to the sound of her breathing while he held every confidence that his charm was working its magic.

"I need my phone."

"Then we should meet soon. Say—tomorrow?" It took a moment before he realized he held his breath, and then another one before he questioned just who exactly was falling under whose charm.

"Tomorrow," she finally agreed. "But I'll call you with the time and place."

His brows rose in surprise while silence filled the line.

"Is that a problem?" she asked.

Damien admired the effortless way she'd taken control of the situation. "What time should I expect your call?"

"Let's play it by ear."

His smile broadened. "I think I can manage that."

"Good," she said. "I'll call you tomorrow," she added.

"I'll hold you to that."

"You do that. Good night."

" 'Night."

Angel ended the call and rolled back onto her small makeshift bed with her arms stretched out wide. "What have I done?" Anxiety rushed from her body in a long exhalation. She was even ready to give herself a large pat on the back when Sean resurfaced in her mind.

Her gaze darted to the digital clock lying on

the floor next to her just as it changed to usher in the new day.

She dragged over a nearby pillow and propped it beneath her head. How on earth did she plan on getting away from Sean long enough to have lunch or dinner with Damien—and without Sean sending a group of his thugs to watch over her?

Tossing against her pillows, she found herself once again wondering if she had made the right decision in moving to Atlanta. Only time would tell.

Just as time would tell her if she was making a mistake in seeing Damien Black again.

Broche stared at the sprawling mansion of Damien Black through a pair of old binoculars. As his gaze roamed over the evidence of Black's expensive lifestyle, his hatred of the man increased tenfold. A year into his retirement, and Broche's obsession with Black had deepened. At this point, he could give a damn about justice or doing the right thing. He wanted a piece of the action.

The Musée d'Orsay had posted a twenty-million-dollar reward for the return of the stolen Cézanne, and Broche envisioned his name written on the check. That would be the way to retire—in style.

For more than a decade, Broche hadn't been able to convince many of his colleagues or his superiors of Black's guilt. The robberies never provided enough evidence to support the certainty he felt in his heart.

But it had taken only his first meeting with the cool and aloof businessman to know that he'd found his thief . . .

Stockholm
Ten years ago

Lieutenant Broche had never been on a yacht, before and he doubted that he would ever forget stepping onto the La Femme Noir. The seventy-five-foot beauty was the most magnificent vessel Broche ever had seen. Out of his jurisdiction and following his gut instincts that the sixty-million-dollar heist from Stockholm's National Museum was connected to the rash of robberies in France, Broche convinced the Swedish police to allow him to play tag during their investigation.

The art theft was the biggest in Sweden's history and was quickly gaining international attention. The thieves were said to have escaped by motorboat by the nearby waterway. Forensic experts were studying the museum for clues, and the police were combing the city, but thus far had come up empty.

The visit on Black's yacht was just routine Q&A. The police visited all vessels docked in the surrounding area. However, when the sleek Monsieur Black waltzed out onto the deck, everything changed.

"To what do I owe this lovely visit?" Black inquired, with unsmiling eyes that darted suspiciously to the four policemen aboard his boat.

Within seconds, Broche's gaze took in the man's seemingly fluorescent white suit, and he felt a pang of envy at Black's extraordinary physical presence. He was handsome to a fault, and Broche knew that Black's apparent wealth had nothing to do with his being a favorite with the ladies.

The head of Sweden's police, Sven Lindstrom, stepped forward, flashed his identification, and offered a hand toward Black. "Please forgive us for the intrusion, Mr. Black. But we just need a few minutes of your time."

Black gave the slightest incline of his head in acquiescence. It was then when Broche felt the tiniest prickle to his spine.

"I'm always willing to help the authorities whenever I can."

For the briefest moment, Broche's and Black's eyes clashed, and a world of information was transmitted between the two men.

He did it.

Broche didn't know the hows and the whys, but he knew.

Black smiled. The smug son-of-a bitch smiled.

A loud knock against the car window jolted Broche awake. When he looked up, he cursed his luck at the sight of an Atlanta police officer glaring down at him.

CHAPTER
7

Broche was led through the doors of the Atlanta Police Department with his hands handcuffed behind his back.

"What you get this one for, Stanley?" a passing cop asked Broche's arresting officer.

"Trespassing on private property," Stanley answered and then directed Broche to an iron chair beside a nearby desk.

Broche took in everything with a critical eye. The hustle and bustle of the precinct was reminiscent of the one he'd work out of for forty years. Most of the criminals being led around in handcuffs held the same contempt for the world in their eyes, while the cops looked bored or irritated at having to put up with the same crap day in and day out.

"Officer," Broche began. "I've explained why I was on Monsieur Black's property."

"Right, right. He's some type of international art thief." Stanley rolled his eyes. "You told me during the ride over. Have a seat."

Broche dropped into his chair. "I'm telling you the truth."

"Everyone always does." Stanley took his seat at the desk and immediately started punching keys on the computer. "Name?"

"Lieutenant Louis Jean Broche."

"Spell your last name."

"Look, if you just let me make a phone call I can clear all this up."

"You'll get your phone call."

Broche's anger rose. "I'm telling you that Damien Black is an art thief, known across Europe as Le Fantôme," he nearly shouted.

"What seems to be the problem here?" a voice thundered behind Broche.

He jerked toward an intimidating and intense-looking black police officer. *"Oui. Je falloir parle avec l'capitaine,"* he spat in rapid French.

One bushy brow shot up on the officer's chiseled expression. "What?"

"L'capitaine. I need to speak to the one in charge," he explained with ebbing patience.

"Ah. That would be me. I'm Captain Johnson. Something tells me that you must be Louis Broche." Johnson looked to Stanley. "Uncuff him."

Stanley blinked. "Sir?"

"Uncuff him. Albertson received a call a few minutes ago. Mr. Black changed his mind about pressing charges."

Broche's eyes widened with surprise. A few seconds later, his wrists were freed.

"Why don't you come with me into my office?" Johnson asked and then led the way.

Broche followed, feeling as though he trailed behind Goliath.

Johnson entered his office and waited until Broche followed behind him. "I believe that you're misrepresenting yourself."

"What do you mean?"

He closed the door. "You're not still a part of the police force in old gay Paree, are you?"

"Not exactly." Broche's throat tightened at being caught in his lie so soon.

"Uh-huh." Johnson plopped down behind a paper-cluttered desk and into a squeaky leather chair. "Well, I don't presume to know how things run in France, but here in America, there's a law against impersonating an officer."

Broche met the captain's cool gaze and knew that the man wanted the truth and nothing less—or he could find himself locked up.

"Maybe I should start from the beginning, *d'accord*?"

Again the bushy eyebrow rose high on Johnson's forehead.

"It is true that I am no longer an officer."

Broche straightened his five-foot-ten frame and puffed out his chest with pride. "I have retired after forty years of service."

Unimpressed, Johnson crossed his arms and waited.

"The reason for my visit—"

"To spy on Damien Black." Johnson sighed and shook his head. "I talked with your former captain last week. I believe he's ahead of you. He went to great lengths to explain your obsession with Mr. Black."

"Mr. Black is an international art thief."

"An accusation you haven't been able to prove," Johnson countered with obvious impatience. "And I've personally taken it upon myself to look into Mr. Black's background and found him to be a model citizen and businessman who donates a lot of time and money to his community."

"That's all a front."

"Apparently a very good one."

Broche was intelligent enough to recognize a stalemate when he saw one. "I'm asking for help, but since you're unwilling, I will leave you to your work." He turned toward the door.

"What proof do you have?" Johnson asked.

Broche's hands froze on the doorknob. "Pardon?" He slowly pivoted toward the formidable captain.

"Proof. Get me something to work with and then I'll see what I can do."

"He's too good to leave any real evidence."

Johnson tossed up his hands. "Then I can't help you."

Broche studied his potential ally a moment longer before he asked. "You said that you did some digging into Monsieur Black's background?"

The captain nodded. "Squeaky clean."

"Run across any clues to how he earned his money?"

Johnson shrugged. "He's a businessman."

"Dig deeper." Broche laughed. "His money apparently doesn't have an origin."

Angel had always considered herself a private person and placing her trust in another individual was a rarity. Which was why she treasured her friendship with her older friend Tonya Caine.

She found Tonya to be an inspiring, interesting, self-made woman who made her first million the old-fashioned way. She married it.

Now her friend had made her mark in the world as a successful art dealer with more than a fair share of connections, which had helped land Angel her latest job at the museum.

Over breakfast, Angel relayed the events of the last twenty-four hours. Her friend's expression went from surprise to suspicion.

"You're not seriously considering going out with this guy, are you?" Tonya's green eyes sharpened as they studied Angel. "You *are* considering it."

"I am my own woman." Angel shrugged. "Besides, I have to get my phone back."

Tonya waved a finger at her. "You're playing with fire and you know it. Now that you've moved back to Atlanta, Sean is going to make it his business to know where you are at all times."

"Don't start." Angel lowered her coffee onto the breakfast bar while she mentally kicked herself. Relocating had seemed like such a good idea at the time. "He needs me," she said under her breath.

"Oh, now it's your job to save him?"

"Somebody has to." Angel avoided her friend's gaze, but from the corner of her eyes, she caught Tonya shaking her head.

"You can't save people from themselves. That's a damnable fact."

"I know, I know." Angel's temples hammered away at her skull.

The kitchen grew loud with silence.

As usual, Tonya's tough façade crumbled at witnessing her friend's plight. "Why don't you come back and work for me?" Tonya asked. "I can't tell you how much it breaks my heart to see you settle for a straight nine-to-five."

"We've already been through this."

"The pay is better."

"Yeah, but the hours are lousy."

Tonya shrugged. "Okay, so you don't want to work for me, so why did you call me over here? I take it you need my help?"

Angel hadn't meant to smile, but there was also no sense in lying to a person who knew her so well. "You know the minute I step out of this door, Sean's thugs will follow me all over town. The only reason Sean doesn't know about Damien now is because he didn't know I was in town early."

Tonya shrugged. "Ditch them. You've done it before."

"Yeah, I can get away, but where can we go that I won't bump into Sean's friends or snitches?"

"Ah. I take it that this is where I come in?"

"Well, I need to get another invitation for the Shafrazzi charity ball."

Tonya stopped her coffee cup midway to her lips as her gaze captured Angel's. "You want to take him to the ball?"

"It's a private affair, and I don't have a date. At least the security would stop my guard dogs at the door."

"It's a twenty-five-hundred-dollar-a-plate function."

"Great. We just raised more money for a good cause." Angel reached across the bar and grasped her friend's free hand. "Do this for me."

Tonya's brows stretched high into her forehead while her displeasure remained written clearly in her features. "Well, there are no guarantees, but if you want him there, I'll see what I can do."

"I'm sorry for the short notice."

Tonya choked. "Yeah, yeah, yeah."

"See. This is why you're my best friend."

"I'm your *only* friend." She winked and then grabbed a napkin to dab the corners of her mouth. "You make sure you tell him it's a black-tie event."

"Done."

Tonya stood up from the stool. "I better get going or I'm going to be late. Thanks for breakfast."

Placing her quandary about her own dress in the back of her mind, Angel walked around the breakfast bar and embraced her friend. "At least my move back means we'll get to spend more time together."

"Yea. Thelma and Louise ride again."

"Hey. Don't knock a classic."

Tonya drew her purse strap across her shoulder. "Whatever. I'll see about getting that extra ticket. You just make sure that Sean doesn't catch you."

A smile bloomed across Angel's face as she waved off Tonya's concerns. "I'm never caught."

"Damn it." Sean slammed down the phone and fought the urge to throw it against the wall. He was out another two hundred thousand dollars. His streak of bad luck was still alive and well.

Flopping back against the pillows on his bed, he could feel his control slip another notch as he drowned in a sea of debt. In the past few months, he had mastered the art of robbing Peter to pay Paul. But what do you do when Peter wises up?

A long, slender, white hand slid across his chest just as a golden head of curls lifted from the pillow beside him. "Are you okay, baby?"

Irritated, Sean brushed her arm away and sat up. "What time is your shift supposed to start?" he asked, already knowing the answer. He hated when women overstayed their welcome.

Carrie either ignored or didn't notice his harsh tone as she, too, sat up behind him. "I switched shifts with Lea. I don't have to be at the restaurant until tonight."

The wonderful feel of her soft breasts pressed against his back did manage to improve his mood. "I have things to do today."

"This won't take long." Carrie's tongue flicked the lobe of his ear, and then blazed a trail down the column of his neck.

The woman definitely knew his weak spots.

"Can't we play for just a little while?" she whispered.

She was an enticing kitten if nothing else, and since he badly needed a distraction, Sean turned toward her and sank his hands into the silky strands of her hair.

"You know I like to play rough," he teased.

Carrie smiled as her nails dug into his skin. "So do I."

Angel parked her rented Toyota Camry in front of Sean's loft and made a quick assessment of her appearance in the rearview mirror. With any luck, this would be a quick visit. She applied an impromptu coat of lipstick to her lips and then watched the same blue Buick Regal that had followed her across town glide into a parking spot across the street.

She rolled her eyes. "Where on earth does he find these people?" Grabbing her purse, she jumped out of her car. After two quick raps on the door, Angel tried the doorknob and was surprised to find it unlocked.

"Hello," she called out as she poked her head around the door. When there was no answer, she pushed inside and tried again. "Hello."

She jumped at a loud thump from upstairs, and then immediately became inquisitive. "Sean?"

A door slammed—then another.

Suspicion tickled her brain as she headed toward the stair railing. "Sean?"

Just then, Sean bolted through the bedroom door while still wrestling with the belt of his robe. "Angel," he announced as though she didn't know who she was.

"Sean." She cocked her head as her eyes

darted to the closed door behind him. "Is everything all right?"

A wide smile ballooned across his face. "Never better." He descended the stairs with his arms outstretched. "Especially now that my best girl is here."

While his strong arms engulfed her, Angel's gaze remained focused on the closed door upstairs. "Is there someone else here?"

Sean ignored her question and asked one of his own. "Have you had breakfast yet?"

Angel pulled out of his arms. "It's noon. You invited me over for lunch, remember?"

His forehead wrinkled in confusion. "R-r-right. That's what I meant—lunch. You haven't had lunch yet."

Her gaze flew back to the door upstairs while she crossed her arms. "Who's upstairs?"

Sean's fingers cupped her chin and then directed her attention back to him. "There's nothing upstairs that concerns you."

His tone made it clear to drop the subject, and after a second, she forced a smile. "In that case, where are you taking me for lunch?"

Sean's smile returned. "Only the best restaurant Buckhead has to offer."

"Lafonte's," they said in unison.

"Besides," Sean went on. "It's time you met everyone. I have a new staff since you were here last."

"Everyone?"

He shrugged. "Sure. Why not?"

"Then why don't we start with the two goons you have tailing me?"

Suddenly Sean's broad smile downgraded to a mere smirk. "What goons?"

Angel shook her head. "Give me more credit than that, will you?" She turned and waltzed to the front door's side window and jerked back the velvet curtain. "Blue Buick Regal. I've christened them Mutt and Jeff."

"Close. Martin and James," he said, shrugging. "And I should fire them for not calling and telling me you were coming."

She released the curtain and then crossed her arms. "Since when do I need to be announced?"

"No woman should show up at a man's place unannounced."

"Even his best girl?"

"Especially his best girl." He winked and then headed up the stairs. "Give me a few minutes to get ready, and then we can head out for lunch."

Angel made a face at his retreating back and then sighed with relief when he'd once again disappeared into the bedroom and to whoever was still lying in wait.

Damien did everything he could to take his mind off waiting for Angel's next call, but nothing worked.

From the corner of his desk, Angel's cell

phone rang. After reading the caller ID, he answered. "So have you picked a time and place?"

"Most people answer the phone with 'Hello.'"

"Hello. Have you picked a time and place yet?" He listened as she laughed and found that he loved the sound.

"As a matter of fact, I have. We're going to a charity ball at Château Élan. It's Wednesday night at eight o'clock. Can you come?"

"I think I can make it." Damien sat up in his chair. "Sounds elaborate."

"It is. Black tie, twenty-five hundred dollars a plate. Can you swing it?"

He smiled. "I think I can manage that."

"Good. I'll make sure your invitation will be at the door. Here, take down this address."

Damien jotted down the information and was already feeling a rush of anticipation.

"Oh, before I forget. Some guy named Rock called earlier. He said it was important that you call him, ASAP."

Damien's grip tightened on the phone, but he said nothing.

"Hello?" Angel inquired.

"I'm still here."

"I take it this guy isn't a friend of yours?"

"Actually, he's one of my best friends."

For the first time, an awkward silence hung between them.

"So." Her voice transformed into a husky whisper. "Do we have a date?"

He hesitated, mainly because he wanted to prolong the conversation. "Since I need my phone just as badly as you need yours, I don't see where I have a choice. Do you?"

"Hey, you're the one with the sticky fingers." Her tone dipped even lower.

"Is something wrong? Why are you whispering?"

She paused and then answered in the same tone. "I have to go. My, uhm—well, I'll just see you Wednesday night, okay?"

Intrigued, his mind focused on what she wouldn't say. "Wait."

"Bye."

"But—"

The line went dead.

Damien pulled the phone from his ear and stared at it. "My what?" he wondered. *Husband, boyfriend, lover?* His brain buzzed, trying to fill in the blank until he tossed the offending phone. Finally, his mood swung upward again. "At least I have a date with an Angel."

CHAPTER

8

Sean was at his best whenever he performed for his best girl. Simply being around her always had a way of making him forget his troubles. And boy, did he have troubles.

With great pride, he introduced her to his friends and staff and enjoyed the way she won them over with her easy charm and beautiful smile. The only time he tensed was when Lea stepped up and offered her hand.

"Sean positively worships the ground you walk on," Lea said, pumping Angel's arm. "Now that you're here, I can see why."

Angel blushed. "The feeling is mutual," she said, and then winked over at Sean.

He tried his best to fight off the wave of embarrassment as everyone's gaze swung in his direction. "I told you guys, I've managed to do something right with my life."

"I know I'll never doubt your word again," Gene, one of his bartenders, exclaimed. "She's quite the beauty."

Angel waved them off. "Don't listen to him. He's done a lot of good things." She paused as she thought for a moment. "I can't think of anything right now, but I'm sure there's something."

Everyone laughed.

Then while a few of the other waitresses seized Angel's attention, Lea made her way over to Sean. "She's lovely."

"Yes, she is." He tossed another glance in Angel's direction. "I'm glad she moved back to Atlanta."

Lea nodded. "Merrick is waiting for you in your office."

His gaze sliced toward her. "And you're just now telling me?"

"I thought you knew. He said that he had an appointment."

The circuits in Sean's brain overloaded just as perspiration glistened along his hairline. "How long has he been here?"

Lea shrugged. "About a half an hour."

He closed his eyes and tried to summon courage. Walking over to Angel, he placed a hand beneath her elbow to gain her attention. "I have to attend to something right quick. Go ahead and sit down and order whatever you want. I'll be back as soon as I can," he whispered.

Angel frowned as she assessed his tense features. "What's wrong?"

"Nothing I can't handle." He flashed her a smile, though he was sure he hadn't fooled her with his fake cheerfulness.

"Don't be too long or I'll order everything on the menu."

He nodded and then kissed her dimpled cheek. "I'll hurry back." He turned toward the few staff members who lingered around. "Take care of her." He unbuttoned the top of his shirt and adjusted the collar as he headed toward his office.

He needed an excuse or some kind of stall tactic that would save his life and limbs once he faced Merrick, but he'd only drawn a blank by the time he'd reached the door to his office. *I'll have to wing it.*

"Merrick," he said, breezing into the office. "I'm so sorry to have kept you waiting."

"It seems to be a nasty habit you have lately." Tevin Merrick looked up from behind Sean's desk with irritation settled into the deep grooves of his face. A man in his mid-forties, he would undoubtedly be considered handsome by most standards.

Sean's smile held firm as he closed the door. "I must have forgotten we had a meeting today."

"You're late on your payment," Merrick cut to the chase. "What do you think I should do about that?"

Sean exhaled. "Just a few more days."

It was the wrong answer, judging by the way Merrick's eyes narrowed and how the room's air thinned, but Sean continued.

The only soft features embedded in Merrick's sharp and chiseled face were his eyes. Though oftentimes intense, their unique shade of honey had the power to entrance. This time, however, a sudden smile broke and also softened his features. "I like you, Sean." Merrick said, standing from the desk. He fastened the lone button in the center of his suit before walking toward Sean. "We've done business together for some time now, right?"

Sean nodded, though now suspicious of the man's amicable smile.

Merrick's massive frame reduced the space of the office. "Seeing that we're *friends,* I'm sure that you would have informed me of any lucrative deals you're trying to cut."

Sean stopped breathing. He was sure of it.

Sliding an arm across Sean's shoulders, Merrick continued with his best-buddies routine. "For example, if you were planning a major heist of some kind over at the museum. You would tell me, wouldn't you?"

Sean's brain shut down. *Lea.*

Merrick's rough laugh scraped against Sean's

skin like nails on a chalkboard, and still Sean was unable to think of a good answer.

"Tell you what." Merrick shrugged good-naturedly. "I'm willing to overlook your little memory lapse in exchange for seventy percent of your take."

"Seventy percent?" Sean tried to bolt from his nemesis's strong embrace, but the arm around his shoulders tightened.

"You don't think it's a fair deal?" Merrick asked with feigned astonishment.

Tread carefully. "It's a little steep." Sean's smile wobbled awkwardly on his lips. "I owe you money, but I don't owe you *that* much."

If Merrick was angered by Sean's answer, it didn't show in his stony expression. "But you don't *have* my money."

No. Sean was definitely not breathing. "True." He boldly removed Merrick's heavy arm from around his shoulders and moved to what he felt was a safe distance.

"What's the take?"

None of your business. "I'm not sure yet."

"What if I was to tell you that the interest on your little loan has just gone up a hundred percent a day?"

"What? You can't do that?"

Merrick's gruff laugh returned. "If you want fair, next time visit a credit union."

"All right, all right. How about if I cut you in for, say—twenty-five percent?"

"It's nonnegotiable."

"The guy I've lined up for this job is taking fifty percent off the top."

"Who did you get?"

"That's confidential."

"There's no such thing."

"There is when you hire the best," Sean said, moving over to his desk.

Merrick shook his head. "I want to know who is taking fifty percent of my money."

"Your money?" Offended, Sean stared at him. "This is my job—my idea. All you need to know is that I trust this guy. And I don't say that too often about anyone."

Merrick studied him. "So you've worked with him before?"

"A few times." As their conversation continued, Sean felt comfortable enough to light a cigarette. "He's from the old school. Honor among thieves and such. Actually, I think you'd like him."

"Then you should introduce us."

Why? So you can steal my own guy from underneath me? "I'll let him know that you'd like to meet. How's that?"

Finally, Merrick's smile turned genuine. "Good. And as far as the seventy percent—"

The door bolted open.

Merrick and Sean reached into their jackets for their guns.

"Sean, what is taking you so—" Angel

stopped in her tracks. "Oh, I'm sorry. I didn't know you had a guest."

The men's hands fell away from their weapons.

"Which is why you should have knocked." Sean came around from his desk and approached Angel with fury simmering in his eyes. "Go back to your table, and I'll join you in a few minutes."

Her chin lifted at his curt tone.

"Sean, Sean." Merrick crossed the room to join the glaring couple at the door. "Aren't you going to introduce me to your beautiful friend?"

"Maybe some other time." Sean's displeasure thickened his voice. "Right now, she's leaving."

Before Angel had the chance to respond, Merrick captured her hand and boldly brought it up to his lips. "What's the rush?"

Caught in the crossfire, Angel shifted awkwardly in her heels, contemplating what she should say. Judging by Sean's expression, she'd be wise to remain quiet.

"If you two are finished flirting," Sean cut in, "Merrick, I believe we still have some business to conclude."

Merrick pulled his large frame erect and slowly released her hand with a wink. "Business before pleasure. What a pity."

Angel smiled with the eerie feeling that she was watching a wolf in sheep's clothing.

"I'll join you later." Sean glared.

Biting back her retort, she tossed Sean a sour look before she exited the office just as quickly as she'd entered.

Once the door had closed, Merrick's boisterous laughter filled the room. "You've been holding out on me."

Sean's backbone transformed into solid steel as all traces of fear disappeared. "Angel is off limits."

Merrick's brows seesawed with curiosity. "Seems we've touched on a sensitive subject."

"I mean it. Stay away from her."

Suddenly the humor evaporated from Merrick's expression. "Are you giving me orders, Lafonte?"

Sean's gaze remained leveled on his nemesis. "You can take it however you like, but no one touches Angel. *No one.*"

"Hello. Earth to Damien." Jerome waved a hand in front of his friend, and then dropped into the chair.

Caught daydreaming, Damien slid on an easy smile. "Sorry." He tossed his pen across the blueprints sprawled across his desk.

"Sorry? Have you even heard a word I've said in the last ten minutes?"

His answer was a wider smile.

"Just great." Jerome's irritation crept along his face. "I love wasting my time."

"Calm down. You were telling me something about the small air vents."

"Small? Try tiny—as in impossible to crawl through. The system in this baby is a hacker's wet dream, and it's going to take me a while to work on this one."

"Well, if anyone can figure it out . . ."

"I wish you'd stop blowing smoke up my ass. It makes me nervous."

Damien shrugged and then stood from his chair. "What about my other request?"

"I don't believe this." Jerome rubbed the deep grooves in the center of his forehead. "I'm getting a bad feeling about this."

"You say that about every job."

"Yeah, but it's not a good sign when you're concentrating more on a woman than on what's at stake, and *that* makes me nervous." He shook his head in pathetic misery. "Definitely not a good sign."

"Relax." Damien chuckled. "We're not going to screw up your parole."

Jerome studied him, and then sighed. "I think you should squash this one, D."

Damien's eyes narrowed. "Is there something you're not telling me?"

"I've said it. Walk away. The girl is bad news."

The air between the two friends was suddenly charged with electricity. "Out with it."

Jerome drew in a deep breath and then exhaled with a shrug when there was no delaying the bombshell.

"Discovering the name of the museum's new art director was a cinch, and once I learned the name, I didn't bother digging any further."

"Why?"

"She's a Lafonte, Damien. Angel Lafonte."

CHAPTER
9

Georgia's Alternative Home for Boys had gone through a number of changes since the days of Damien Black. One was that its location had moved from the heart of Atlanta to a sprawling ranch a hundred miles south. While Broche traveled down the home's unpaved dirt road, he held little hope of finding anything that would help him.

He wanted to better understand the man he hunted. What made Black tick? What had led him into a life of crime? He'd read about Damien's stint in the group home, but he hoped a visit would help him better understand what wasn't on paper.

The mile-long driveway with numerous potholes and endless clouds of dust had Broche believing that his small rented Honda lacked shock suspension. After a few minutes, a line of white, box-shaped trailers materialized. He parked next to a line of parked cars and got out. Seeds of doubt flourished with his slow glance around the premises. This couldn't be the right place, he thought.

He entertained the idea of jumping back into his car, but what the hell—he was already there.

With the nicotine in his bloodstream reaching a dangerously low level, Broche retrieved a cigarette from his jacket and proceeded to light up.

"There's no smoking on the property." A gruff voice attacked him from behind.

Broche jumped as though he'd been caught planting a bomb. When he turned around, he was startled to discover that the voice belonged to a short, stout, older woman. "*Je regret, madame.*"

One of her gray brows arched inquisitively before her beady brown eyes performed a slow drag over his attire. "Where you from?" she asked bluntly.

"France," he said, flashing a patient smile. He expected a stream of tobacco to exit the side of her mouth at any moment.

"Is that right?" The second gray brow rose, transforming the woman into a walking, talking comic book strip.

"*Oui, madame.*"

"Well, what business do you have with us?"

Broche took another glance at his surroundings and determined he didn't have much to lose on this longshot. "Actually, I was trying to find out information about a boy who used to live here many years ago—well, not here, but at the original facility in Atlanta."

The woman's brows returned to their normal state, but her eyes held their suspicious glint. "How long ago?"

"Nearly twenty-five years."

She crossed her arms as she emitted a low whistle. "Heck, you're not asking for much, are you?"

He laughed. "I guess I am."

Her thin lips tilted downward as she gave him a careless shrug. "I doubt you're going to find what you're looking for here." She walked past him to head toward the trailer's ramp. "Our records don't go back that far."

Broche followed her. "What about employees? Anyone employed here that long?"

She slowed to a stop and glanced back at him. "Yeah. Me."

Angel drummed her fingers on the tablecloth while she waited for her brother to join her. Something was wrong. She'd never been more certain of anything in her life. But getting her big brother to admit his troubles were somewhere in the realm of impossible.

When she finally saw Sean appear from the back of the restaurant, she released the air trapped in her lungs. Trailing behind Sean was Merrick.

"I hope I didn't keep you waiting too long." Sean forced a smile.

Her attention, however, remained glued to the massive man behind Sean. "Will you be joining us?" she asked.

Merrick smiled. "If only I had the time."

Sean's face darkened, but he said nothing.

Merrick smacked his large hand against her brother's back. "But who knows, maybe next time."

Again, Sean remained mute.

She formed her own tight smile. "Yes, who knows?"

He gave her another appraising look, and then winked. "Until then."

He departed during the table's overwhelming silence, acting as though he didn't notice.

She leaned back in her side of the booth and crossed her arms. "You want to tell me what that was all about?"

"I'd rather not." Sean raised his hand and waved over a waitress.

Angel waited patiently while he ordered his usual martini. When they were finally alone again, she continued her interrogation without missing a beat. "I want to know about Merrick."

"All you need to know is to stay away from him."

"Maybe you should be telling yourself that."

"Trust me, I have."

His drink arrived, and the table fell silent again.

In Angel's head, Tonya's voice reminded her that it wasn't her job to save her brother—especially when he insisted on doing himself in.

"Do you owe him money?"

"Drop it."

"Maybe I can help."

"I mean it, Angel."

She tossed down her salad fork, and its loud banging drew a few curious stares from the surrounding tables. "Will you stop treating me like a child and talk to me?"

Sean's furious gaze challenged their onlookers before it landed on Angel. "The only thing I'm doing is what I've always done, and that's look out for your best interests. Stay away from him."

Never a withering rose, Angel continued. "Since he's so dangerous, why was he in your office?"

"He was there because I didn't listen to my own warning. But my God, you will."

"So you *do* owe him money," she concluded. "How much?"

"Let me worry about that." He lifted his glass and guzzled his drink.

Over the years Angel had seen Sean during the best of times and definitely through some bad ones. There was something different about this. She had a bad feeling about Merrick. Judging from her brother's demeanor and the strange look in his eyes, Angel knew Sean was scared.

"Please allow me to introduce myself," Broche said, and quickly gave the woman his name.

"Marge Westerbrook." She accepted his extended hand and pumped it with remarkable strength. "Why don't you come on in and take a load off while I take care of a few things?" She turned to enter the trailer.

Broche frowned at her back and tried to decipher what she'd said.

"Well, are you coming?" she asked, holding the door open.

"*Oui*." He jumped into action and followed in behind her. Once inside, he was surprised by the large space. Inhabiting three separate corners were three women behind paper-cluttered desks. However, they all looked up with genuine smiles and gave friendly hellos.

"Can I get you something to drink?" Marge asked.

"No, I'm fine."

She shrugged and led Broche around a bend to an enclosed office.

The woman was in desperate need of a good

filing system—and a good cleaning crew.

"Please excuse the mess," she said as if reading his mind, though she failed to offer an excuse such as that the housekeeper was on vacation—or had died. Of which he had no trouble believing the latter.

"So what's the big interest in one of our former children? Is he in some type of trouble?"

Broche pulled his gaze from three moldy Styrofoam cups lined up on the desk to meet her inquisitive stare. "What makes you ask that?"

She shrugged again. "I'm a pessimist by nature, I suppose. Plus, you don't look like you're trying to hand out any awards."

Broche laughed, but then sobered when Marge's expression remained deadpan. "There isn't trouble." *Yet.*

Marge eased into her chair; her hard gaze refused to leave him. "Then why are you here?"

"Just looking for some information."

"For?"

He smiled.

She didn't.

"Uh, actually I'm doing a piece," he said, hit with a sudden inspiration. "This man is a real success story. He's turned into a very prominent businessman."

"Oh?" Her gray brows rose skeptically. "What's his name?"

"Damien Black," he said, and watched carefully for a response. He didn't have to wait long.

A broad smile finally graced the older woman's face, and Broche was surprised by just how much the simple act softened her features. "Ah, Damien. You're here doing an article about Damien?"

"So you know him?"

"Of course I do. We all do." She laughed. "He comes to visit us quite regularly."

"You're kidding."

She laughed at his shock. "Oh, no. Mr. Black has always been there for us, especially over the years when state funding has been reduced to little more than a joke."

"Really?"

She nodded vigorously while her smile grew wider. "We had a bad apple involving one of our counselors, which resulted in some rather embarrassing trials. He was pretty much our knight in shining armor."

Broche's brows furrowed. "Could you be a little more specific?"

Marge exhaled and leaned back in her chair. "The short version: One of our female counselors had a fling with one of the seventeen-year-old boys. The result was a baby."

"Oh, I see."

Marge rolled her eyes. "Well, when the truth came out, everything pretty much hit the fan.

There was an investigation, and come to find out it wasn't the first time our cradle robber had struck. It was a mess."

Broche grew tired of trying to connect the dots. "And how did Black help you with this?"

"The state punished us by pulling its funding. Black became our sole sponsor."

Broche blinked.

"Pretty amazing, isn't it?" she asked, misreading his shock. "He also moved us from a crime-infested area to this beautiful three-hundred-acre ranch."

"That's . . . something." Broche adjusted himself in the chair.

"It was incredible, actually. We had to start all over and win back the trust of the state. We still have residential programs where we accept children from the Department of Family and Children Services, as well as from the Department of Juvenile Justice. Damien came up with the idea of having animal-assisted therapy for those who don't respond in a clinical setting. That's something he knows a lot about firsthand."

The throwaway remark about Black grabbed Broche's full attention. "How so?"

Her face contorted while she mulled over her next words. "Let's just say when Damien first came to the home, he was no angel."

"Really?" *Finally, the good stuff.*

Her laughter returned. "For a short time back then, I thought his name should have been Black Demon."

It was Broche's turn to laugh.

"He absolutely hated authority," Marge went on. "Which resulted in numerous fights with the faculty and children alike. Then he joined a small group of boys and seemed to settle down."

Broche allowed the short story to sink in a bit before another question formed in his mind. "How old was Damien when he came to the home?"

Marge thought about it for a minute before she gave him another shrug. "I don't recall—young."

"What happened to his parents?"

"Mother ran out. Devastated him, really."

"And his father?"

"Federal prison. After he served his time, the state awarded him custody of his son again."

Broche's eyes widened. "You know, doing my research I was never able to pull anything up about his parents."

"Ah, that's probably because Damien shortened his last name some years ago. I believe his last name was actually Blackwell. I guess it was his way of separating himself from his past. Can't say that I blame him."

"What was his father in prison for?"

She looked dubiously at him for a moment, and then shrugged. "Ah, hell. It's all public record. If I remember correctly, I believe he was some type of art thief."

CHAPTER
10

The night of the charity ball, Damien took special care in getting ready for his date. In fact, he was nervous. But after changing into his tux, he rushed to meet his belle of the ball.

Damien loved speed—and there was no substitute for the adrenaline rush he experienced whenever he got a chance to rip around Georgia's interstates. Behind the wheel of his Lamborghini, his problems with the world melted away. It felt good to be in control of something that held so much power. Of course, there were better things he could've invested his money in, but he doubted if they would've been as much fun.

He smiled as he took another turn and then accelerated to over a hundred miles an hour. He was rocketing away from his problems, from the pain of his past, and from the widening emptiness of his existence.

The old photograph from his address book flashed in his mind, and once again he wished he could go back and talk to his younger self. But remembering the kid he'd been, the trip wouldn't have garnered any results. Ten-year-old Damien Black was as hardheaded as they came.

Back then, Damien blamed himself for everything: his mother leaving, the divorce, and his father's incarceration. Counselors, therapists, and teachers always told him that none of it was his fault, but he was convinced that he knew better.

Mothers don't walk out on their children.

Later, when his father returned from prison, he tried to explain that his mother left because she couldn't deal with her husband being a thief. Damien accepted the answer, though it didn't answer why she'd left *him*.

Drawing in a deep breath, he released the past and tried to focus on the problem at hand: Angel Lafonte.

Common sense told him to walk away and cut his losses. But damn if he could respond to reason. If anything, he was more intrigued by the web woven between brother and sister. Why would Sean hire him to steal from the very museum his sister worked in?

One conclusion was that she was involved.

His last image of Angel on the steps of the High Museum surfaced from his memory. Again he was struck by her wholesomeness, her beauty, and he quickly dispelled the notion.

No, he decided. Angel Lafonte was no thief. She was an innocent who had a devious brother.

Within the sweeping panorama of the north Georgia foothills, and a world away from the bustling city's high-rise palaces of concrete and steel, sat Château Élan. For Damien, the landscape was reminiscent of France's countryside and just as breathtaking.

At valet, he entrusted the keys to a barely legal-to-drive teenager and pretended not to hear the revving of his engine as the car sped away. Boys will be boys.

After a few questions to the hotel staff, he learned that the Shafrazzi charity ball was being held in the Da Vinci Room and headed in that direction.

He joined a crowd of people milling outside the Da Vinci Room and saw men lined up to take their invitations. However, he didn't have his.

"You must be Damien Black."

Damien turned toward a melodious feminine voice and was surprised when a familiar face stepped from the crowd. "Have we met before?" he asked, certain that they had.

"I don't think so," she said, studying his face. "I was told that you'd have a check for me?"

"Of course." Damien reached into his jacket while his lips curled. He was sure that he'd met the salon-coiffed blond, but let it go. He handed over a twenty-five-hundred-dollar check, and she in turn gave him an invitation.

She smiled. "Enjoy your evening." Without further ado, she disappeared into the crowd.

"You must forgive Tonya."

Damien turned again, and this time was stunned at the vision before him.

Angel's lips slid wider. "I keep telling her she needs to work on her people skills."

Large, beautiful brown eyes twinkled while a captivating smile clamped onto his heart like a steel vise. "You're beautiful," he said. His gaze swept along her thick, black hair that lay iron-straight against her shoulders.

Angel blushed. "The same could be said for you. You clean up well."

Damien's gaze fell to the red silk strapless dress that hugged her hourglass body like a second layer of skin, and then traveled up to the heart-shaped diamond necklace resting above the valley of her breasts.

"I don't think I'll be able to take my eyes off you all night."

She looped her arm possessively through his as another flush of color crept into her cheeks. "Careful. I might hold you to that."

The heat of her touch didn't go unnoticed by Damien, neither had the heavenly scent of her perfume as it wafted lazily around his head. In that dress, Angel was the definition of a seductress. What he wouldn't give to empty the crowded ballroom and have her all to himself. What fun he could have peeling her out of those clothes.

Just before they reached the Da Vinci Room, their invitations were taken.

Slyly, she leaned forward and whispered, "Stop looking at me like that or I'm never going to get through this evening."

Damien's brows arched with amusement. "Stop looking at you how? Like you're the most beautiful woman in the room?"

"More like I'm not wearing anything at all," she corrected with a subtle laugh.

"A man can dream, can't he?" he asked.

"I can see now you're going to be quite a handful, Mr. Black."

He nodded, and then decided to feel her out a bit. "I'd hoped by now we could be on a first-name basis, Ms. Lafonte."

She blinked as suspicion clouded her eyes and caution stiffened her body. "I see you've been doing some research."

"Just a little something to pass the time." As a waiter walked by, Damien retrieved two flutes of champagne. "I hope you don't mind."

"The champagne or your digging into my private life?"

"The champagne, of course."

Their gazes met, and Damien quickly grew confident that Angel wasn't truly upset. His hunch proved correct when she accepted the offered glass with a grin.

"You have me at a disadvantage," she said.

"How so? You already knew my last name."

"And that's all. There was no invasive research into your background."

"Really?" he asked.

Their gazes locked.

She was the first to look away. "I might have known that you're a successful businessman of some kind."

"Hence, how you knew I could afford a twenty-five-hundred-dollar-a-plate function, I'd imagine."

She laughed. "Something like that."

"You two still huddled in a corner?" Tonya forced her way between them. "Let's not forget the whole purpose of this party." Her eyes landed on Angel.

"I hope to have a good time," Damien said.

Tonya's cool gaze shifted to him, and the room's chill factor dipped ten degrees.

"Mr. Black, the Shafrazzi Gallery appreciates your generous donation to the American Cancer Society. They're always in need of good sponsors. I'm hoping that they can count on you more in the future."

Angel rolled her eyes and laid a hand against

her friend's shoulder. "Ease up on him a little, Tonya. He's not as dangerous as he looks."

Damien couldn't stop the smirk that hugged his lips. "A model citizen, I'd like to think."

Tonya's frostiness didn't let up. "Gee. I didn't know such people went around stealing women's cell phones."

"Okay." Angel squeezed between them. "It's time I split you two up," she said, laughing and pushing Damien away.

"Angel," Tonya warned.

"We'll mingle. We'll mingle," she promised.

"Who is she—your publicist?" Damien asked when Angel maneuvered him to a safe distance.

"Sometimes," Angel joked, and then took a deep gulp of her champagne. "But mostly she's just a good friend who had a lot to do with me getting my current position at the museum. There're a lot of art dealers here tonight, and she wants to make sure people know my face. But I've never really been good at networking."

"She doesn't like me."

"Yeah, well. She's like my brother in that regard. Both are very protective of me."

Damien sipped from his glass while allowing his gaze to caress her face. "Actually, I can see where they're coming from. If you were mine, I'd do my best to protect you, too."

Her brows lifted. "Even if I'm not interested in being protected?"

"Ah, Angel." A man's brash voice destroyed their friendly repartee.

Together, Damien and Angel turned and greeted Albert Jones, a distinguished art dealer from New York. Damien recognized him from various functions, but Mr. Jones had never been one with a good memory and accepted Damien's hand as though for the first time.

"I still think the best way to get a bunch of rich people together is to throw a party," Albert joked good-naturedly.

Despite its being a bad joke, Damien and Angel laughed. Soon Angel introduced him to a Mrs. Barker, and then the nearly deaf, ninety-nine-year-old Ms. Vassar. The evening had now lulled into a slow grind as handshakes and dull conversations took center stage.

"I need to get some air," Angel complained, feeling light-headed.

Damien gently took her by the arm and led her onto the patio.

The moment she drew in a deep breath, she could feel tension leave her body. "Thank you," she whispered as she rubbed the muscles along her neck. "It's a good thing you're here."

His lips twitched into a smile. "The nice thing about being around you is that I get to play hero a lot."

"Or thief," she countered jokingly.

"That, too." He played along.

"Which reminds me." Angel perked up and

opened her small purse. "Don't you think it's time we exchanged phones?"

Damien patted his pants pockets, and then his jacket's breast pockets.

"What is it?" Angel's eyes narrowed suspiciously on him.

"About your cell phone—"

"Yes?"

"Seems I might have left it in my car. I'll have to give it to you when I take you home."

Her stern look was ineffective while amusement twinkled in her eyes. "Who said anything about you taking me home tonight?"

Damien pretended to be confused. "This is a date, isn't it?" He glanced toward the heavens to avoid showing his own amusement. "Now, I know it was a little unconventional for us to meet at the party. It's a small technicality that I'm willing to overlook, but I was definitely under the impression that this was our first date."

"A twenty-five-hundred-dollar date?"

His gaze returned to hers. "It's been worth every penny so far."

She laughed as another flourish of burgundy stained her cheeks. "I see flattery comes naturally to you."

He moved toward her. "I was just being honest."

A few more couples filtered out onto the patio, and Damien and Angel instinctively moved closer to maintain their privacy.

"You strike me as a man who has a trail of broken hearts behind him."

"Funny. I was just thinking the same about you."

She laughed at the absurdity. "Hardly."

"Forgive me if I have my doubts."

In an instant, Angel became serious. "I'm not interested in being just another woman among many."

Damien lifted a hand to caress the side of her face. "Finally something we can agree on."

A million bolts of electricity shot through Angel; she was unequipped to save herself from Damien's charm. "You scare me, Damien," she said.

He leaned forward until he could feel her warm breath against his face. "There's no reason to fear me." He could almost taste her lips, but he denied himself the pleasure.

She stared at his mouth but didn't speak.

His smile heightened a notch before his brows furrowed. "Did we ever solve the matter of me driving you home?"

She stepped back and broke the spell. "That's not possible." The weight of his stare drew her gaze back to him. "It's not what you think."

Damien erased the small distance she'd made. "And what am I thinking?"

His closeness robbed her of breath. "That there's a man in my life."

"And there isn't?"

"No." She blinked and shook her head. "Well, yes."

"Oh?"

She shook her head again. "I mean, not in that sense." At his laughter, she grew more flustered. "Let me start over."

"Please do. I'm a little confused myself."

Angel took a deep breath to steady her nerves when it occurred to her that Damien was enjoying his effect on her. She stiffened her backbone as she met his gaze again. "As I told you earlier, I have a very protective brother."

"Do you live together?"

"Let's just say he makes it his business to know where I am—and who I'm with."

"Sounds like an interesting guy." Damien drained the rest of his champagne. "Should I be worried?"

"Only if you have something to hide."

Damien smiled.

She finished her drink as well and then handed him the empty flute. "Do you mind getting me another?"

"It would be my pleasure." He accepted her glass. "Don't go anywhere."

"I'll be right here."

Turning, Damien maneuvered his way back into the ballroom and found a waiter with fresh drinks when a now familiar voice reached his ears.

"Having a good time?"

He faced Angel's friend Tonya. "As a matter of fact, I am." He beamed at her with a confident smile. "And yourself?"

"I don't come to these things to have a good time." She took one of the flutes of champagne from his hand. "Thank you."

"Then why do you come?"

"A girl has to make a living." She tilted up her glass and in one quick guzzle drained its contents. "That hit the spot."

Damien couldn't make up his mind whether to laugh or run. "How come I get the feeling that you're not really interested in if I'm having a good time?"

She shrugged. "Maybe because you're as smart as you look."

This time he did laugh. "All right, then. What do you want?"

"To warn you."

He covered his surprise with another smile. "Warn me about what?"

"Not what but who."

"The brother?"

Tonya nodded. "She told you about him?"

"Not in so many words, but I think I can handle myself."

"You're not the first man to think he could go up against Sean—and myself."

Damien chuckled, thoroughly enjoying their

conversation. "So you make it a point to warn off all Angel's suitors?"

"Just the dangerous ones."

Their gazes locked.

"I'm many things, Ms. . . . ?"

"Caine."

"Ms. Caine, I'm many things but I'm not dangerous. You have nothing to fear." He nodded. "Enjoy the rest of your evening."

"Angel is like a sister to me," Tonya continued, not ready to be dismissed. "She might play a tough game, but she's fragile."

"I think she's a lot stronger than you and her brother give her credit for."

"She's been hurt before, and it's been a while since I've seen her carry on the way she has tonight."

"I have no intentions of hurting her."

Tonya's lips thinned as her emerald gaze scrutinized every nuance of his features. "But what are your intentions, Mr. Black?"

"Tonight I'm trying to get to know a very beautiful woman. I plan to have her home at a decent hour while dodging her brother's spying eyes. Does all of that meet with your approval?"

She finally smiled. "I'd have to say that it does."

Damien experienced a heady rush of déjà vu. "Where have we met before? I don't normally forget a face."

Her features relaxed again as her laughter took on a lyrical quality. "This is where I say good night, Gracie." She tossed him a wink and once again sauntered off into the crowd.

CHAPTER
11

Hours ago, Broche had lost Damien somewhere along Interstate 85. His rented contraption didn't stand a chance against Black's Italian sports car. Now as he circled back to wait outside the man's home, his thoughts tangled with all he'd learned from the group home. Tomorrow he would have to find a library to see if he could find information on Damien's father.

With his limited resources in Paris, Broche was never able to access much information about Damien. It would have helped if he had a criminal record of some kind. Through a long line of friends and confidants, Broche did learn of a juvenile record, but such things were sealed by the United States legal system.

For the most part, Broche's investigation consisted of small business articles whenever the billionaire purchased new companies or property.

"Billionaire." Broche spat and shook his head. There had to be a way for him to get a piece of the action. It was only fair.

Damien walked onto the patio with two new drinks and was surprised to find no trace of Angel. He made a second lap, carefully weaving between couples, only to have the same result. Surely he hadn't been gone that long.

He made a quick glance at his watch and confirmed that he'd been gone for only a few minutes. When he realized that his anxiousness was turning into a panic, he smiled. *She's really worked a number on me.*

Returning to the ballroom, he spotted a flash of red silk from the corner of his eyes. In the next second he zeroed in on Angel as she conversed with a handsome gentleman. A strange rush of emotion had Damien assessing every detail of the man's appearance.

Angel laughed at something the man said, and Damien propelled forward and quickly erased the distance between them.

"There you are," Damien said, joining the couple and handing Angel her new drink.

When her beautiful eyes shifted to Damien, they immediately salved his jealousy. "Thank you." She smiled and moved closer to him. "I'd like to introduce you to a former coworker of mine, Craig Mitchell. Craig, Damien Black, my date for this evening."

Damien's gaze and interest slid to the grinning gentleman before he offered his hand. "A pleasure to meet you."

"The pleasure is all mine," Mitchell said, with genuine affection. "I'm going to write this day down in the history books. I was beginning to believe Angel was all work and no play." His gaze warmed as it returned to her. "But it would be a shame for such beauty to go to waste."

Damien's arm draped possessively around Angel's waist. "I can assure you that none of her attributes are wasted on me."

The men's gazes clashed while their smiles remained intact.

"Craig is one of Tonya's associates."

"Ms. Caine?" Damien asked.

"That's right," Mitchell confirmed. "I'd actually started the same time Angel and Gary signed on. What was that, four years ago?" He looked at Angel.

"Somewhere around there."

Gary? "Is that right?" Damien said and looked to Angel as well and was puzzled by her loss of color.

Mitchell nodded. "I'm sure this new job at the Atlanta High Museum will work wonders for her. But I already miss her."

"I consider myself a very lucky woman," Angel said with a strained smile.

Damien gave her an affectionate squeeze. "I'm sure you'll do great."

She leaned into him.

"So, what kind of business is Ms. Caine in?"

Craig's gaze swung between the couple before he and Angel answered in unison.

"A little of bit of everything."

Angel and Craig looked at each other and smiled.

Damien frowned.

"Well." Craig cleared his throat. "I hope we'll get the chance to talk again soon. I look forward to us playing catch up." He leaned over and placed a kiss against her cheek. "Call me."

"I will," she promised, easing from Damien's arms to kiss her friend goodbye.

Damien had no choice but to simmer while he watched.

At long last, Angel turned to Damien with wide-eyed astonishment. "What's with the look?"

"What look?"

"That." She smiled. "For a minute there I thought I was going to have to give you guys boxing gloves."

He shrugged. "I can take him."

Laughing, she rested against him. "I would have never thought you had a jealous streak."

"There's a lot you don't know about me," he said. His serious gaze held hers, and the rest of the world melted away.

"Really?" She inched closer. "And what are my chances of getting to know the real Damien Black?"

"I'd say the chances are pretty good." He tilted his head to the side. "Of course, that would require you agreeing to a second date."

She went to pull away, but Damien's arm locked her into place.

"Don't tell me I have to steal something else to coerce a second date." His eyes fell to her diamond necklace. "Maybe something a little more valuable?"

She shook her head as her body quaked with laughter. "You're starting to worry me."

"Say you'll go out with me again."

"Most people wait until the end of their first date before making plans for the second one."

"I told you before I'm not like other people."

"It's starting to sink in."

He loosened his hold around her waist. In a million years he wouldn't be able to explain his actions tonight. "Would you like to dance?" he asked. He needed to do something to defuse the heat boiling between them.

She shied away. "That's not such a good idea."

"Why not?"

Angel lowered her gaze as another blush colored her cheeks. "I can't dance."

Glancing down at her high, cross-strapped red shoes, he mistook her meaning. "Do your feet hurt?"

"No." She laughed. "What I meant was—I don't know how to dance."

Surprise and disbelief coursed through Damien. "Nah."

"Really." She nodded in emphasis. "Two left feet. Trust me."

"Perhaps you just had the wrong teacher." Damien gulped down his champagne, relieved her of her glass, and then set both flutes onto a passing waiter's tray. "Everyone can do a waltz."

Angel's eyes pleaded with him. "Please don't do this."

"I know there's rhythm in that body somewhere." With a confident smile and a firm grip, he escorted her to the dance floor. He almost relented at her terrified expression, but instead he pulled her body up against his and whispered, "Trust me."

She exhaled, and Damien felt her body relax.

"Look at me," he further instructed.

Angel lifted her gaze while a slow smile fluttered at her lips. "I'm going to make a fool of myself."

Damien chuckled. "I would never let that happen." He lifted her arms and stepped back into position. "Now follow my lead."

"I'll try." She drew in a deep, steady breath and watched as Damien nodded and counted softly in three-quarter time. And just as she feared, she stepped first and inadvertently crushed his foot with her sharp heel.

Damien jerked in surprise, but quickly recovered with a laugh.

"Oh, I'm so sorry." She pulled back her arms and balled her hands at her sides. "I'm awful at this."

"It's okay. It's okay." He reassured her and pulled her back into his arms.

Again, she tried to pull back. "Hey, if you stop now, you can save yourself." She glanced around to see how many people were looking at them.

"You can do this," he said, repositioning their stance.

"But—"

Damien kissed her.

It was likely the first time that heaven had touched the earth. And its effect on Angel was a glorious rapture that harmonized in perfect tune with her soul. The taste of him was more potent than any alcohol and more addictive than any Godiva chocolate.

As his lips withdrew, the slow dawning that their bodies were gliding effortlessly in time with the music sank into her consciousness.

"We're dancing."

"Of course we are." He leaned over and claimed another kiss.

This one seemed sweeter than the last and

just as intoxicating. Holding on to any stream of thought was impossible, and Angel found herself willing to float in an abyss of wonderment.

"You're a man full of surprises," she whispered, coming up for breath. "I'm definitely going to have to watch myself around you."

Damien laughed. "It's good to know I wasn't the only one affected."

She pulled back and stared up at him. "Do we know what we're doing?"

"I don't have a clue."

"That's good to know. I'd hate to think you're following some jaded routine."

"Put your mind at ease. I'm just trying to rack up enough points for that second date. You know—the one you haven't agreed to yet."

Angel sighed. "You have no idea how much work is involved in keeping my brother out of my business."

"Maybe I can help. I've been known to be very resourceful when it comes to things of this nature."

Her brows arched delicately. "Is that right?"

He nodded. "I want to see you again."

Heady from the power he'd just handed her, she wasn't ready to agree to another date. She would, of course, but not just yet. "Let's see how the rest of the night goes. I want to know whether you're a man of your word and will actually return my phone."

"In that case," he chuckled, "I'm just going to

consider it a done deal. Next time I get to plan the evening."

She laughed and caught a glimpse of their reflection as they floated past a mirror. They made a striking couple, she thought with a smile.

After another twirl around the floor, Angel caught sight of Tonya.

A series of bells chimed overhead and slowly the orchestra's music died away.

"Can I please have everyone's attention?"

With one arm draped around Angel's waist, Damien turned toward the stage, where a sophisticated Asian woman stepped in front of a microphone.

"I trust everyone is having a good time," she said to the crowd. "My name is Anna Laing and I'm with Shafrazzi's Art Gallery."

A small cluster of men walked onto the stage and began setting up a canvas of some kind. Another army of security men with stern faces, black tuxes, and wire draped around their ears took their positions around the stage.

"We at Shafrazzi's have some great news we want to share. As many of you know, we're excited about the new paintings we'll have on exhibit this spring." She clasped her hands while excitement glowed in her face. "However, there is one painting that we are particularly proud to have acquired. It's one of Peter Paul Rubens's greatest masterpieces," she boasted, and then turned to signal her assistants.

The men unveiled the painting.

Anna proudly announced, "*The Massacre of the Innocents*."

Shock rocketed through Damien and rooted him in place. "I'll be damned."

CHAPTER
12

"Are you all right?"

Damien forced his gaze from the painting when Angel's concern penetrated his shock and the surrounding applause. "I'm fine," he said, smiling.

Her brows gathered. "Are you sure? You look as though you've seen a ghost."

He laughed and tightened his hold around her waist. "I'm positive." He tossed another glance at the Rubens.

"I forgot you were into art," she said, leaning into him. "Are you a Rubens fan?"

"Something like that," he said, still unable to believe his luck.

"It's beautiful," she said.

Damien nodded.

"And expensive. You wouldn't believe how much the owner paid to obtain it."

"Seventy-five million," he answered absently.

She glanced up at him. "How did you know that?"

He blinked and shifted his attention back to her. "I must have read it somewhere."

Their gazes locked.

Another round of applause surrounded them, and Damien realized that they'd missed the rest of the speech.

"Will you excuse me? I need to make a call."

She stepped back. "A call? Are you sure nothing is wrong?"

He resisted the urge to kiss her. "I assure you nothing is wrong. I just remembered something I need to take care of. It shouldn't take but a moment." He grew uncomfortable beneath the weight and intensity of her stare.

"Okay." She smiled, but it failed to reflect in her eyes. "Lord knows if I don't do some more networking, Tonya's going to kill me."

"Five minutes," he said, wanting to convince her that everything was all right.

"I'll be here," she promised.

The music struck up again, and Damien reluctantly turned and left his dance partner on the floor.

He made a beeline out of the Da Vinci Room and into the lobby. But when he reached into his jacket, he remembered he didn't have a cell phone. "Damn."

After a quick search, he found a row of pay phones and called his best friend.

"You've got to be kidding me," Jerome's groggy voice filled the line after he heard Damien's story.

"Can you believe it? The very painting my father went to jail for stealing is right here in this very building."

"Forget the painting. I can't believe you still went out with that Lafonte chick. Do you have a death wish or something?"

Damien frowned into the phone. "What does that have to do with anything? We're talking about destiny. We have to do this one."

Jerome expelled a long sigh. "You want to steal the one painting that landed your dad in jail? Are you crazy? Haven't you ever heard of history repeating itself?"

Damien ignored the question. "Do you know what your problem is?"

"I'm sure you're going to tell me."

"You won't admit that you miss this job as much as I do." At Jerome's laugh, Damien pictured his friend shaking his head in denial.

"Is that what all these jobs are about—to see whether we have what it takes to stay in the game?"

Damien smiled.

"Uh-huh. You know what?" Jerome asked. "I think we need to call everything off and you need to seek a therapist."

Damien waited a moment before asking, "Are you finished?"

"This is the part where you blow me off again, isn't it?"

"I'm not twisting your arm."

Jerome sighed.

Damien laughed. "We can do this job. Trust me."

"So how's your date going?"

"Good night, Jerome."

"Fine. Don't tell me. I'll see you at your place tomorrow."

"Deal." Damien ended the call with a confident smirk. He turned but abruptly stopped in his tracks at the sight of Angel standing three feet from him.

She held up his cell phone. "I figured you might need this."

Suspicion narrowed Damien's gaze. How long had she been standing there? "Thanks, but I just called the old-fashioned way."

Her lips twitched upward as the sparkle returned to her eyes. "Serves you right."

Damien forced himself to relax before he approached her and reached for his phone.

Angel snatched it back. "I was just going to loan it to you." She opened her purse and slipped it back inside. "But since you don't need it anymore, I'll just hold on to it until the end of the night."

"Fair enough." He chuckled and slid his arm back around her waist. "Should we rejoin the party?"

"Sure. They're getting ready to move everyone to the other room for dinner."

If Angel was uncomfortable with the familiar and intimate way he held her, it didn't show. In fact, if Damien wasn't mistaken, she leaned into him.

Together they returned to the party arm-in-arm.

Damien, lost in the scent and feel that was undeniably Angel, had a hard time controlling flashes of sexual images that cropped up in his mind. Maybe it was her delicate appearance that made him want to muss her a bit.

"You know, you have a wonderful knack for avoiding talking about yourself."

"Do I?" he asked, trying to hide his amusement. "Maybe I'm trying to keep that mysterious thing working for me."

"You're doing a good job."

Any chance of intimacy was dashed when Damien and Angel were led to their dinner table with four other couples.

Almost immediately Angel tensed, and Damien saw firsthand how difficult networking was for her. Taking it upon himself to ride to the rescue, Damien blended into the conversations with offhand witticisms and won the crowd over. After a while, Angel visibly relaxed.

"You two make such a lovely couple," was the most frequent compliment. It was also one Damien agreed with.

As the night wore on, Damien was more than ready to leave and spend some one-on-one time with his date.

Angel leaned toward him. "What do you say we blow this taco stand?"

He winked. "I'd say you got a deal."

"Great. Let me just tell Tonya."

As they stood from the table, Damien struggled to hang on to his smile. Given the frosty attitude he'd received from her mysterious and evasive friend, he wasn't sure how he felt about Tonya Caine.

She laughed. "It'll just take a moment. She was, after all, my ride here."

"No problem," he said.

"She's really a wonderful person," she stressed. "I'm sure once you get to know her, you'd love her."

I doubt that. "I'm sure you're right." Wanting to erase her concern, he gave in to the gravitational force pulling him forward and kissed her.

His body reacted as though it recognized the missing half of itself—a part he didn't want to let go. However, reason seeped into his consciousness and warned him if he continued to kiss her this way, he was going to embarrass them both.

Angel savored the aftertaste of his lips while her eyes remained closed for a fraction longer than their kiss. When she finally opened them to stare into his onyx gaze, she could feel her soul being pulled forward. "You're a great kisser," she whispered.

He gently caressed her cheek. "I think I've met my match."

Desire swept through her with an intensity that scared her. "I'll be right back."

Damien nodded. "I'll be right here." He winked.

She turned and prayed that her knees and feet still worked. Locating Tonya was easy. Surviving her friend's glare of warning was another matter.

"What do you know about this guy?" Tonya asked, pulling her to the side.

"Don't start. Be happy for me. I'm having a good time."

"What about your brother's thugs?"

"I told you. Sean called them off."

"What if he didn't? The minute you walk out of here on Black's arm, Sean will have his name, rank, and serial number," she hissed.

Frustration soured Angel's mood. "No one followed us out here. I checked." She forced a smile. "Lighten up. It's just a date."

Tonya sighed. "I'm just as bad as your brother, aren't I?"

"Not quite, but you're getting there."

"Sorry." Tonya shook her head. "But after what happened to Gary—"

"I understand." Angel's lips tightened. "I'll call you tomorrow."

Tonya nodded and squeezed her friend's hand. "Have a good time."

Angel walked away with an image of Gary floating through her mind. What if Sean hadn't called off his watchdogs? How would he react now if he discovered she was interested in someone?

"Angel?"

She turned toward the tap on her shoulder. "Yes?"

"Are you okay?" Damien asked. "You just walked right past me."

"Oh, I'm sorry." She shook her head and cleared her troubled thoughts. "Are you ready to go?"

"Whenever you are." He slid his arm around her.

She loved it when he did that. The simple act offered her a level of security that was foreign to her. She also loved the light musk of his cologne. It was undoubtedly a scent that would follow her into her dreams.

They strolled from the party, stopping occasionally to say their goodbyes to people they'd met.

"I think you're getting better at this," Damien said, once they'd cleared the doorway.

"I'm just following your lead," she admitted. "You're a natural with people."

"I'll take that as a compliment."

"As you should."

They moved from the lobby and stepped out into the cool night air. Out of habit, Angel glanced around, expecting Mutt and Jeff to still be huddled somewhere with a live-feed video camera. When she didn't see them, she sighed and tried to relax.

"Good evening, sir," the young valet said to Damien as he handed over a ticket.

"Are you cold?" Damien asked, already removing his jacket.

She hadn't realized she was shivering and nodded to accept the jacket he quickly draped around her shoulders.

"Thank you," she said. However, the instant heat rushing through her body was generated from the intensity of his warm gaze and the soft brush of his hand rather than the jacket.

"Actually," he said, smiling down at her, "I kind of like the way it looks on you."

Angel smiled, but failed to respond when a silver Lamborghini pulled up. At first sight of Damien's car, Angel's breath caught in her throat. She'd never thought of a car as being sexy, but that was the single word that had jumped into her head.

One of the valet drivers stepped out of the car wearing a broad grin. "She was definitely the highlight of my night," he said, handing Damien the keys and receiving his tip.

Damien chuckled and placed a hand against the small of her back. "Are you ready?"

"Sure," she said, before she looked sheepishly over at her date. "May I drive?"

Amusement sparkled in Damien's eyes as he plopped the keys into her open palm. "Be my guest."

A giddy excitement rushed through her as she stretched up onto her toes and kissed his cheek. In the next second she rushed around to the driver's side in a near sprint.

The moment she slid into the leather interior, she was seduced. "I'm in love."

"With me or the car?" Damien asked as he climbed into the passenger seat, but he stopped her before she could respond. "Don't answer that. I don't think my heart can take the crushing news."

She laughed as she adjusted the seat and mirrors, then placed the key in the ignition. The car came to life with one flick of her wrist, and the power it exuded possessed her.

Damien buckled up. "Do you know how to drive a stick shift?"

With a wink, she buckled up and shifted into first gear and sped away from the hotel. Cruising down the long, dark, winding road, Angel let the window down and enjoyed the feel of the wind blowing her hair. "This is amazing," she said, smiling over at him. "I could drive for hours behind this wheel."

Damien adjusted himself in his seat so he could watch her. "Are you a car aficionado?"

Her gaze returned to the road. "The only thing I know about cars is that you need to change the oil every three thousand miles." She laughed. "But this is more than just a car. This is . . . freedom."

"Freedom," he repeated with a raised brow.

She nodded and then glanced at him again. "Don't tell me that you've never felt it." Her hands adjusted on the steering wheel as though she wanted to feel every inch of it.

"Oh, I definitely know what you're talking about. I have the speeding tickets to prove it."

"I believe it," she said, laughing. When she approached the turn for the interstate, she opted to stay on the back roads of the sprawling countryside. "Let's just drive for a while," she said, meeting his questioning gaze.

"Whatever you like."

"Now that's what a girl likes to hear."

He laughed and shifted his chair for more legroom. "This is the first time I've ever sat on this side. Maybe I can get used to being chauffeured around by a beautiful woman."

"How well do you tip?"

"I guess that all depends on what's included in the service."

Her eyes widened. "Was that a sexual innuendo, Mr. Black?"

He chuckled. "That depends."

"On what?"

"On whether you're offended."

She pretended to be angry but she couldn't quite manage to stop her lips from turning upward. "I've got to watch you, don't I?"

"I plead the Fifth." He glanced around and grew concerned about their isolated area. "Do you have any idea of where you're going?"

"Not a clue."

He swiveled to face her. "How many roads did you turn down on?"

She shrugged. "You've got me."

The headlights grazed the tail of a deer completing its trek across the road.

Incredulous, he stared at her for a few seconds. "Aren't you afraid of getting lost out here?"

"Not at all."

The road suddenly turned into a steep incline, and Angel hugged the curves with the smooth grace of a professional driver.

"Okay." Damien relaxed again. "If you're not worried, then neither am I."

She laughed. "You look worried."

"More like concerned."

"Same difference." She slowed down and turned onto a small shoulder and parked. "Now isn't this beautiful?"

Before them, a full moon appeared to be within reaching distance, while below, a large lake that resembled a black mirror sat surrounded by a gorgeous canvas of various shaped trees.

"It's breathtaking." He unbuckled his seat belt and stepped out of the car.

She turned off the car and stepped out, too.

"I take it you've been out here before?" Damien asked as he moved to the front of the car and sat on the hood.

Angel slid her hands into the pockets of his jacket as she drew in a deep breath. "A few times." She settled in a spot next to him. "An old friend of mine used to own some land a few miles from here. Once I came out for a visit and got lost, but I discovered this magnificent view." She glanced out over the landscape. "It's a great place to come and think."

"What did you come out here to think about?" he asked softly.

Shocked by the sudden threat of tears, Angel took a moment to compose herself. "Nothing and everything, I suppose." She hoped he hadn't heard the quiver in her voice.

He didn't respond, but she felt his stare.

A gust of wind whipped around them and quickly reminded her of just how little she had on. She huddled deeper into his jacket just as he draped his arms around her.

"Thank you for bringing me out here," he whispered.

Their eyes locked and completed the magic swirling around them.

The long-forgotten swarm of butterflies returned to her stomach, and she had to remind herself how to breathe.

"Why do I feel as though our paths were meant to cross?" he asked, leaning into her.

She didn't trust herself to answer while she watched the slow descent of his head. At the soft touch of his lips and then the gentle invasion of his tongue, Angel was transported to another time and place—where there were no worries or cares of this world.

He pressed her back so her entire body lay across the warm hood of the car before he peeled open the jacket.

As his lips deserted hers to burn a trail down the column of her neck, she opened her eyes to a canopy of stars. Rapture gripped her, and she didn't want it to let go.

His hands slowly inched up from her waist.

She moaned, while her pulse hammered everywhere at once. But she didn't protest—she couldn't . . . she wouldn't.

Encouraged, Damien's mouth and hands

grew bolder. He wanted all of her. He needed all of her. His mouth returned to her soft lips and he was lost.

The kiss became desperate, ravenous, tongues tangling, teeth nipping.

Angel turned away from his lips to draw in some much-needed air.

Their gazes locked in one long, intense, and measuring stare before she whispered, "We have to stop."

Her words were like a splash of cold water, and he groaned with regret as he pulled himself away. "You're right. I'm sorry."

Angel sat up and quickly smoothed out her rumpled dress. "There's no need for you to be sorry. I enjoyed it."

He smiled awkwardly. "That's good to know."

Angel sucked in a deep and unsteady breath. She couldn't believe how easily she'd pushed Gary to the back of her mind, nor could she believe how close she was to asking a man she hardly knew to make love to her.

She shivered when a cool breeze whipped around her body, but then smiled when he slid his jacket back around her shoulders.

"Thank you."

"You're more than welcome."

She dropped her gaze when his eyes intensified in their scrutiny.

"May I ask you a question?" he asked, folding his arms.

"Sure," she said, bracing herself for anything, but found that she was still unprepared when his question hit her.

"Who's Gary?"

CHAPTER

13

Angel's eyes stung as her heart muscles constricted painfully in her chest. She'd done it again. She'd somehow pushed the man she'd sworn to never forget to the back of her mind. Why was it so easy to do around Damien? "Gary was my fiancé," she finally answered, pulling away.

Her answer was met with a grave silence, and when she looked up at Damien, she found it difficult to gauge his reaction.

"What happened?"

The tenderness in his tone threatened to destroy the dam holding back her tears. "He was killed in a car accident."

His hand slid over to hers. "I'm sorry."

She smiled awkwardly and removed her hand as Gary's cocky grin floated to the forefront of her mind. "We met at the American University in Paris. We were both art majors. He loved the Renaissance period while I was crazy about French Impressionists." She laughed.

"Édouard Manet, Claude Monet . . . Edgar Degas?"

She brightened. "I keep forgetting that you're an art fan. Where did you study?"

Damien's laughter rang deep and loud. "I guess you can say I acquired my B.A. in art history at the local library."

Angel's brows heightened with new curiosity. "You're not a college graduate?"

"No. My father told me at a young age that there was no point in paying a large university just to make me pick up a book."

"That's an interesting way of looking at it."

"It was his way to get me to think outside of the box."

She drew his jacket close around her body. "He sounds like quite a character."

He shrugged as he thought about it. "He was. He wanted nothing to do with conventional thinking. Never saw any fun in it, I suppose."

She turned curious eyes toward him. "Are you like your father?"

Damien glowed. "More than I care to admit."

"And your mother?"

Though his smile remained in place, its radiance diminished instantly. "I don't know. I don't remember much about her."

Angel's keen senses realized she'd struck a nerve, and she quickly decided to drop the subject, but he surprised her by continuing.

"My mother left my father and I when I was nine." Damien's gaze traveled up toward the stars. "She never called, wrote, or anything. It was just one big magic act. Now you see her, now you don't."

Pain hollowed out his voice and even caused a tightening in Angel's vocal cords. "I'm sorry to hear that. It must have been hard for you."

He shrugged but kept his eyes glued to the heavens.

A list of questions strolled through Angel's mind but she was unsure if she should voice them. Instead she decided to share more of her own heartache. "When I was eleven, I lost *both* of my parents. Believe it or not, to another car accident. It's a recurring theme in my tragic Shakespearean life."

"How awful for you." Damien centered his attention back on her. The fine sheen around his onyx gaze tugged her heartstrings.

It was her turn to shrug and pretend that the past didn't bother her. "It's okay. I fared pretty good—considering." Her thoughts turned to Sean. "I know I don't give my brother enough credit, but given the circumstances, he did a good job."

"What's the age difference between you two?"

"Seven years." Angel smiled at his frown. "Or was that your sly way of asking how old I am?"

"Saw through that, did you?"

His lips turned up again, and to Angel it felt like sunshine after a storm. "It was pretty thin," she agreed, grinning. "But if you must know, I'm twenty-six."

"Twenty-six." He nodded. "I think I can work with that."

Amusement twinkled in her eyes. "Is that right? Well, what about you?"

"I'm . . . older." He chuckled.

"Older?" She crossed her hands over her chest. "Care to be a little more precise?"

"Thirty-six."

Angel's hands fluttered to her heart in exaggerated shock. "Oh, my. That old?"

Damien's smile disappeared as he straightened up. "I'm not *that* old. I'm sure I can still learn a few tricks in order to keep up with you."

"I highly doubt that," she boasted, laughing. At his responsive frown she leaned into him for a reassuring hug, but quickly found herself entrapped by the man's powerful dark gaze.

There had to be something wrong with the cool night air. What else could explain her sudden light-headedness or the strange stirring of her blood? While she stared at Damien, she couldn't help but feel as if she were looking at a missing part of herself. That didn't make any sense . . . did it?

"Would you mind if I kissed you again?" he asked.

The question caused an instant hunger pang in the pit of her stomach. Angel didn't trust herself to speak and instead shook her head.

Another smile fluttered across his full lips as his head descended. His warm breath brushed against her cheek, and a bolt of electricity charged through her when his soft lips landed on hers. Her body melted beneath its power.

Damien prided himself on being a man of great patience and restraint, but all of that went out the window whenever he touched this amazing woman. He couldn't get over how good she tasted or how wonderful she felt in his arms. The very thought of what it would be like to make love to her elicited a low groan of longing within him.

Her hand glided along his chest and his breath thinned in anticipation of her next move. The first and then second button of his shirt slid undone. Her soft, slender fingers slid against his bare chest and left a trail of fire in their wake.

Milk chocolate skin, soft and firm, smooth and fragrant. If he wasn't careful, he could lose himself in this woman. Problem was, he had no idea how to go about being careful—not when everything about her felt this good.

Angel marveled at how he was able to make her body come alive. *More* echoed through her head like a religious mantra. He could make her body feel *more*. She just knew it.

The idea of begging him to stop this slow torment crested her thoughts just as his free hand glided past her waist and around the sensitive curve of her hip.

Surprised by her wanton behavior, Angel realized she was just seconds away from offering herself to Damien right there on the hood of his car. However, it was he who broke their kiss.

"I better get you home," he said in a ragged whisper. "Or else I'm not going to be able to stop next time."

She smiled while conflicting emotions raged inside her. A part of her wanted desperately to finish what they'd started while another part scolded her brazenness.

"Are you okay?" he asked, tipping her chin up so that their gazes met.

"Yes," she managed to say, but no more.

Damien's beautiful eyes searched her face for the truth and then rewarded her with a grin of satisfaction at what he saw.

Not since junior high had Angel felt like such an open book. All her emotions on display for casual perusal.

He kissed her again, this time a quick and

softer version of the two previous ones. "I feel the same way."

He pulled away with a knowing wink and then helped her off the hood of the car and over to the passenger seat.

After Damien closed her car door, Angel took the brief reprieve to regain at least some of her composure. All questions and reprimands regarding her behavior were placed on hold and forced to the back of her mind.

Damien opened his door and slid in behind the driver's seat. Before he started the car, he glanced once again up at the sky. "From now on whenever I look at a full moon, I'll think of you."

A warm blush heated her cheeks. "I have a feeling it's going to be the same way for me."

His smile returned with another wink before he started the car. "Now how do we get off this mountain?"

Angel instructed him through the back streets of north Georgia until they reached the main highway, and then she gave him directions to Tonya's hideaway mansion in Alpharetta.

"I live not too far from here," Damien said as his car hugged another curve.

"Meaning?"

He shrugged but kept his eyes on the road. "Meaning that you're more than welcome to stay at my place."

Those damn butterflies returned and then

swarmed her insides. "I don't think that's such a good idea."

He glanced over at her. "I meant in separate rooms."

She laughed and rolled her eyes. "Sure you did." Angel shook her head, but couldn't believe the idea appealed to her. What was going on with her? "I think it's best that you drop me off at Tonya's place."

"So when will I get to see your place?"

Never. "I don't think that's such a good idea, either."

"Your brother?"

"My brother," she agreed, and then left it at that. A few minutes later, Tonya's estate came into view. "There it is."

"When can I see *you* again?" he asked.

Angel drew a blank. "I don't know." She wasn't sure whether she wanted to see him again. Okay, maybe she did want to, but that, too, wasn't a good idea. In fact, she was sure it wasn't.

Damien turned into the private driveway.

She drew in a breath but refused to glance over at him while a small battle continued within her.

"Angel?"

The car rolled to a stop, and she could feel Damien's heavy gaze. It would be nice to see him again.

"I'm not going to lie. I had a wonderful time tonight."

Damien drew a deep breath. "But?"

She attempted to smile, but the corners of her lips refused to curve upward. "It's just not a good time for me to pursue anything right now." She glanced over at him and realized it was a mistake. Her speech was forgotten and her heart grew heavier with guilt.

"Gary?" he asked.

Angel nodded. "Not to mention the headache of dealing with my brother."

"You never know. He might like me."

She laughed and rolled her eyes. "Not likely."

Nodding, Damien dropped his gaze. "Then I guess this is it?"

"I'm afraid so," she said, and then reached for her purse. She withdrew his cell phone and handed it to him.

He stared at it for a moment before accepting. Quietly, he reached over to the glove compartment and withdrew her phone and gave it to her.

Her eyes burned as the threat of tears blurred her vision. "Thank you."

Damien opened his door and stepped out of the car. As he waltzed around it, Angel's heart squeezed. She did want to see him again . . . but that was wrong, wasn't it?

He opened her door and helped her out.

Angel wanted to rewind the clock and start again, but as they walked toward the front door, she couldn't catch his eyes.

Just great. I really screwed this up.

At the door Damien faced her again. "Well, for what it's worth. I had a great time."

"Me, too," she said softly. *Say something.*

A small smile lifted the corners of his lips. "Are you sure there's nothing I can do to change your mind about this?"

Now. Angel swallowed and felt another sting of tears, but she quickly blinked them away.

"I didn't think so." He exhaled, and his large shoulders deflated a few inches.

Angel removed his jacket from around her shoulders and handed it to him.

He draped it over his arm. "Can I at least have a good night kiss?"

Angel managed to nod before leaning up on her toes and receiving the sweetest kiss she'd ever tasted. Lazily, her hands slid up and covered his heart. Its fierce pounding matched her own. Her hand drifted down and around his waist. How was she going to walk away from this?

Damien pulled away, and Angel's body screamed in protest. He brushed away a tear she wasn't aware had fallen, but before she could say anything, he kissed its dewy track. "Good night, Angel."

" 'Night," she whispered against his lips and

slid her hands behind her back. She watched numbly as he turned away from her. She remained rooted in front of Tonya's door while he returned to his car, and even watched as he drove out of view.

Behind her, the front door opened and Tonya's voice floated out to her. "So what's the verdict? Are you going to see him again?"

Turning, Angel faced her with a smile and held up Damien's wallet and cell phone. "Absolutely."

CHAPTER
14

The next morning while still lounging around in his black silk pajamas, Damien related most of the night's events to Jerome.

"She stole your wallet and cell phone?" Jerome laughed, falling onto the leather sofa in Damien's study. "You've got to be kidding me."

Damien laughed and shook his head. "She could have taken the wallet at any time while she wore my jacket, but the cell phone, she had to switch during . . . well, while I was busy."

"And you didn't know?"

He shook his head. "No clue."

Jerome's eyes lit with admiration for a woman he'd never met. "Maybe there's something to this soul mate thing. Even though the idea still frightens me."

"Yeah. She's not like anyone I've ever met. She's beautiful, sensitive, kind—"

"And dangerous," Jerome added. "She's still a Lafonte who also has sticky fingers."

"You say that like it's a bad thing."

Jerome rolled his eyes. "Hey, you may find this game of petty thief you two are doing amusing. I, frankly, find it disturbing. Why can't you two ask for dates like normal people?"

Damien waved him off. "Come on, she probably just switched the phones as a sort of payback. How can you not think it's cute?"

"Therapy. You both need therapy. If you two hook up and get married, trust me, your children are going to need therapy, too."

"Whatever, man."

Jerome took a sip of coffee and then studied his friend over the rim of his cup before he asked, "Does this mean that we're not taking the job from Sean?"

Damien settled his elbows on the edge of his desk and rubbed his chin as he contemplated the question. "You know this whole thing doesn't make sense. Why would he steal from his own sister?"

"Hey, it's not the strangest thing we've seen in this business."

"True." Damien agreed. "But still. After talking with Angel and her friend Tonya, I got the impression that Sean is very protective when it comes to his sister. So for him to actually be the one to betray her—"

"Makes him a snake in the grass?"

"That's putting it mildly."

"So where does that leave us?"

"Still retired for the moment." Damien decided suddenly. "But I'm still curious about this brother and sister duo."

"I guess this means that you're going to see her again."

Damien held up Angel's cell phone. "Absolutely."

Two weeks passed before Angel summoned the nerve to call Damien for their second date. During that time she rode a constant roller-coaster ride of emotions. Could she find love the second time around? Was she ready to find out?

Working at the Atlanta High Museum was nothing but a blur of activity. Her hands were full preparing for the delivery of the Edgar Degas collection arriving in two months. With it being her first project as the new art director, she was obsessed with every detail.

Work also helped keep her mind off her loneliness, and that had to be a good thing. Then one night a pair of deep onyx eyes haunted her dreams and evoked a longing so painful it physically hurt.

"I thought you'd never call," Damien said the

morning she finally made the call. "I was starting to feel like a fool for not reporting my wallet stolen."

"You were going to sic the cops on me?"

"It would have been hard."

She smiled as she settled back against a mound of pillows on her bed. "Well, I'm glad you didn't. I don't know how I would have explained myself."

He chuckled and caused an army of goose bumps to march across her body. She didn't know why, but she missed him. What the heck did that mean?

"So, is there any chance of you being available tonight?"

"Boy, you sure don't believe in giving a man a little more notice, do you?"

Laughing, she stared up at her bedroom ceiling. "Is that a no?"

"Actually, it just so happens that I am free this evening."

"Well, what do you know?"

"Plus it's my turn to decide where we're going."

Angel hesitated. "Should I be worried?"

"About me?" he pretended to sound offended. "I'm as harmless as a kitten. Nothing will happen unless you want it to."

An erotic image of her and Damien making out flashed through her mind, and her heart skipped a beat.

"Hello. Are you still there?" he asked.

"Yes, I'm here." She stood from her bed and waltzed over to the window to peek outside. "You do remember my certain circumstances?" she asked, staring at the same blue Buick Regal parked across the street. Her guard dogs had returned. She was just barely able to make out her brother's thugs nestled inside.

"You're being watched?"

"As always, but I can shake them."

"How?"

"Usually a trip to the mall does the trick. It's real easy to lose them in a crowd. Most likely one will follow me inside while the other watches the car. I'll dash in, lose the one trailing me, and then bolt to the other side of the mall and take a taxi or a bus to another destination. Simple."

"Sounds like you've done this before."

"One of many tricks up my sleeve." She melted at the sound of his soft chuckle.

"Have you ever just asked your brother to stop having you followed?"

"Every chance I get." She shrugged and walked away from the window. "The only time I felt safe from his prying eyes was in Europe. Of course, it meant I had to move a lot, but Sean's resources and connections were limited, and it took him a little while to find me."

"Surely this can't go on forever."

"My thoughts exactly. But until I can knock

some sense into him, this is the only way I can maintain any level of privacy." She sighed and then tried to lighten the mood again. "So where are we going tonight?"

His sexy laugh filtered once again through the phone line, and Angel found herself falling in love with its sound.

"Tonight is going to be a surprise. So bring your best dress and let me handle the rest."

CHAPTER
15

The old mall routine with Mutt and Jeff went just as Angel predicted. One would have thought Sean would've warned his men of this simple maneuver by now, but c'est la vie.

Her taxi rocketed through Friday evening traffic with ease while her talkative driver carried on about high gas prices. She tried her best to participate in the conversation, but it was difficult to pretend interest while she was on pins and needles about her second date with Damien Black.

For the most part she was surprised by the effect he had on her. He had resurrected emotions she was sure died along with Gary in that fatal car crash. In the year since his death, she lamented restlessly about the direction of her life. Was she going to continue running to the far corners of the world so she could evade her brother's reach or was she finally going to face him and demand her space in society?

What would her brother do if he found out that she wasn't such an angel? What would he say if he found out that she, too, had a love of danger or that she was attracted to dangerous men? And Gary Powell had been such a man.

She laughed. Maybe the old saying that good girls loved bad boys was true. Was Damien Black a bad boy?

For the most part, she believed that her brother didn't mean any harm. He was a man with enemies. Enemies who wouldn't mind harming someone Sean loved to even a score. No doubt that Merrick was such a man.

She frowned as she reflected on this.

"Here we are," the cabdriver said, turning onto the Black estate. "Wow. Who lives here—a superstar or something?"

Angel's eyes widened at the beautifully man-icured lawn as they drove the down the curvy driveway. When the house finally came into view, she sucked in a breath at the towering mansion fit for a king. "Maybe a superstar does live here."

The moment the taxi pulled to a stop, the front door to the house opened and Damien stepped out dressed to the nines in a powder blue linen suit. The soft color seemed to enrich his dark skin and even brighten his smile.

The cabdriver jumped and opened the door for Angel.

She looped her large tote bag onto her shoulder and stepped out. Moving as though she was in a trance, she realized that was definitely underdressed.

"Hello and welcome," he said, taking her hand and lifting it to his lips. "I've been waiting for you."

"This is your place?" she asked, finally finding her voice.

"One of them." He looked to her driver and extended his hand in greeting. "Thanks for getting her here safely." During the handshake, he slid the driver his pay, and then returned his attention to Angel.

Angel heard the man gasp before he began to trip over his words. "Yes, sir. Thank you, sir. It's been a pleasure, sir. Is there anything else I can do for you, sir?"

"No. I think that will be all."

"Yes, sir. Have a nice evening, sir." Finally his eyes shifted back to Angel. "You, too, ma'am."

"Thank you," she said mildly curious about just how much Damien had paid him.

Damien swept out his hand to lead her toward his car. "Shall we?"

She labored briefly on whether she should ask to drive the sleek Lamborghini when the sound of jingling keys caught her attention.

Turning, she saw the outstretched keys dangling in front of her.

"I figured you might want to take her for a spin."

"You read my mind." She smiled and reached for the keys.

The taxi driver honked as he sped past them.

"I'd say that you made his day," she commented as she gave the man a quick wave.

"Probably. Are you ready?"

"I brought a change of clothes." She glanced down at her low-riding jeans and pink cashmere halter top. "I figured this wouldn't raise suspicions about my trip to the mall."

"I think you look pretty hot with what you have on." He winked and then escorted her to the house.

When the door opened, Angel moved inside a breathtaking foyer. In the center, a glass and sterling silver table held a silver vase with a spectacular spring bouquet. She glanced around, trying to take in the size of the house, but ended up shaking her head in disbelief. "This is unbelievable."

"I'm glad you like it."

"Like it?" She laughed. "I love it. This place is beautiful."

He smiled and then glanced at his watch. "Perhaps when we return, I can give you a full tour. But right now we're running late for our date."

"Oh." She blinked. "Just lead me to a bath-room."

"Follow me." Damien glided across the silver and white marble floor and halfway down an elegant hallway with spectacular paintings.

"Picasso, de Kooning, and Cézanne," Angel listed with awe. "You really know your stuff."

"All anyone needs is a library card." He winked again and then pushed on what Angel perceived to be a wall.

She gasped in surprise when the wall actu-ally slid back and revealed a large bathroom.

"I'll wait for you out here," he said. "There's a white button next to the light switch. Just press it to open and close the door."

She nodded and moved slowly into the room.

Damien waited until the door closed before he chuckled to himself. Knowing women as he did, he suspected he had a bit of a wait ahead of him. He walked around the corner to his study and figured he'd better call the restaurant.

Forty-five minutes later when he was just get-ting bored with twiddling his fingers, he heard Angel out in the hallway.

"I'm coming," he called, standing from his desk.

She suddenly appeared at his door. "There you are. I wondered where you were."

His brows lifted at the sight of her slender body in a white floral gown with a halter neck. Her hair was once again iron-straight and rested against the glow of her shoulders. "Wow. You look fantastic."

"You think so?" Slowly, she spun around so he could take in the full effect of the dress.

"Definitely." He joined her at the door and impulsively brushed a kiss against her lips. "You look good enough to eat."

Her cheeks darkened a deep burgundy. "Thank you, I think. Oh, and this belongs to you." She returned his wallet and cell phone.

"Thank you. I think I'll give your phone back at the end of the date."

"Any particular reason why?"

"No." Damien offered his arm and she gently looped hers through. "I hope you're ready for the evening I have planned for you." He led her from his study and back down the opulent hallway.

"Are you going to at least give me a hint where we're going?"

"And ruin the surprise?"

"Not even a small hint?"

"Okay." He opened the front door. "We're going to dinner."

Stepping out into the warm glow of the fading sun, Angel's eyes once again fell on his car. "Do I still get to drive?"

"As long as you still have the keys."

She held them up.

"Then I guess you get to drive."

This time with a renewed wave of excitement,

Angel leaned over on her toes and gave him a light peck.

Damien's eyebrows rose in pleasant surprise. "Hell, I have a whole fleet of cars in the east wing garage. You're welcome to drive those, too, if it'll garner the same results."

Angel simply laughed while he opened the car door. As she eased behind the seat, his gaze traveled down the length of her gown and down to her nice rose-painted toes. He had no doubt in his mind that she was the woman for him.

Angel waited while he strode to the passenger side before she started the car. "Where to, Captain?"

He clicked on his seat belt. "Follow the driveway out of the estate and then take a left onto Holloway."

"Aye, aye, sir." She winked and followed his instructions.

Damien smiled and shook his head as he eased back in his seat and enjoyed being chauffeured around by a beautiful woman. When Angel made the left out of the property, Damien caught sight of the small white Honda parked across from the estate.

Broche. He frowned and glanced into the side-view mirror just as the Honda pulled off and followed them.

Angel fell in love with one of Damien's favorite restaurants, Panos and Paul's. The elegant setting and wonderful food won her over. The man sitting across from her was quickly doing the same.

"Well, you definitely know how to pick a restaurant."

"I'm glad you like it."

"I love it. I'll have to come back here again."

"Ah, ah, ah. This is our first real dinner date so it's *our* place. That means you can never bring another man here."

"Is that right?" Angel took another sip of her wine. "Does that also mean that you've never brought another woman here before?"

"Actually, no. I've only been here twice before, and both times they were business dinners."

She studied him as if trying to decide if he was telling the truth. "All right, but what about my brother? Can I bring him?"

He hedged. "Well, since he's in the restaurant business. I guess you can bring him at least once."

Angel's expression soured. "How did you know that he was in the restaurant business?"

Damien's breath caught. He was surprised by his foolish blunder. "I asked you about going there once and you said something about being there a lot. So, I made the assumption . . ."

"Oh." She nodded and took another sip of her wine. "Then in that case, I'll only bring my brother here once, and after that, I'll only come here with you."

"Good."

She laughed. "Now, if you would excuse me, I'm going to dip into the powder room for a minute and I'll be right back."

"Certainly." Damien stood as she stood up. When she walked away from the table, his eyes traveled down her backside, and he could feel a tightening in his heart muscles.

Once she'd disappeared from sight, his gaze drifted and fell on a white gentleman on the opposite end of the restaurant. He recognized the balding gray-haired man instantly.

"This is ridiculous." With long, purposeful strides, Damien drifted across the restaurant and over to Broche's table.

"*Seul dîner?*" Damien asked, stopping next to his nemesis and smiling despite himself.

Frosty blue eyes lifted to meet Damien's while a thin wiry smile hooked the corners of Broche's mouth. "Oui, Monsieur Black. I'm eating alone. Fancy meeting you here."

"Mind if I join you?" Without waiting for an answer, Damien pulled out the vacant chair opposing the ex-cop.

"And what of your restraining order?"

Damien sat. "It doesn't seem to stop you from trespassing on private property."

"True." Broche chuckled. "Maybe because I know that one of these days I'm going to catch you in the act. That will be something, eh?" He splayed his hands out as if reading a marquee.

"'Lieutenant Broche captures the world-famous Fantôme.' Nice, eh?"

"I would have thought that a man your age would have stopped believing in ghost stories by now."

Broche's expression soured. "I will get you. That is, of course, unless you care to cut me in."

Damien laughed. "You're not soliciting a bribe, are you, Lieutenant Broche, or should I say ex-lieutenant?"

"Call it what you want." Broche tossed down his napkin. "What kind of figures do you pull on a job? A million—two million?"

"I don't know what you're talking about. I'm a retired financial wizard. Don't you read the papers?"

"Ha! Hogwash!"

Damien shrugged. "It's true. I spend my days playing with expensive toys in erotic locations that you only dream about." He smiled as he watched the Frenchman's jaw clench.

"I've worked all my life following the straight line of justice, only to retire with little more than two good suits and no matching socks. Then I see someone like you, slinking around in the dark and daring the world to expose him. Why should you be the only one to roll around in millions?"

Damien studied him. "Lovely speech."

"I'm glad you approve."

"But there's a problem with your plan . . . of catching me, that is."

"Oh?"

"There's the thing about me being retired."

Broche laughed. "A man like you can't stay retired for long. You always struck me as the type who enjoyed the thrill of the chase. Do you not?"

The smile on Damien's face froze. The man did know him.

Broche's gaze shifted over Damien's shoulder and then returned to meet his stare. "Your young lady friend has returned. Surely you'd want to get back to her."

Damien pushed back his chair and stood. "I'm sure I'll be seeing you around."

"You can count on it." Broche winked.

Turning, Damien suppressed his annoyance and anger. By the time he returned to his table, he was ready to concentrate on his date.

"There you are." Angel smiled. "I was beginning to think that you bailed on me." She glanced over his shoulder and then lifted her wineglass in salute to someone. "Is that man a friend of yours?"

Damien turned around and saw Broche holding up his own wineglass. "No."

"Oh." She lowered her glass. "Weren't you talking to him a few minutes ago?"

"Would you two like to hear what's on the

dessert menu tonight?" Their waiter stepped in and saved Damien from responding.

"Oh, no, no," Angel said. "I couldn't possibly eat another bite."

"Are you sure? We have a wonderful chocolate cheesecake that will bring tears to your eyes."

"Well, if you're going to put it that way, then I'd love a slice."

Damien laughed. "What a great wall of resistance you have."

"Had it been chocolate or cheesecake, I would've been able to turn it down. But no woman in her right mind can resist the fusion of the two."

"And what about you, sir?" The waiter turned his attention to Damien.

"I'll have what the lady is having."

"Good choice, sir."

"I'm going to hate myself in the morning," Angel complained.

"I doubt that. You're an athlete. Didn't you tell me in the car about loving to rock climb, parachute, and run?"

She nodded. "I love anything physical."

Damien brows hiked. "Is that right?"

A warm flush of color that he was beginning to love rushed into her cheeks.

"I didn't mean it like that."

"Sure you did. It was your way of flirting with me." He shrugged his shoulders. "I don't mind. I was sort of turned on by it."

"What? I was doing no such thing."

"You weren't trying to tell me that you enjoy having sex?"

"No."

"So you don't like sex?"

"No. I mean yes. Of course I do."

"So you have sex a lot?"

"Yes. I mean no. Wait . . . you're confusing me." She shook her head to clear her thoughts. "What just happened?"

"We were talking about you wanting to sleep with me."

Angel frowned. "We were not."

"Then I guess I'm the one that's confused." Damien shrugged, and then laughed when she threw her napkin playfully at him.

"A woman has to be careful around you."

Two slices of chocolate cheesecake arrived. Angel's eyes lit up at not only at the decorative chocolate glaze and extra shavings, but also at the large portion size.

"Oh, I think I've died and gone to heaven."

"I've been thinking the same thing all night."

Angel turned her sparkling gaze on him. "I'm starting to think that you have a book on all the perfect things to say."

"I'm just being honest."

"I think that's what scares me," she said seriously.

Their gazes locked.

"There's a lot about you that scares me, too,"

he said. "Since the moment I saw you in the museum I felt as though a long search had ended. Which doesn't make sense because I wasn't aware I was looking for anything."

She drew in a breath. "I felt that way, too. But . . ." She looked away.

Damien waited, but his heart grew impatient. "Yes?"

Exhaling a long sigh, she shook her head. "I keep telling myself that I should feel guilty for these new feelings or thoughts . . . that I'm somehow betraying Gary's memory by dating so soon."

"How long has it been?"

"One year next week."

He nodded, but then slowly shook his head. "I don't have an answer for that. But I do want you to know that I've thought about you every day since we've met. I keep thinking of ways I could conveniently bump into you or find some excuse to call. I've never been like that before."

Her smile seemed to sparkle as she looked back up at him. "Have you ever been in love before?"

"No. This is my first time."

Awkwardly, she laughed off his answer. "You don't know me."

"I love what I know so far."

"Which is what?"

"That you're kind, smart, loyal, and beautiful."

Angel sucked in a breath. "You're giving perfect answers again."

"I'm being honest again."

When she reached for her wineglass, Damien caught the slight tremor in her hand. "I'm making you nervous. I'm sorry."

"I'm fine." Angel drained the rest of her drink before fluttering another smile at him. "It's just . . . well, there's still a lot you don't know about me. I'm not this perfect person you just described."

"No. You're a damn good pickpocket. How could I not fall for you?"

"You have a few sly moves yourself."

"Stick around and I'll show you a few more." He winked.

Angel smiled. "I just might do that."

CHAPTER
16

After dessert, Angel and Damien made their way out of the restaurant. When the car was brought around, Angel bypassed the chance to drive again and quickly slid into the passenger seat. Her door lowered and clicked closed. However, Damien didn't readily get into the car. She glanced out of her window and witnessed a strange moment when Damien glared at someone coming out of the restaurant.

More people filtered outside, and Angel couldn't tell just whom Damien was angry with. A few seconds later he joined her in the car.

"Is there something wrong?" she asked.

"Everything is perfect."

The smile he gave her made her doubt what she'd witnessed. In turn, she shrugged it off. "All right, then where are we going now?"

Damien buckled himself in and revved the engine to life. "I figured we drive back out to the mountains. To that spot that you like so much."

Something like a match sparked to life and a warm glow radiated throughout Angel's body. "That would be nice."

He reached for her hand and brought it to his lips. The spark became a fire.

She watched the road as he navigated through Buckhead's Friday night traffic. She even scrunched down in her seat when they passed by the busy Lafonte's. When she noticed Damien's eyes darting to the rearview mirror several times, she turned around in her seat and glanced at the cars behind them.

Alarm bells blared in her head. "Is someone following us?"

"Uh, no." He turned off onto the highway. In the next second, they rocketed past the other cars as if they were standing still.

Angel laughed. "Well, if they were they aren't now."

Damien glanced over at her and winked.

"You're not boring," she said. "I'll give you that."

"I'll take that as a compliment. Dating me is more like an adventure."

"More good news." She squeezed his hands, and it somehow eased the residue of guilt she still had about dating.

"Who knows," Damien went on, "you might even shed your good girl image."

She rolled her eyes, and her laughter deepened. "Do you always judge a book by its cover?"

His gaze shifted to her. "Are you saying that there's a bad girl buried in there somewhere?"

"Buried, no. Camouflaged, yes."

Damien's brows rose in mild surprise. "You're not boring, either."

"Damn right."

Their laughter blended like music as they sped north.

Damien displayed his good memory when he exited off the highway and turned down the numerous roads that led back to Angel's favorite spot.

"Here we are." Damien announced, killing the engine.

They unbuckled their seat belts and climbed out of the car.

It was another brilliant moon accompanied by the same blanket of bright stars. If Angel didn't know better, she would've thought she'd stepped back in time and was given the chance to relive their first night out there.

"It's beautiful," Damien sighed, drawing in a deep breath. "I'm starting to love it here as well." He moved to the front of the car and leaned back against the hood.

Angel sat next to him. "I'm glad you like it." A light breeze ruffled her hair.

"Cold?" Damien removed his linen jacket and proceeded to drape it around her shoulders before she responded.

"Thanks," she whispered. Her eyes crept up to meet his dark gaze, and once again she was sucked into a strange vortex of emotion. Before she knew it, she said the first thing that crossed her mind. "Make love to me."

Damien blinked and looked as though he didn't trust himself to speak.

"Right here. Right now," she said.

Stunned, Damien couldn't stop staring, nor could he calm the fierce beating of his heart.

He wanted to make love to her, no doubt about it, but he wasn't sure if she was truly ready.

She pushed up from the hood of the car and moved so that she stood before him. "Don't you want to make love to me?" she asked. The note of innocence in her tone belied the soft invitation in her eyes and her bold actions.

Her hands reached out to his shirt and slid open the first button, and then the second.

"More than anything." The honest response poured from his lips as if he were a sinner in a confessional booth.

"But?" she asked, undoing the third and fourth buttons.

"But?" he repeated dumbly. Had there been a "but"?

Her hands roamed against his chest, shed free of the shirt.

Then he remembered. "But what about Gary?"

She exhaled slowly. "He's gone. This is about you and me."

Reason abandoned him while her hands stroked flesh and muscle. "Are you sure about this?" he asked.

"I'm positive." Angel's warm breath blew against his ear and sent shivers down Damien's spine. He turned his face away from the cause and brought his lips in instant contact with hers.

His heart was already pounding, a hard primal beat as he crushed their bodies together.

Her small feral purrs echoed against his ear like soft music. He removed his jacket from her slender shoulders and reached to the back of her gown.

She laughed breathlessly with her mouth to his throat.

"Here, let me," she said, reaching behind her neck and unhooking the halter-top portion of her gown.

The sight of her full, perky breasts brought every muscle in his body to attention. "Jesus," he whispered.

She chuckled at his reaction and allowed the rest of her dress to fall and pool at her feet.

Damien's sanity teetered as his need to taste her creamy flesh overpowered him.

She stepped closer to him and away from her dress, and their lips sealed in a hungry yet tender kiss. His tongue slid in, teasing and tasting her until her head was full of flashing colors. Angel had known it would be this way. Had known from the moment she'd laid eyes on him.

She reveled in this part of herself that she'd spent a year ignoring. She wanted and needed to experience all the emotions he elicited.

Damien allowed one breast to fill his ravenous hand while the other filled his mouth. *Magnificent.*

Consumed by passion, Angel drifted her head back to allow her hand to roam over the smooth muscles of his back. *More* echoed through her head like a religious mantra again. He could make her body feel *more*.

The detail of how he removed the rest of her dress from her body was a mystery; and to be honest, she didn't care. All she knew was that the heat from the car's hood was pleasantly welcome against her skin.

With a deep groan he abandoned one taut nipple for the other and winced at the feel of her nails against the hard ridge of his shoulders.

"I need you." The whispered plea tumbled from her lips.

Damien lifted his head to meet her stare. He'd never seen anything sexier than the goddess clad in red lace panties, a matching garter, and high-heeled shoes.

Reaching into his back pocket, he quickly removed a condom from his wallet and placed it on the hood. His eyes then dared her to take things to the next level.

Angel understood. How she kept her hands from trembling while she stretched them out to his pants had to be nothing less than a miracle. She returned her gaze to his handsome features and tried to gauge whether he was shocked by her behavior. However, his smoldering eyes only reflected an intense desire that left her breathless.

A lazy grin curved the corners of his mouth a fraction before he pushed up from the car to tower above her.

She trembled while waiting for their lips to connect, and when they did, a series of explosions shook her body to its core.

Angel's hand slid up and around his neck while his hands drifted south of her back to give her bottom a gentle squeeze. She loved the way her mind spun with rapture, and she loved how her breasts swelled painfully against his chest.

Damien's caress softened before they moved to the warm V beneath her panties. This time when he squeezed, his finger eased inside her.

Her body quivered at the small invasion.

"You're ready for me," he stated.

How could she not be? The man had set her body on fire.

Damien battled whether to take what he wanted—needed—now or to prolong this sweet torment. But as her hands fell from his neck to stroke the width of his back, and then grew bolder still to plummet beneath his pants again, he was reminded that the choice was not his to make.

His lips deserted hers as he buried his head against the scented curve of her neck. He gritted his teeth against the surge of heat that added steel to his erection. The want was so strong that it squeezed the breath from his chest.

Suddenly he was kneeling before her and sliding her panties down from her hips. He smiled when the material unveiled the small nest of curls between her legs, and he placed a kiss against her inner thigh. He slid the lingerie farther and peppered more kisses down her leg.

Angel could barely move to step out of her underwear. Once it was removed, she became self-conscious of the way his gaze roamed over her body.

"Beautiful," he murmured.

He stood, wrapped his arm around her waist, and lifted and placed her onto the car's hood. In this space and time, she was all that mattered.

A soft moan tumbled from Angel's lips as her body arched in open invitation. Twining his fingers in hers, Damien raised her hands over her head and seized her mouth for a slow, burning kiss.

This time when his lips left hers, they trailed kisses along her throat and collarbone, and then lower still to her bare and trembling breasts.

She gasped and instantly arched her body when his tongue encircled a tan peak. Throbbing and aching, she pushed her breast against his hot mouth.

Damien moaned with approval. While still feasting on a taut bud, he moved his hand downward, between their bodies, and dipped his fingers inside her.

Angel whimpered, and her pulse raced as his lips mimicked the slow, arousing rhythm of his hand. His sweet torture went on for what seemed like forever before her body strained for release.

"That's it, baby. Come for me," he encouraged.

She cried out as her orgasm slammed into her.

He held her tight until her breathing returned to normal.

"I hope you don't think that I'm through with you," he said, before raining more kisses from the valley between her breasts down to the warm bud between her legs.

At his tongue's bold intrusion, Angel filled

her lungs with the night's cool air while her eyes widened at the canopy of stars above them. Her eyes glistened with tears as she gave in to the hot sensations he aroused.

After a long while, a weak trembling began in her limbs and then a feverish yearning.

Again his tongue touched her swollen flesh, tasting her, and igniting her senses. When his mouth closed around the bud with exquisite pressure, Angel squirmed away.

He quickly gripped her hips in an iron hold and refused to let her go.

Her frenzied senses went crazy, and she bucked and clawed at his hands. Exploding, she cried out his name, as waves of ecstasy quaked through her.

He released her then when she lacked the energy to move and was just barely able to breathe.

How quickly the tides had turned. She had started this game being the seducer, yet he, in fact, turned out to the master of seduction.

Angel pulled herself back up into a sitting position, only to come face-to-face with Damien.

Her cheeks flooded with color. "Don't look at me like that."

"Like what? Like you're the most beautiful woman in the world?" He leaned forward and kissed the center of her forehead.

She stifled her disappointment in the weak show of affection.

He placed another kiss on the tip of her nose.

For a brief moment their gazes locked, and she knew there was more to come.

Sensations of longing and desire surged through her body as his lips descended. At the delicious feel of his warm breath across her parted lips, her own breathing thinned.

He kissed her slowly, tenderly, and shivers coursed through her when his tongue delved inside. After a moment, his hot mouth slid lower.

Her breathing sharpened painfully when he found the rising swell of her breasts. Wherever his fingers touched, her skin seemed to burn.

Instantly all the fires he'd aroused earlier rekindled, and in no time she felt certain she was melting from the inside out.

Suddenly, roughly, he dragged her bottom to the edge of the car's hood. He stood, and she gasped as his steellike erection saluted her. Remembering the condom packet he'd placed on the hood, she reached her hand out to her left and retrieved it.

Damien waited patiently while she tried to peel open the packet with trembling fingers. After a while, he laughed. "Here, let me help you with that."

"I've got it." She moved her hands away, determined to do this herself. A second later, she withdrew the condom with a victorious smile. "Got it."

He leaned over and kissed her forehead. "Yes, you do."

Now she was faced with the next pleasurable task of sliding him into it. Her gaze returned to his impressive size, and she self-consciously drew in a deep breath.

Gently she reached out for him and was aroused not only by the length and width of him, but also by his silky texture.

He drew in a shuddering breath. "You're killing me," he said, referring to her deliberate slowness.

"Just a little taste of your own medicine," she said.

"Is that right?" He flashed her another crooked grin before he reached down and finished the task for her.

"Hey," she complained, smiling.

"Hey, yourself. You're going pay for that little stunt."

She laughed as he leaned her back.

His mouth returned to worship her body. A tremor rippled through her when he slid a long finger into her quivering flesh and found her wet.

Her head moved restlessly from side to side, her gaze occasionally snatching images of the moon and stars.

The fingers were bolder now, exploring her with hot, slick strokes, the smooth thrusts a sweet, delicious torture.

Writhing, she arched against his hand, seeking ease for the pulsing ache between her thighs.

"Look at me, Angel," he commanded.

She obeyed.

Their gazes locked as he lifted her hips off the car and eased the silken head of his shaft inside her.

She stiffened and gasped as her body struggled to accommodate his size. Tears sprang to her eyes. He was holding her so gently, and his eyes were so soft.

Her legs wrapped around his hips to get as close as possible.

Slowly he began to rock, and brilliant flames colored the darkness behind her eyelids. She drew him deeper while racing toward an inferno that would consume her.

"Damien . . ." His name fell like a prayer from her lips. She was no longer conscious of her surroundings, only of Damien, of his dark skin and even darker eyes, of his increasing rhythm, his growing moans and possessive thrusts.

He had become her world, the center of a spiraling madness that held her in its turbulent grip. With a renewed intensity, she arched her body and rocked her hips in the same madding pace as he drove into her.

In the next instant, he lifted her off the car. Her arms flew around his neck, and her legs locked behind his hips. With amazing strength, Damien bounced her against him.

She could barely breathe and could hardly think, but she took great enjoyment watching his face contort with pleasure and pain.

Her strangled cry of release blended in erotic harmony with his hoarse roar as he pressed her back onto the car. She reveled in the violence of his explosion, cherishing every pulse beat of his manhood still buried inside her.

For a few moments afterward, their labored breathing filled each other's ears.

"My God, you're amazing," Damien said in a ragged whisper.

She smiled against the curve of his neck. "I think we might have frightened away the animals."

He chuckled. "Trust me. They were the least of my worries."

Her brow arched with surprise. "You don't strike me as the worrying type."

"It's been known to happen from time to time." He kissed her.

Playfully, Angel pushed him off her. Sitting up she looked around the ground for her discarded panties.

"What are you doing?"

She blinked. "Looking for my clothes so I can get dressed."

The humor vanished from his eyes. "Who said that you could do that?"

She laughed. "I didn't realize that I needed permission."

"Then I'm telling you now."

A hypnotic languor stole over her, while a slow heat built inexorably between them. He reached up and caressed his fingers alongside her jaw and gently lifted her face up to his. "I'll let you know when I'm through with you, agreed?"

She drew in a shaky breath. "Agreed."

CHAPTER
17

Angel uncurled her body and stretched as far as she possibly could before falling limp against the pillows once again. A soft moan fell from her lips before a lazy smile drifted across her mouth.

Last night must have been a dream. No man possessed that sort of stamina.

However, as she fought her way through her groggy haze, she slowly became aware of the soft ache from her breasts and between her thighs. And then she realized she was definitely not lying on her own bed.

Her eyes fluttered open.

Yards of ivory silk instantly came into focus, but it didn't clear her confusion. Where was she?

She sat up in the center of a king-size, mahogany poster bed and gasped when the top sheet fell and revealed her nudity. Clutching the material back to her chest, she glanced around at her magnificent surroundings.

Furniture made of the same rich mahogany gave the room a strong masculine feel, while the soft colors of cream and gold hinted at a sensitive soul. The room had to be the size of her first studio apartment, equipped with its own colonial columns. Her artistic eye found two Monets and one Cézanne.

"Impressive," she whispered, smiling. As she leaned back against mounds of soft pillows, the memory of last night's events returned. This was Damien's bedroom.

But where was Damien?

Judging by the amount of sunlight streaming through the windows, Angel was willing to bet she'd slept through the morning.

"I should be ashamed of myself," she scolded with a light giggle. Damien wasn't an ordinary man.

She closed her eyes and drew in a deep, cleansing breath. Her body still tingled and ached, but damn if she didn't feel good.

Almost drifting into another round of sleep, Angel mustered the strength to climb out of the large bed. When her feet touched the cool marble floor, she performed a quick search for her clothes, but was greatly disappointed when she couldn't find so much as her shoes.

At a loss for what she should do, she grew uncomfortable at the idea of parading around the room in her birthday suit.

She marched back to the bed and snatched the top sheet when she heard something fall to the floor. She quickly wrapped the silk sheet around her like a toga and rushed to the other side.

Her brows gathered at the sight of a large white and gold package. Picking it up, she discovered her name written in perfect penmanship on an attached envelope.

She sucked in a corner of her lip as she plucked the card out and anxiously read:

> *To my dearest Angel,*
> *You are indeed heaven sent.*
>
> —*Damien*

Her smile ballooned wider as she now rushed and tore open her package. She laughed aloud at the sight of a floral print circle skirt, a black knit top, and a pair of black cross-strapped shoes. All were in the right sizes.

"I could get used to this." She stacked everything back into the box, and then rushed to find the bathroom without tripping over her extra-long toga.

The first door she opened led to a large, extremely organized walk-in closet. In fact, the space was easily the size of her own bedroom at her new townhouse. She moved inside and allowed her gaze to roam the neatly pressed dress shirts, the iron-straight trousers. Sweaters were separated from turtlenecks while jeans were separated from khakis.

"This settles it. He can never come to my junky place."

"I see madam has finally awakened."

Angel jumped and dropped the box before swinging her startled gaze to a calm, older, white gentleman near the closet door. "You startled me," was all she could think to say. She knelt down and retrieved her things.

He nodded slightly. "Sorry, madam. My name is Nigel. I'm Mr. Black's personal assistant." He lifted the tray he carried higher for her viewing. "I was asked to see if you might like something to eat."

Her stomach's growl was loud, long, and extremely embarrassing. When it finished, she flashed him a timid smile. "Food sounds great."

The man struggled not to smile. "Very well, madam." He turned from the door and walked to the nightstand beside the bed.

She rushed out of the closet, careful to avoid

any nasty tumbles or yanking her sorry excuse of a dress from her body.

"Uh, where is Damien now?"

"I'm sorry, but he's unavailable at the moment."

She blinked at the man's cold answer.

"But I will tell him that you've inquired about him."

"Thank you."

He smiled, but she could tell it was something he didn't make a habit of doing.

He walked away from her in quick, soundless steps.

"Oh, one more question," she said, before he'd managed to slip out of the door.

"The bathroom?" he guessed with another disturbing smile.

She nodded.

"Third door on your right," he said. Warmth finally introduced itself in his gaze.

"Thank you," she murmured.

Nigel nodded, and then slipped out of the room.

"Interesting," she mumbled, turning her attention to the tray of food. She nearly melted at the sight of ripe strawberries, diced cantaloupe, buttered biscuits, bacon and eggs, and her all-time country favorite—grits. She was definitely back in Georgia.

Succumbing to temptation, Angel seized a

plump strawberry, dipped it into the small serving of cream, and moaned in pure ecstasy when its sweet juices exploded in her mouth.

She shoved her new clothes aside on the bed and then lost herself as she devoured everything on her plate. When she finished, she was grateful Damien hadn't been around for her transformation to a gluttonous pig.

This time when she gathered her things and moved toward the bathroom, her movements were much slower and more lethargic. The bathroom was fit for a king. It appeared Damien denied himself nothing when it came to luxury.

However, she opted for a quick shower as opposed to a long bubble bath. Still, she had fun playing with the motion-detecting showerhead.

While she worked the soap into a nice lather, the song "Giving Him Something He Can Feel," poured out of her as though she were singing before a packed stadium. She even had fun with shimming her shoulders and rocking her hips as she belted the song's last chorus.

At the sound of loud, measured, claps echoing off the walls, she clutched a hand across her heart and quickly poked her head out the shower door.

"Wonderful show," Damien said, smiling. "Why don't you come out so I can tip you properly?" He winked and crossed his arms over his chest as he leaned back against the door.

He looked as handsome as ever, dressed head to toe in black.

"Oh. You finally remembered me." She closed the shower door with a smug smile and rushed to finish rinsing off.

She listened as his footsteps crossed the tiled floor and stopped just outside the shower. When he opened the door, their gazes met through the mist and steam.

"I can never forget you," he said. "I would never want to."

Her body jerked in reaction to his confident smile, and as his eyes lowered to view her body, every nerve tingled with excitement.

"Why didn't you wake me when you got up?" she asked, turning off the water.

"Because you looked like you were enjoying your sleep. Well, at least it sounded like it anyway." He moved back as she stepped out of the shower.

"Are you trying to say that I snore?"

"Just a little bit. It's cute really."

She snatched a towel from the rack. "I do not." Embarrassment burned the tips of her ears.

"If you say so." He took the towel from her hands. "Please, allow me." He blotted off her shoulders and then kissed them. "Has anyone ever told you that you have great skin?"

She closed her eyes against the sensations he was causing as the towel glided down to the small of her back, and then gently around the curve of her butt.

"I think you might have mentioned it last night," she whispered.

He turned her around, and her eyes were instantly drawn to his.

"I love how soft it is." The towel slid across her collarbone. "I love how it darkens whenever I pay you a compliment."

His lips lowered to extract a kiss while his hands cupped her wet breasts.

Her body hummed with pleasure.

Damien dropped the towel and gave in to the heady taste of Angel's sweet mouth. God help him, but he wanted to take her again. To hell with his appointments and responsibilities. Surely he had time to appease his newfound addiction.

Captain Johnson couldn't wait until his vacation. This year he and the missus were spending ten glorious days in Hawaii. In his mind he could already picture himself sipping drinks with plastic umbrellas on the beach and watching his wife demonstrate the latest moves from her hula class.

Those daily images were what gave him the extra spring in his step in the mornings on his way to work. However, his mood soured the instant he strolled through his office door and found Broche waiting for him.

"It's you again."

"You knew I'd be back." Broche uncrossed his legs, stood from his chair, and offered his hand in greeting.

Johnson ignored the hand and went around to his desk. "What can I do for you this time?"

Broche dismissed the insult with a smile, and then reached for the briefcase he'd stored beside his chair. "I've discovered some new information on Black."

"New won't impress me near as much as something *stronger* to support your case."

"Mr. Black's real last name is Blackwell." He removed a new manila folder. "I visited the boy's home where he grew up." He withdrew a copy of an old newspaper clipping. "Turns out he's the son of the late James Blackwell—an art thief." He tossed down the paper on Johnson's desk. "How much are you willing to bet that the apple doesn't fall too far from the tree?"

Johnson picked up the paper with a large picture of an older, distinguished-looking African-American man with intense eyes. The caption read: *To Catch a Thief.*

Broche smiled. "I see I have your full attention now."

"I'm listening." Johnson lowered his large frame into his chair.

"Good." Broche settled back in his chair, feeling he was back on his game. "After this latest discovery, I was able to do some research on the father."

"And?"

"And apparently justice failed to keep Blackwell behind bars. It seems his son has the same good fortune."

"Let me guess. They were unable to find enough evidence to link him to the crimes."

"You're familiar with the case?"

"I only know what was printed in the papers." Johnson tossed the copied newspaper clipping across his desk. "As far as this Mr. Blackwell being the greatest criminal mind the art world has ever known, that's a label an embarrassed law enforcement and sloppy journalists attribute to him because—"

"Because they couldn't catch him," Broche finished for him. "You could hardly be considered the best if you were caught."

Johnson shook his head. "I think we're seeing two different sides of a coin here. I say Black is innocent until proven guilty, and you say he's guilty until proven innocent. What makes you so damn sure about this?"

"My gut," Broche declared. "I've spent most of my life on the force, and my gut has never led me astray. Never."

The men's gazes clashed.

"What about you?" Broche asked. "How often do you rely on your instincts in this line of work?"

Johnson drew in a breath, hating that the Frenchman had finally struck a chord.

Broche tossed up his hands. "I don't know what to say to convince you I'm right about this. A thief is a thief whether he's caught or not. And the only way we're going to catch this Black is to set the trap ourselves."

CHAPTER

18

Jerome kept dozing off while waiting for Damien to return. Frustration described Jerome's feelings about having time wasted. When he first arrived that morning, he had been shown to the study where he waited over an hour.

Since when did Damien start sleeping late?

After he finally arrived, it was pretty much a repeat performance of the last time. Damien's mind was clearly focused on something else—or someone else.

Jumping up from his chair, Jerome shook the sandman's dust from his eyes. "This is ridiculous," he said, snatching up his jacket. He stormed toward the study's door, but jumped back when it jerked open.

"Sorry about that," Damien said, breezing through. "Now where were we?"

Jerome blinked as he watched his friend brush past him to head toward his desk. "You mean an hour ago?"

Damien glanced up, his smile wide. "Was it that long?"

"Uh-huh."

"Damn." Damien winced. "Sorry, man. I had some other business I needed to attend to. Forgive me, 'cause I know you're getting a little upset with me on this."

Smooth-talking Damien always knew how to diffuse a situation. Jerome tossed his jacket back across the leather sofa and then he noticed something. "Weren't you wearing all black this morning?"

Damien looked down at his pristine white cotton top. "Yeah, I, uh, had to change. I got the other shirt wet." His smile returned.

"Whatever, man." Jerome glanced at his watch. "Let's just get this over with. I have an appointment with Amber at two o'clock."

"You're bringing your third wife in on this?"

Jerome drew in a deep breath and pinched the bridge of his nose as he counted to ten. "I told you that this morning."

With a furrowed brow, Damien slumped down into his chair.

"What's going on with you, man?" Jerome huffed. "Amber works for Putman Securities. She can get us what we need on the museum's floor plans."

"But what about the restraining order *you* have on her?"

Jerome waved off his concern. "We'll work something out."

"Can she get you the security codes?"

"I'm still working on that."

Damien remained dubious. "I don't understand why you want to do this. I thought you loved retirement."

"I do, but I got to thinking, and I don't see why we can't pull one last job."

Damien finally smiled. "You miss the adrenaline rush, don't you?"

"More like the money." Jerome exhaled. "That land I bought out Coweta County turned out to be a dud. Man, I don't know what it is about me and all these bad investments. Unlike you. You have the Midas touch when it comes to investing."

"And marriages."

"Yeah, that, too." Jerome leaned back in his chair. "I don't know how to say this but . . . I need this job. Besides, don't you still want to go for the one painting your father didn't get?"

Damien nodded thoughtfully. "What's the news on Broche?"

Jerome shrugged. "I'll have to get back to you on that."

Concern quickly trickled through Damien. "Whatever you do, don't lose tabs on him."

"Consider it done."

Damien sighed as his thoughts drifted to the

beautiful angel awaiting him. He also thought of his mother and father and how she couldn't live with a man who stole for a living. Would coming out of retirement cause him to repeat history?

"Yo, D. Are you listening to me?"

"Yeah. Sorry about that."

"So what do you say? Are you in?"

Damien mulled the offer over. "The Shafrazzi's Art Gallery should be a walk in the park compared to the museum job."

"Of course we could always do both."

For the second time that day, Angel stepped out of the shower. At the rate she was going, she'd never make it back home—though she wasn't complaining. However, she needed to check in with her brother before he sent an army to comb through Georgia looking for her.

Sean's overprotectiveness had always been a problem for Angel ever since their parents were killed in a car accident. She was eleven and he'd just turned eighteen.

Their parents had left them with nothing—mainly because they didn't have anything. After Sean begged, borrowed, and hustled for the money for funeral costs, he packed her up and moved them from the projects of Shreveport, Louisiana, to Atlanta.

Through the years, Sean wore many hats:

brother, best friend, and even father. It was the last role that the now twenty-six-year-old Angel had a problem with. She no longer required a father figure, but she would always need her brother and best friend.

College was never a dream Sean had for himself, but it was a religious vision he held for Angel. For a long time she allowed Sean to control her life.

Until she fell for Gary Powell.

Angel exhaled and finished blotting her body dry. Sadness washed up against the shores of her emotions as a snapshot of an old boyfriend resurfaced from her memory.

Whether she was truly in love or just sowing her wild oats, she didn't know. Hell, it was college and she was finally out from underneath her brother's large thumb.

Angel stared at her reflection in one of the bathroom's mirrors.

"I don't want to think about this now," she mumbled, reaching for her box of clothes. She searched through the garments again and realized there weren't any undergarments.

"I don't believe this." She laughed under her breath.

She rushed to put on what few clothes he did provide and tried not to feel self-conscious about not having anything on underneath her short skirt. When she was through dressing, she returned to the adjoining bedroom and was surprised to discover the room had been cleaned.

Red silk sheets replaced this morning's ivory while the handsome furniture now shone with a fresh coat of polish. Did the man also employ the fastest cleaning crew in the East?

With nothing to do, Angel eased into an incredibly soft chaise longue and waited for Damien's return. However, sitting around in one place had never been Angel's forte. She grew bored, so she stood up and started rummaging around.

She discovered a plasma television that descended from the ceiling, a great stereo system that apparently had invisible speakers, and even took time to study the beautiful paintings mounted on the bedroom walls.

What time was it? The man owned everything but a clock.

Crossing over to the bedroom door, she poked her head out into the hall to see if Damien was on his way back.

There was no sign of him.

She stepped out and glanced around. The place would put a five-star hotel to shame with its eye-popping splendor. It was immaculate, but perhaps a little impersonal.

Walking around, she was impressed at how each enormous room morphed into the next with only a few mini-hallways that showcased magnificent contemporary paintings. After thirty minutes of wandering, she was convinced she was lost.

Why would a bachelor need this much space, she wondered. The place seemed large enough to house the entire Kennedy clan. Well, maybe half of them.

"May I help you, madam?"

Angel muffled a scream as she nearly jumped out of her skin. Turning, yet again she met the calm, cool eyes of Nigel. "You have to stop scaring me like that," she insisted.

"Sorry, madam," he said. "Where you looking for Mr. Black?"

"Uh, no. Not really." She flushed. He had caught her snooping.

"I see." Nigel's gaze dulled with disappointment. "I'm quite sure my employer would rather he gave you a personal tour as opposed to you perhaps roaming around and getting lost."

There, he had successfully scolded her.

"Where is Damien?" she asked, forcing her own tight smile.

"I'm sorry, but he is indisposed at the moment."

Here we go again. "Yes, but *where* is he?"

"He's in a meeting. If you'd like, I can tell him again that you would like to see him."

"That's all right. I can do it myself."

Nigel blinked at her sudden directness. Finally he gave her a slight nod. "Downstairs, madam."

There are stairs? A vague memory of Damien carrying her up a spiraling staircase resurfaced. "Thank you," she said, turning around but not moving in any direction.

"If madam would follow me," he said, riding to her rescue.

Despite their short spar, Angel liked the frosty butler. And something told her that he liked her, too.

Damien opened his study door to walk Jerome out when he nearly smacked into Nigel.

"Ms. Lafonte would like a word with you."

Jerome groaned but didn't get a chance to speak before Angel moved around Nigel.

"Sorry to have bothered you," she said, smiling.

Damien's lips automatically twitched upward. "No bother." He glanced to Nigel. "Thank you. I'll take care of her from here."

"As you wish." Nigel bowed, and then quickly disappeared.

Jerome cleared his throat.

Damien picked up on the hint. "Angel, I would like for you to meet an old friend of mine, Jerome McCleary. Jerome, Angel Lafonte."

Jerome snaked around Damien and seized Angel's hand. "It's nice to meet you." He leaned forward and kissed her knuckles.

"It's a pleasure to meet you, too." She laughed.

Tapping his friend's shoulder, Damien tried his best to stifle his annoyance. "Weren't you about to leave?" he inquired.

"Uh, yeah." Jerome lowered her hand and released it. "I was just leaving."

Angel continued smiling. "What a shame. Maybe we'll run into each other at another time."

"I sure hope so."

Damien had stomached all he could. "Angel, would you mind waiting here while I walk him out?"

"Certainly." She looked to Jerome. "Again, it was nice meeting you."

Jerome's smile turned goofy as he bobbed his head. "Same here."

At that Damien gave his friend a good shove through the study door and then walked him through the vestibule to the front door.

"My God, why didn't you tell me how gorgeous she is?" Jerome exclaimed in a hushed tone.

"Didn't think it was important."

His friend kept glancing over his shoulder toward the study. "Not important?" He shook his head. "Now everything makes perfect sense. I'd risk Sean's wrath for a chance to hit that, too. Did you see the way her top hugged her chest?" His voice dipped lower. "I don't think she's wearing a bra."

"Goodbye, Jerome." Damien opened the front door.

Jerome chuckled. "All right. You don't have to tell me twice. I'll leave you two alone." He crossed the threshold. "Don't do anything I wouldn't do. And if you do, take pictures."

"I'll keep that in mind."

Both men laughed and said their goodbyes.

When Damien returned to his study, he found Angel strolling around and assessing everything. "Sorry I kept you waiting."

She glanced up and flashed him another breathtaking smile. "No problem. I hated to interrupt your meeting, but it's time I got home."

"Home?" He frowned, crossing the room. "But I'd hoped we could spend the rest of the day together." He took her into his arms. "Wouldn't that be nice?"

"It would be wonderful." She accepted a quick kiss. "But impossible."

"Oh, don't do the responsible thing. Let's just have a day of fun and leisure—food, wine, and sex." His hand ran along the side of her hip.

"Oh?"

"And not necessarily in that order." He wiggled his brows.

Angel shook her head. "You definitely know how to tempt a girl, don't you?"

"I know a little sumthin' sumthin'."

She laughed at how his use of slang clashed with his personality.

"Did you know you forgot to purchase underwear for me?"

"I never forget anything."

Angel laughed. "You're bad."

"But you knew that." He kissed her again. "C'mon, what do you say?"

CHAPTER
19

Angel was having the time of her life.

It was a bright sunny day, and after Damien provided a personal tour of his estate, he proposed a nice dip in the pool.

"I don't have a bathing suit," she objected.

"Who needs suits?" His arm slipped around her as they stood near the Olympic-size pool. "Clothes will just get in the way."

The sparkling blue water beckoned, cajoled, and dared her to dive in. The fact that she'd never gone skinny-dipping before was an added incentive. "I don't know," she hedged, and threw up a roadblock. "What if someone sees us?"

Damien laughed and made a grand sweep of his arm. "Like who?"

"What about Nigel?"

He shrugged. "I'll tell him not to come out here." Stepping back, he pulled off his shirt.

Angel's gaze dropped to his broad shoulders and six-pack abs. A sweltering heat rose within her. "You're doing it again."

"Doing what?"

"Making it impossible for me to say no."

His eyes twinkled above his smile. "I don't want you to say no. He toed off his shoes. "I do, however, want to see that gorgeous body of yours wet again."

There were many ways she could take his last statement, and she blushed at each of them.

"I'll go talk to Nigel and bring us back some refreshments." He winked and then walked away.

She shook her head. Would she ever be able to tell this man no and mean it?

True to his word, Damien returned a few minutes later, dressed in a white terry-cloth robe, carrying towels, an additional robe, and a large tray with drinks and bowls of fruit.

"You haven't undressed yet?" he inquired with a wide grin. "Does this mean I get to watch you perform a private striptease?" He sat the tray down on a glass table.

"Hardly." Angel laughed as she joined him at the table. "Or did you forget about my rhythm-less body?"

Damien's eyes slanted in her direction. "From what I remember, those hips have plenty of rhythm." As if to remind her, his hands settled on her waist and dragged her closer.

His slow grinding against her hips made her breathless, while the friction of her bare breasts against her knit top caused them to ache and swell.

"See," he said, his lips a mere wisp away from her own. "You have great rhythm."

At that moment, if the man had told her she could fly, she wouldn't have a single reservation about jumping off the Empire State Building.

They continued dancing to imaginary music, and it took Angel a moment to realize that Damien's hands had found the small zipper in the back of her skirt. By the time she realized what he was doing, the light material slid off.

He swallowed her gasp of surprise with a kiss.

She nearly wept at the feel of his strong hands squeezing and caressing her bottom. It was amazing how this man wielded power over her—amazing how he made her experience things as though it were her first time—and amazing still how she loved every bit of it.

Slowly, his hands traveled north and slipped beneath her top. Their light brush against her spine weakened her knees, and she leaned into him for support. Soon after, his roaming hands came around her body, and each claimed a firm breast as its own.

Angel whimpered against his lips. Last night

was the first time she'd made love beneath the open sky, and today she was willing to do it in broad daylight.

Her shirt was pulled over her head and discarded by the poolside in one quick swipe. Now she stood before him wearing only a pair of high heels. His gaze swept over her and darkened with desire.

Damien crushed her against him. His kiss was violent in its tenderness and brutal in its sweetness. She moaned at the feel of his steel erection pressed against the apex of her thighs.

Her breasts peaked and ached as she glided her fingertips through the exposed V of his robe. In no time at all, she discovered his belt held no knots and came loose with a quick tug.

Her hand returned to his flat stomach and very close to another interesting part of his body. She wanted to touch him, caress him, and become a part of him. How could she be this brazen and out of control?

Finally she gave herself permission to explore his body, but was surprised when his hand clamped down on her wrist.

"What do you think you're doing?" Damien smiled against her lips.

Did she have to answer that? "I, uh . . ."

"Yes?"

The teasing lilt in his voice furthered her embarrassment and she pulled back and took a swat at his shoulder. "You're evil."

With a boisterous laugh, Damien's head rocked back.

She couldn't help but laugh, too. "Fine," she said, kicking out of her shoes. "We're supposed to be swimming, remember?"

He shrugged out of his robe.

His long, defined legs drew her, as did his impressive washboard stomach and his nicely shaped butt. Yet his manhood had a beauty all its own and was his most compelling feature.

"I'm ready when you are." That said, he sprinted toward the pool and dove in as though he were about to rescue a drowning victim.

She watched as he swam along the bottom before bobbing up to the surface.

"Come on in. The water's fine."

Angel played it safe. She walked to the pool's edge and dipped in the tips of her toes to test the water. "It's freezing," she declared.

"That's why you just jump in. Your body adjusts to the temperature faster that way."

She ignored him and proceeded to enter the pool by way of the stairs. With each step, her teeth chattered. When she finally made it knee-deep into the pool, she gave serious thought to chickening out.

Damien made his way over to her, and she quickly splayed out her hands in defense mode to keep him away from her.

"That's all right. I can do this on my own," she shouted with distrust.

"What?" He kept moving toward her. "I just want to help."

The water still felt too cold around her knees, and she took a retreating step back. Her nervousness, mixed with the devilish glint in his eyes, made her tremble.

Then everything happened so fast. Damien lunged out of the water, his arm sweeping at her knees.

Screaming, she pitched forward and landed unceremoniously over his right shoulder.

"Gotcha," he announced and playfully smacked an upturned cheek.

Indignant, Angel pounded his back with her fist. "Put me down!"

Damien laughed and moved farther into the pool. "Are you sure about that?"

She froze, remembering the cold water.

"You want me to put you down?" he asked again.

"No, no, no."

"Good." He smacked her cheek again.

She jerked and clenched her jaw at the instant burn. Beneath her, his body quaked with laughter. "I'm going to get you for this," she swore, laughing.

"Not until after I have my fun." Smack!

When she bucked with all her might, Damien lost his balance and they both went down.

Shock numbed her body, and it took her a few quick seconds to remember to kick her way back to the top. Breaking through the water's surface, she gulped down as much air as her frozen lungs would allow.

Something clamped onto her ankle and then dragged her back under. Submerged, she opened her eyes to see a grinning Damien.

This meant war.

The cold water and her spanking were forgotten. Angel had a new agenda: teach Damien a lesson. At first, his strength was enough to maintain the upper hand. Occasionally, they surfaced for air, but went right back into their game of dunk.

Being a Lafonte did allow her one luxury in life: the ability to fight *dirty*.

About the fourth time Damien dragged her under, Angel dove straight toward him and clamped her own steel vise around the family jewels.

Still stubborn, Damien wouldn't relinquish his hold on her ankle. So, with great regret, she yanked.

Instantly free, Angel relived her glory days as a competitive college swimmer and zoomed away from Damien before he could recover.

They played for hours, both constantly seeking revenge for one prank after another.

Angel was first to call a time-out. She was sure if she stayed in the water much longer she'd turn into either a pickle or a Popsicle. Climbing out, she donned Damien's robe, grabbed a drink, and collapsed into a lounge chair.

Could the day get any better than this?

She sipped her drink and watched as Damien performed a few laps around the pool. She admired every ripple of muscle in his legs and arms.

"How long are you planning to stay in there?" she shouted.

"I'm just waiting for you to jump back in." He slowed down long enough to answer.

Now that she had reached land again, she held no desire to return. "I think I'm going to call it a day."

He stopped swimming and fixed her with his best puppy-dog expression.

"That doesn't work on me," she informed him.

He navigated to the pool's edge and poked his lip out for further emphasis.

"No."

Convinced she wouldn't be persuaded, Damien pulled himself out of the water.

Angel continued to admire every inch of him as he moved toward her. Despite spending the last two hours in cold water, Damien remained an impressive size.

Grabbing one of the towels he'd brought, he blotted his face dry and then wrapped it around his hips. "Are you having a good time?" He picked up the bowl of fruit and joined her on the chair. He remained sitting up and facing her while she lounged back.

"I'm having a great time. But you know you're going to have to take me home soon. I'm probably already in enough trouble."

He shrugged and then leaned forward to kiss her. "You know," he said, pulling away. "You could always call your brother from here."

"I prefer to answer the question of where I've *been* as opposed to where I *am*."

"All right. I'll take you home tonight."

"This evening," she countered.

"Seven o'clock," he negotiated.

"Six."

"You sure know how to drive a hard bargain." He shook his head and peeled open her robe. "Of course, six doesn't leave us with much time." He selected a plump strawberry and held it to her lips.

Obeying the silent command, Angel bit the juicy fruit in half and then met his hungry gaze as she chewed with deliberate slowness.

Damien took the other half of the small fruit and lowered it to encircle her jutted nipples. When they finally glistened beneath a sweet glaze, his mouth lowered for its first taste.

Angel's eyes drifted to half moons as her head lolled back. Sheer pleasure created magical, threadlike connections to every pore, muscle, and blood vessel in her oversensitized body.

He took his time lapping up the sticky substance and bringing her to the brink of madness.

The next fruit he selected was a small vine of grapes. Again, he held it out to her mouth and fed her two of the delicious green orbs.

"Let's just put this away," he said, moving the bowl from his lap and setting it on the tile a few inches away from them. He returned his attention to her and helped reposition her legs so that he now sat comfortably between them.

Her eyes narrowed with suspicion as he still held the grapes.

He plucked one and placed it between his teeth and leaned forward for a kiss.

Angel giggled when grape juice squirted into her mouth and laughed harder when he purposely tried to smear more of the juice all over her lips.

Suddenly the kiss changed. It was no longer playful but hungry.

His mouth ravished hers, and then drained the life out of her with his thrusting tongue. She was vaguely aware of the fire blazing in the wake of his hand as it lowered.

At his fingers' soft invasion, she gasped and arched against him.

Damien chuckled against her neck.

Angel opened her mouth to respond, but could only manage a strangled gasp.

His body rumbled with amusement as he discarded the grapes and once again repositioned to hover above her, however briefly.

While his hands continued playing with her, his tongue eased down the center of her neck, the valley of her breasts, and dipped lightly into her navel. His warm breath wafted against the nest of curls between her legs and then against her feminine lips.

Her hands balled at her sides just as her breath thinned in anticipation of his next move.

Damien flicked his tongue once, twice, and then a third time over her slick rosebud. Each time her body jerked and tried to squirm away.

"Where are you going?" He slid his hand beneath and around her thighs to drag her back toward him and drove his hot tongue inside her.

His firm grip didn't stop Angel from trying to buck aw   but her struggles heightened their erotic gar .

Angel que: led, moaned, and squealed again. Flinging her head from side to side, she surrendered to the most cataclysmic orgasm of her life.

When it was over, her face scorched with embarrass ent.

But Damien wouldn't let her off so easy. He crawled back up the chair and slid his hands into the pocke   of the robe she still wore. He retrieved a condo n and quickly rolled it on. Taking his erection in hand, he placed it at her entrance, no further. "Look at me, baby."

With tear-filled eyes, she did as he asked.

Slowly, with a long, drawn-out groan, Damien entered her. He watched with great joy as her eyes dilated and her mouth formed a perfect circle.

He hit the chair's lever and their bodies dropped to lie in a straight line. It was a tight fit, but Damien was determined to make the small accommodations work. Supporting himself on straight arms, corded neck arched, Damien moved inside her with slow, excruciating rhythm.

Angel raised her hips to meet his thrusts pound for pound. She caressed his perspiring face, his wide, shoulders, and his heaving chest. Their pacing was perfect. Neither was in any rush to end the wild sensations coursing through them that went beyond a primal lust.

Finally his strokes quickened and grew rough, causing the chair to bounce and threaten to break.

She wrapped her hands around his neck as well as her legs around his hammering hips. Every nerve quivered to life, every impulse centered on the need to absorb him.

A scream tore from Angel's throat and a low growl ripped from his soul as their combined explosions left them trembling weakly in each other's arms.

For long seconds afterward, she lay stunned beneath him.

Once he gained control of his breathing, he shifted so he could rain kisses along her face. "How do you feel?"

"Wonderful," she whispered.

"Great." He kissed her again. "I want you to always feel that way when you're with me."

Angel's heart squeezed as she reached up to still his face and met his gaze. "And what about you? How do you feel?"

"The best I've ever felt in my entire life."

She smiled. "Good. I want you to always feel that way when you're with me."

He smiled and then leaned in for another kiss.

For the past twenty-four hours, Sean had been the hottest thing in the Horseshoe Casino. Right now he didn't have time to think about how Angel shook the tail he had on her or the fact that he hadn't heard back from Damien on whether he was going to accept the museum job.

With each roll of the dice, he felt his financial noose loosen. Gone were any anxieties and doubts about the trip to Las Vegas being a bad idea. Finally his yearlong losing streak had ended.

"Lady Luck is my girl tonight," he boasted to his sudden crowd of fans. They, in turn, cheered him on.

It was impossible for Sean not to feel the eyes of the box men, floor men, pit boss, shift boss, and casino manager on him—not to mention all of those eyes behind the cameras. But he didn't care. When you're hot, you're hot.

Somewhere around three A.M. Sunday morning, he left the craps table while he was ahead. Before he made it to his complimentary suite, he decided to try his luck at a real man's game: poker.

The casino manager was all too happy to get him a spot at a high-stakes table. And then a funny thing happened: His luck continued.

At four A.M., he had enough to pay Merrick back. By six he'd doubled it. When eight o'clock rolled around, Sean had no choice but to call it a night. He simply couldn't keep his eyes open any longer.

By the time two tall, slender, ebony beauties volunteered their services for the morning, Sean was on cloud nine. He gave no thought to his sister's whereabouts or how the restaurant was faring.

But before he boarded his plane Sunday night, Sean had lost it all.

Tevin Merrick always got what he wanted.

Sometimes it meant he had to be patient, other times it meant someone had to die. He was comfortable with both. Up until yesterday, getting rid of his old pal Sean Lafonte was a forgone conclusion—then he met Angel.

A crafty smile twisted into place as he leaned back in the sauna's sweltering heat. Who would have thought that smug son-of-a-bitch was hiding such a jewel?

Everything about Angel seemed to be in total opposition to her brother. She had class, grace, and style.

Then there were her eyes. He didn't understand how they sparkled with innocence and jaded intelligence at the same time.

He would need a plan to win her over—a damn good one.

First, he needed to know all about her, but so far his people hadn't been able to turn up much.

So maybe his only plan of action was to go through Sean. Merrick cringed at the thought. Everything about Lafonte rubbed Merrick the wrong way. Sean had made too much money, too fast.

However, Merrick took great pride in being the grand puppeteer in the fall of a potential empire. While Sean had the ability to make a lot of money, his gambling problem prevented him from keeping it.

Then again, if everything went well on this museum job, Sean stood to be his next best friend. Hell, for a possible nine-figure profit margin, why wouldn't he be?

Merrick drew a deep breath, finally tired of

his thoughts chasing one another. All he could do now was sit and wait—and pray to God that Sean wouldn't screw up . . . again.

Angel never made it home that evening. How could she possibly give up the most comfortable bed ever created? Plus the thought of leaving the security of Damien's strong embrace didn't settle well, either.

Wine, food, and sex were what he'd proposed, and that's what he delivered—with no complaints from her.

After yet another mind-altering orgasm, Angel fell back among the pillows begging, "Rest, rest. I need rest."

"All right. Just for a few minutes." Damien chuckled as he eased next to her.

"What do you do—run on batteries or something?" She pushed away from him, but didn't move too far.

"Duracell *is* my middle name."

"Now you tell me."

They laughed, and then snuggled closer together.

Damien closed his eyes and inhaled the soft floral scent of her hair. This was what it meant to be alive.

"You know I'm going to regret this in the morning," she moaned.

He leaned over and kissed her shoulder and

gently glided his hand along the erotic curve of her hip. "Maybe you should call in."

"I've only been on the job a week."

"Okay," he laughed. "Maybe that's not such a good idea."

"It's a terrible idea." She inched closer and kissed the tip of his chin. "You're lucky that you don't have to drag into an office anymore."

Damien's head rocked back with a bark of laughter. Being a suit-and-tie man went against the very fabric of his character.

"What's so funny?" she asked, smiling.

"Nothing." He chuckled.

Propping up on her side, she stared down at him. "Do you miss your job?"

He smiled up at her inquisitive stare. "Sometimes."

She glanced around the bedroom. "One thing for sure, it provided you a very good living. Ever thought about coming out of retirement?"

Another chuckle. "Sometimes."

"Then you should consider going back to work. I mean, one can only lounge around for so long. I'd imagine I would get bored with nothing meaningful to do."

Damien thought it over and nodded.

"How did you get into sales and acquisitions anyway?"

He stalled. "Well, I sort of fell into the biz because of my father."

"Really?"

"As well as my grandfather."

Her eyes widened. "So you're following a family tradition?"

"That's one way to look at it." Damien propped up on his pillow as well. "When I was younger, I didn't want to be anything like my father. I thought I hated everything he represented, but in the end I'm his mirror image."

Their gazes held for a long moment.

"Do you hate him now?" she asked.

"No," he answered without hesitation. "To hate him is to hate myself . . . being that I turned out just like him. I miss him though."

She pressed a kiss against his lips, and he could taste the salt of her tears. "I know just what you mean."

His heart broke for her. While he'd lost one parent at young age, she'd lost both. "Do you remember much about them?" he asked.

Sniffing, she nodded. "I remember silly stuff. Like I remember them dancing cheek-to-cheek to old Motown records and my mom constantly burning fried chicken." Angel laughed. "Actually, she used to burn a lot of things."

"Not a good cook?"

"Probably the worst. But we always ate it with a smile."

Damien smiled at the warm image she painted. "Are you anything like her?"

"Are you asking if I can cook?"

He shrugged. "They say it's the way to a man's heart."

"You have a chef."

He released another rumble of laughter. "Let's stick to the question."

"Yes, I can pretty much cook anything—except for fried chicken." She laughed. "Who knows? Maybe it's a mental block or something, but I always seem to burn it."

"That's okay. I can live without fried chicken."

"No, no. I have to cook it for you and if you really care for me, you'll eat it."

"That's an interesting test."

"Maybe, but it's a good one."

He agreed and tilted up her chin. "I have a few of my own tests. So far you're passing with flying colors." He kissed her and savored the taste of her lips.

"What about you?" she asked, pulling away gently. "What do you remember about your parents?"

The first thing Damien thought of was the tears. It was just before his mother left. He'd walked in on her in her bedroom, and she was sprawled across the bed sobbing. "I don't remember much," he said, avoiding Angel's gaze. "I just know that my father loved her until the day he died. He told me that he knew within minutes of meeting her that she was destined to be his wife. He fancied himself a hopeless romantic."

"Love at first sight?" she asked, absorbed in his story.

"That's what he said." Damien's gaze returned to hers. "Do you believe in such a thing?"

Put on the spot, Angel blinked as she stammered, "I-I don't know." At Damien's silence, she drew in a deep breath and mulled the question over. "I certainly believe one could feel an instant attraction to someone—a stranger, I suppose."

"Like us?" he asked.

She hesitated and then nodded. "I guess we had a certain chemistry on our first meeting."

"That's putting it lightly." He laughed. "Look where we are."

Angel flushed and settled back down on the pillow. "Good point."

But was it love? he wondered.

Damien gazed down at her lush body bathed in soft moonlight. "What time do you get off tomorrow?"

She smiled and reached up to caress his face. "I don't know—about five, I suppose. Why?"

He shrugged to force an air of indifference. "Maybe we can have dinner together."

Her hands lowered to trace the lining of his lips. "Dinner?"

He kissed the tips of her fingers. "Or maybe lunch?"

"Lunch is definitely out of the question, but I

can swing dinner. I just have to shake a few people first."

He kissed her again.

As the night wore on, Angel was well aware that she needed to get some shuteye, but she was enjoying their pillow talk. In the end, she managed to squeeze in one hour of sleep before it was time to get up for work.

Damien made it even harder for her to do the right thing. And when he joined her in the shower, she almost relented for a repeat performance of the day before.

Another outfit was presented to her, this one a nice Armani business suit—complete *with* underwear.

"You're spoiling me," she said, marveling at her reflection in the mirror.

Damien, still dressed in his morning robe, moved up from behind her and draped a beautiful string of pearls around her neck.

Angel gasped.

"Whatever you do, don't tell me that you can't accept it."

That was exactly what she was about to say. "They're so beautiful."

He kissed the back of her head as he continued to admire her in the body-length mirror. "Just like you."

"You make me feel beautiful."

Their gazes met in the mirror as Damien's arms slid around her waist.

"I'm going to ask you again. Are you sure you don't want to stay home with me?"

"Of course I *want* to stay." She leaned back into his embrace. "I just can't."

He nodded, but remained unhappy about her decision.

Breakfast was prepared and waiting for them out on the patio, and when she was ready to leave, she was surprised that a lunch had been prepared in a new shiny, silver lunchbox.

"There you go spoiling me again."

"I hope you don't mind." Damien kissed her.

"And if I said I did?"

"I wouldn't believe you." He led her out of the house and over to the garage.

"You'd be right not to." She kissed him. "Are you sure you don't mind me taking one of your cars?"

"Nah. I trust you." He winked.

They strolled around his collection of high-performance cars a few times before Angel settled on the Lamborghini.

"What can I say? I like it for sentimental reasons," she cooed.

Laughing, they strolled back toward the house for the rest of her things. The dress she had worn to dinner had been dry-cleaned, as well as the outfit he'd given her yesterday.

The car was brought to the front of the house, and when she was all packed, they stood next to the car trying to say their goodbyes. "Oh, one final thing," he said, reaching into his robe's pocket and withdrawing her cell phone.

"Ah, I'd almost forgotten." She opened her purse and gave him his phone back as well.

They both turned to the sound of a car traveling down the long driveway toward the house.

"It looks like you've got company," she said.

Damien frowned. "I wasn't expecting anyone." He continued to watch the car as it approached. He didn't recognize or know anyone who drove an older-model Mercury Sable.

The car's tinted windows made it impossible for him to make out the driver, so he waited with a patience he didn't feel to discover the identity of his visitor.

When the car finally stopped and a man's giant figure emerged, the world tilted on its axis.

"Good morning, Black," the man greeted with a lopsided grin.

Damien didn't smile. "Good morning, Rock."

CHAPTER
21

Rock removed his shades when he stopped within inches of his old friend. As always, it was difficult for him to gauge Damien's dark expression, so his gaze instead slid to the stunning woman at his side.

"Aren't you going to introduce me to your lovely friend?" he asked, smiling.

Damien drew in a deep breath and then glanced down at his companion. "Angel, I'd like for you to meet an old friend of mine, Rock."

She extended her hand. "Hello. We talked briefly the other day on Damien's cell."

"Ah, yes. I remember." Rock nodded as he accepted her hand. "I thought I'd dialed the wrong number." He glanced back at Damien, but his expression hadn't changed. "I hope this isn't a bad time."

"You know you're always welcome," Damien said with a fair dose of sarcasm.

"Well," Angel said, during the ensuing silence. "I better get going. I don't want to be late."

Damien pulled his gaze from Rock to flash a warm smile at her. "Call me when you get a chance."

She nodded and smiled when he leaned in for a quick kiss.

Rock's brows shot up. In the past, he'd seen Damien with more than his fair share of women, but there was something different about him with Angel.

She glanced at Rock. "It was nice meeting you."

"Same here." His lips twitched into another smile as he watched her climb into the driver's seat, and damn if she didn't have the best pair of legs he'd ever seen.

He stood next to Damien as the car pulled off from the house. "She seems nice," he finally said when the car disappeared from view.

Damien's gaze once again shifted to him. "Cut the crap. What are you doing here?"

"Checking on you. You haven't returned any of my calls."

"I've been busy." Damien turned and headed back into the house.

Rock followed. "Rumor has it that you're back in business."

"Who told you that—Jerome?"

"Does it matter?"

"May I take your jacket?" Nigel asked.

Rock jumped with his hand immediately landing on the gun inside his jacket.

Damien quickly placed a halting hand atop his. "It's just Nigel."

"You shouldn't sneak up on people like that." Rock relaxed, but tossed a warning stare at the frightened man.

Visibly shaken, Nigel swallowed. "I'll make sure I remember that." He looked to Damien, who allowed him to excuse himself.

Damien exhaled and shook his head as he led the way to his private study. "Okay," he said, closing the door behind Rock. "Out with it."

"Out with what? I already told you why I'm here. You on the other hand are being evasive."

"Why? Are you here for a job?" As soon as Damien asked the question, a rumble of laughter pealed from his chest.

Rock laughed as well. "We don't work well together. We never did."

Despite the smiles, their gazes deepened in intensity as they continued to play cat and mouse.

"But I have to admit," Rock continued, "It's good seeing you again." He looked around. "And seeing that you're still doing well for yourself."

Damien nodded. "You know me. Nothing but the best."

"No matter what the cost?" Rock caught the instant spark of irritation in his friend's gaze and even took pleasure in watching Damien's body stiffen. "Okay, maybe that's a low blow."

"I had nothing to do with Pete's death."

"You led him into the life," Rock accused. "You led all of us."

The spark in Damien's eyes became a full-blown fire. "You give me way too much credit."

Tension layered the space between them and showed no signs of letting up.

"Why did you come here?" Damien asked. "I hope it wasn't to play this blame game because there isn't going to be a winner."

Damien was right, Rock knew. In fact, he should have never hurled the accusation of Pete's death at Damien in the first place. Pete, his younger brother, was a grown man who made his own decisions; unfortunately, he made some very bad ones. Rock stared at the man whom he loved like a brother and realized that it was time to let go of all the years of animosity.

Taking a deep breath, he held his hands up in surrender. "You're right. I didn't come to play this game. I came to warn you."

Sean crawled out of bed with a massive hang-over. At any moment, he was sure the fierce pounding in his head would do him in. It might even be a welcome reprieve, but Lady Luck beat the hell out of him in Vegas.

Thankfully, last night was one of the few times he'd gone to bed alone. The last thing he wanted was to wake up with the task of trying to get a woman to go home.

After vomiting the remaining contents of his stomach, he made it to the shower, and then tried to resemble something akin to the human race.

He desperately wanted to pay Merrick back so he wouldn't have to go through with this heist. Normally, he wouldn't have given a second thought to robbing the museum; but now that his sister worked there, he had to deal with guilt for the first time in his life.

Of course, Angel would never know about his part in the robbery, but damn the irony.

Finally, when he left the confines of his bedroom to head downstairs, he received the shock of his life.

"Ah, good afternoon," Merrick's unmistakable voice stopped him in his tracks.

Sean's gaze jerked to his nemesis, lounging comfortably on his leather couch in the middle of his studio.

"I hope you don't mind that I let myself in."

Sean swore his heart stopped as the blood rushed through his head and sobered his thoughts. "What are you doing here?"

Merrick's wiry smile widened as he uncrossed his legs and stood. "I wanted to see you."

Their gazes crashed while the air thickened around them.

"Now that you've seen me," Sean said, descending the rest of the stairs, "I guess you can leave."

The black glint in Merrick's eyes shone like polished marble. "I also came for a favor."

It struck Sean as funny that he didn't sound like a man who wanted or needed a favor. In fact, he sounded like a man about to demand something—something Sean feared he would be forced to provide.

"But first," Merrick added, his smile taking on a devilish quality, "How was your trip to Vegas?"

It was pointless to act surprised; Merrick had eyes and ears everywhere.

"I can't complain." Sean faked a careless shrug.

"Tsk, tsk, tsk." Merrick shook his head. "A fool and his money shall always part."

Sean's hands balled at his sides. The itch to throw the first punch threatened to overload his senses. As he glared at Merrick, Sean knew the man was having fun toying with him.

"What's the favor?"

"I want a date with your sister."

"Over my dead body," he grumbled without hesitation.

Merrick's smile hinted that his death could be arranged. "What's the matter? You don't think I'm good enough?"

"Damn right." Sean's anger seemed to give him strength.

"I'm hurt." Merrick placed his large hand across his heart. "And here I was thinking that if things happened to work out between your sister and I, it could be the beginning of a beautiful relationship—or better yet partnership."

Sean's sharp retort screeched to a halt and teetered on his tongue. "What kind of partnership?"

"For starters we could wipe out the debt you owe me."

"Wipe out?" Sean's heart leaped at the possibility.

"And even restructure your percentage on the museum heist."

"How much?"

"Your guy wants half off the top?"

Sean nodded.

"Then we can split the remaining . . . fifty-fifty."

With writing off the five million he owed Merrick, the calculator in Sean's head quickly tallied . . . a five-million-dollar profit.

"I think I'm being more than generous, don't you?" Merrick asked.

Five million dollars.

"Now, I'm not saying things have to lead to

marriage," he said, straightening his jacket. "But a simple . . . understanding will do." His gaze returned to Sean's.

"Understanding?"

"Yes," Merrick's lips widened. "An arrangement. I'll see to it that she's well taken care of: money, clothes, whatever she wants. In exchange, Angel is my mistress."

Sean stiffened as his hands balled once again at his sides.

"So what do you say?" Merrick extended his hand. "Do we have a deal?"

CHAPTER

22

"April showers bring May flowers" was certainly true for the city of Atlanta. The city came to life with various colors, but all went unnoticed by Angel. She spent the day arguing with everyone dealing with the Degas collection, from the shippers to the museum's publicity department.

Angel arrived home late Monday evening practically too exhausted to slide her key into the door of her townhouse. She crossed the threshold with her mind still wrapped on the job ahead and stopped in her tracks.

"Well, it's about time."

Angel gasped and swiveled toward the voice. "Sean," she exclaimed. "What are you doing here?"

He shrugged with a lazy grin. "I just dropped by to see you. That's not a crime, is it?"

She drew in a deep breath and forced herself to relax. "No, but breaking and entering is the last time I checked."

Sean walked over to her at the door and delivered a quick peck against her cheek. "I called. Do you ever turn on your cell phone?"

She mimicked his smile. "The battery is dead. I haven't had a chance to charge it."

Sean glanced over her shoulder to the driveway. "Damn. How did you get a car like that?" He rushed outside to take a look.

Angel remained at the doorway with her stomach tied into knots. "A friend loaned it to me."

Sean eyes shot over to her. "A friend loaned you *this* car? What sort of friend?"

Her eyes narrowed on him. "Don't start. I've only been in town a few weeks." She continued into the house.

Her brother came back to the door, his eyes still darting to the car. "That's a beautiful piece of machinery. Is it Tina's?"

"Sean," she warned with a sharp look as she peeled out of her suit's jacket.

"Nice outfit," Sean commented, closing the door. "I never pictured you as an Armani girl, but . . ." He nodded as he continued to check her out. "It looks good on you."

Her smile turned genuine. "Thanks." She removed her heels.

"Well?" Sean asked.

"Well what?" She glanced at him with a blank expression.

"Does the car belong to Tina?"

"You mean Tonya."

"Yeah, whatever."

"No. It belongs to my new secret lover," she said sarcastically and walked around a stack of boxes in the middle of the foyer to head toward the kitchen.

Sean's heavy footsteps followed her to the kitchen. "What? You better be joking."

"Can I get you something to drink?" she asked.

"What, diet water or something?"

She laughed. "No, I have juice."

Sean cringed. "No thanks."

Angel shrugged and quickly grabbed bottled water for herself. When she looked at Sean again, it became clear that something was amiss. "What's wrong?" she asked before analyzing whether she wanted to know.

Their eyes locked.

Now she definitely didn't want to know. His sobered gaze was warning enough that she wasn't going to like his answer.

"I need a favor," he said.

Sean never needed a favor—especially from her. She opened her bottle and took a deep gulp.

"It's a pretty big favor," he added.

Angel leaned against the refrigerator and braced herself. "What is it?"

Suddenly he looked uncomfortable and kept shifting his weight. "I need you to go out with an associate of mine."

Stunned, she stared at him.

He curved his lips into a smile, but they just wobbled at the corners before taking a nosedive. "Look, Angel, I know I'm out of line for asking you to do this, but—"

Angel shook her head and moved away from the refrigerator. As she stormed past her brother, he reached out and grabbed her arm.

She snatched it back. "I'm not one of your *girls*," she snapped and turned away. "I don't do entertainment."

Sean snaked out in front of her, blocking her exit. "One of my girls?" His face contorted with anger as he clamped his hands down hard on her arms. "What's that supposed to mean?"

"Just what I said." She jerked away. "You have some nerve—"

"Don't you dare turn your nose up at me." His grip tightened. "I've sacrificed my life to make sure that you've always had the best of everything. *I* made sure you were fed. *I* put clothes on your back."

"Don't give me that. I never asked for a damn thing."

"But you took it, didn't you?" His voice lowered to a hiss. "You enjoyed the life I provided. As far as I'm concerned, it's time you started pulling your weight."

Angel couldn't believe what she was hearing. "So to pay you back, I have to turn tricks?"

Sean stared at her. His anger dissipated as his grip loosened considerably. "I would never ask you . . . I would never put you in that situation."

"Then what is this about? Why do I have to be involved with one of your associates?"

Now irritation creased his forehead. "Dealing with my *associates* helped pay for your expensive education. I made sure you were safe, protected you from men who were trying to use you, though you were too naïve to know it."

Heat blazed up Angel's body. "You bastard," she hissed. "Gary loved me."

Sean's harsh laugh felt like a punch.

"Love? Gary Powell loved two things: money and himself."

She struggled to jerk out of his grip. "You don't know what you're talking about."

He laughed again. "Your precious Gary worked for me, Angel. I bet he never told you that. I hired him to watch over you. He didn't tell me that he was also banging you."

Another hard jerk and her hands came free. "You're a liar," she screamed and reared her hand back to deliver a hard blow across his face.

Sean blocked the blow and wrestled to subdue her hands. "It's the truth. When I found out the truth, I roughed him up a bit, but I *didn't* kill him. I know that's what you think, but I didn't. I had nothing to do with his car accident."

She struggled against him, her tears flowing freely. "Liar."

"Angel, I mean it," he snapped; his desperation finally penetrated her angry fog. "I didn't kill him."

She stopped fighting and slumped against him.

"Angel?"

"Get out," she said in an alarmingly calm voice.

"Angel—"

"I *said* get out."

"But we need to talk—"

She jerked out of his arms with renewed strength. She grabbed the bottle of water she'd dropped and threw it at him. "Get out!"

Angel rushed to the kitchen counter and grabbed a plate and hurled it at him. "Get out of my house now!"

Sean ducked and dodged more plates and a few glasses as he dashed out of the townhouse.

The door slammed behind him, and a final dish crashed against it.

Angel dropped to her knees in the middle of the hallway and buried her face in her hands. Her body trembled as tears soaked her fingers and palms. "Please, God. Say it's not true," she moaned.

Gary couldn't have been one of her brother's hired thugs. He just couldn't have. Even as she made her prayer, she knew Sean had told her the truth, but she continued to pray anyway.

CHAPTER
23

Damien couldn't believe he'd been stood up. He'd flown in his favorite chef from New York for the night, hired a violinist from the Atlanta Symphony Orchestra, and had most of the house covered in rose petals.

All for nothing.

At the stroke of midnight, he sent everyone home. He was too upset to be embarrassed and too embarrassed to call Angel.

"Maybe she just forgot," he mumbled, but the thought only made him feel worse.

He found himself in his study with no memory of how he'd arrived there and decided to pour himself a drink. It had been hard enough getting through the day—with the Rock's sudden appearance and Jerome's hassling about him finally falling in love.

"Love." He laughed and shook his head. What he felt could hardly be classified as love. He just liked her. She was attractive, intelligent, and good in bed. Actually, she was great in bed.

Anyway, it didn't mean that he was in love. His gaze fell to the amber liquid swirling in his glass. So she could walk with the grace of a ballerina, and when she smiled it was as if he were in the presence of a silver screen legend. None of that meant anything.

Damien downed the rest of his drink and then poured another one. He stole her phone; she took his wallet and now his car. "How do you like them apples?"

There was a knock at his door, and he had to smile when Nigel poked his head inside.

"Is there anything else I can do for you, sir?" Nigel asked.

"Nah." Damien waved him off. "You can call it a night."

"Very well, sir." Nigel nodded and slipped back out of the door.

"Hey, wait a minute," Damien called out, pushing from his chair.

Nigel reappeared. "Sir?"

"You were married for some thirty-odd years, right?"

Nigel gave what was perhaps the first genuine smile Damien had ever witnessed.

"Thirty-five years, sir."

Damien blinked. "Wow."

Nigel's smile grew wider. "I married my high school sweetheart two days after graduation."

Damien remained impressed as he crossed his arms. "Two children?"

"Twin girls." The man glowed. "Both teachers just like their mother."

Damien knew that breast cancer made Nigel a widower so he was careful to avoid that subject. But he was curious about something else. "When did you know that your wife was the one?"

"The one?" Nigel echoed, sliding his hands into his pockets and rocking on his feet.

The uncharacteristic movement surprised and amused Damien. "Yeah, when did you know? How did you know?"

Nigel gazed off for a moment while he thought about it. "I'd have to say the moment I laid eyes on her in the high school cafeteria." His expression turned dreamy. "I can still picture her laughing and surrounded by her friends." His smile dropped a notch. "Of course, they were laughing at me. It seems one of the bullies in school thought I looked better wearing my lunch as opposed to eating it."

Damien couldn't help but laugh at the instant imagery. "Not too popular at school?"

Nigel shrugged. "Ah, but it was worth it. Gillian had a beautiful laugh. The kind you fall asleep dreaming about."

With his laughter diminishing to a soft smile,

Damien looked at him with admiration. "You were lucky."

"Extremely."

Damien nodded, but as Angel's image returned, so did his confusion. He, too, liked the sound of Angel's laughter. It wasn't like the customarily high giggle women usually used around him, but more like a head-back, hearty, Julia Roberts–type that infected everyone.

"What else?" he asked.

Nigel shrugged and moved farther into the room. "Her fragrance," he said, lost in memory. "Whenever I held her in my arms, she always smelled like jasmine. Always."

Damien chuckled. "Strawberries."

Nigel's brows shot up with amusement.

"I know," Damien said. "You don't meet too many women who smell like strawberries."

"Indeed."

They laughed and then fell silent before Damien continued.

"So, is that it? Laughter and strawberries?"

Nigel turned. "What else do you need?"

Sean woke up the next morning with another hangover and entwined in a mass of female body parts. He'd invited Carrie and Lea over to salve his woes. The booze was good, the sex was great, but nothing could erase his guilt.

Prying himself free from the bed, he stumbled to the bathroom. Sean emptied his stomach into the toilet and then tried to revive himself in a blazing hot shower.

He had finally done the unthinkable. He was trying to sell his sister to save his hide.

Tears stung his eyes.

Merrick materialized in his head. The man's sly grin twisted a knife in Sean's stomach, and another wave of vodka and Thai food bolted from the bottom of his stomach.

He dropped to his knees, waiting for the spasm to stop while trying not to drown. Then came the tears. When had he turned into this man? How could he ever look his baby sister in the eyes again?

He had vowed to protect her, and now he was offering her up to the wolves. Miserable, he couldn't figure a way out of this mess.

Angel cringed at her reflection in the bathroom mirror. Her eyes were red and puffy from a night of crying. Just great. Now she could sleepwalk her way through work.

After she'd had a shower and a second cup of coffee, Damien's features crept through her fog of depression and she gasped.

"Damn." She hopped up from the breakfast bar and rushed out of the kitchen to find the cordless phone. She had forgotten about their date.

A few moments later, just as she finished punching in Damien's number, the front doorbell rang. With the phone tucked against her ear, she sprinted to the door. "Who is it?" she called out while waiting for the line to connect, but she couldn't hear her visitor's answer for the loud ringing in her ear.

She unlocked the door and pulled it open just as a shrill sound came from the other side of the door. Her eyes lifted and welcomed the sight of her devilishly handsome lover.

His cell phone stopped midway to his ear when he saw the phone in her hand. His brows lifted in question, and she nodded and disconnected the call. "What are you doing here?"

She tugged him inside and glanced around outside in search of the blue Buick Regal. When she didn't see it, she sighed in relief. "You know I may be watched."

"I took a chance."

"I wish you'd check with me next time," she snapped.

Damien blinked. "Sorry."

Angel peeked out the glass panel next to the door for a final check when her gaze shifted to the sleek black limousine in front of her townhouse just as it started to pull away.

"One of the rare times I have someone drive me around," he commented, glancing around the foyer. His eyes darted to the many boxes surrounding them. "Still unpacking?"

She nodded. "I guess you came to pick up your car," she said, closing the door behind him.

"I thought it was a good excuse to see you." He laughed. "Unless you need to keep it for a few more days?"

"Oh, no. That's not necessary." She waved off his offer. "About last night—"

"Don't worry about it," he rushed in. "I figured a band of terrorists had kidnapped you and were holding out for a ransom. In fact, that's the real reason I came over—to see if they left a list of demands."

She laughed but it sounded forced.

Damien's brows inched high; no doubt he caught the note of insincerity.

Silence pooled around them.

"Is something wrong?" he asked.

Now she forced a smile. "No, I just . . ." She huffed. "It's nothing. I'm sorry about last night."

He moved in close. "Something *is* wrong. What is it?"

"Nothing. My brother and I had a little argument last night, that's all."

"About your whereabouts this weekend?" Concern marred his features.

"Actually, he never asked me about that." She thought for a moment. "Who knows, maybe he was out of town himself. Probably Vegas."

Damien's features clouded. "Does he go there a lot?"

"Is the Pope Catholic?"

A frown carved his lips. "So what *did* you fight about?"

Strangely, Angel opened her mouth to tell him, but luckily common sense choked off her voice. "Nothing. Trivial brother and sister stuff," she said.

His frown deepened, and she pretended not to notice. "Anyway," she continued, closing the small space between them, "I hope you can forgive me about standing you up." She stretched onto her toes and gave him a light peck on the cheek.

He stared at her; his frown easing a little before his head dipped in for a quick kiss. "Why are your eyes so red?"

Dropping her weight onto her heels, she released a long sigh. "I haven't had much sleep the last few nights."

The comment won a sheepish smile. "I guess I might have had something to do with that."

"Maybe a little." Her arms fell back to her sides. "Now I need to get ready for work. I don't want to be late."

"Hmm. Well, we wouldn't want that." He looped his hands around her waist to pull her back. "However, we haven't discussed how you're going to make up last night to me."

She allowed him to nestle her back against his firm chest, while his strong arms locked against her flat stomach. His heat and strength enveloped her, and the security of his embrace elicited an undeniable sense of home—of belonging. The sweet feeling brought the threat of tears to her eyes. If she'd been wrong about Gary, she could easily be just as wrong about Damien.

"You don't happen to know my brother, do you?"

"What?" He appeared startled by the question.

"Never mind." She brushed the question off as being ridiculous.

"What did you have in mind about me making up last night?" she asked, smiling. And then giggled when he nibbled at her ear.

"I want you," he whispered huskily.

His words evoked an erotic image and in turn caused her heart to pound with desire.

Damien's lips traveled from her ear to the sensitive spot he'd discovered at the nape of her neck. "Can I have you?"

Angel's breath thinned as her eyes drifted closed. Her head shouted that she needed to get to work, but her heart's trumpet blare demanded for her to say, "Yes."

His hands unlocked and instantly tugged at her robe's belt. The plush material opened, and his hands dipped inside. His touch was a gentle caress and a pleasurable torture.

He spun her around to face him. His dark, lazy gaze took its time roaming her body before a hand lifted to slide her robe from her shoulders.

Angel loved the way he looked at her. It gave her an incredible sense of power. She could make him say and do anything she wanted. Right now, she wanted him to make love to her. She wanted his body to erase her newfound doubt.

She moved closer, eliminating the already sparse space between them. It was then when she heard his shallow breathing. Smiling, she nipped at his lower lip.

With a groan, his lips settled on top of hers in blatant ownership.

Angel grabbed hold of him so that she wouldn't fall. When his tongue swept inside her mouth and rubbed erotically against hers, her body dissolved in his arms.

Damien's hands moved down her spine, rubbing, caressing along the way. He cupped her backside and lifted her onto her tiptoes until they were intimately rubbing against each other.

When their mouths parted, her lips tingled from his gentle attack.

"Is there a bed in this place?"

"Upstairs."

His brows lifted a fraction before he swept her into his arms. "Good, let's go try it out."

Maneuvering around boxes and oddly placed furniture, Damien and Angel made their way to her bedroom. They laughed as he worked his way around even more boxes to reach her queen-size bed.

He placed her gently in the center of the mattress and made quick work of eliminating his clothes.

At her raised brow, he remembered the most important item and removed a condom from his wallet. She smiled and lifted her hands toward him.

He went to her, starving for her touch.

Desire made Angel blissfully carefree. She simply couldn't get enough of Damien. The heat of his skin made her nipples hard, and she arched against him, begging without words for him not to stop his sweet torment.

Her breasts gained some relief when his mouth covered one in a rough suckle. The pleasure consumed her. His hand took hold of her other breast and gently rubbed the pads of his fingers across her sensitive nipple.

She sucked in a long breath and dug her nails into his shoulder blades.

Damien grunted against the painful pleasure she gave and then moved farther up her delectable body. Her skin was soft and smelled of strawberries. He slanted his mouth against hers, and her lips parted. Once again, her arms looped around his neck, her hands splayed against the back of his head.

Slowly his hand moved down between their bodies. He caressed her breasts and then traveled farther for his fingers to brush her navel. Their lips remained sealed as he shifted positions so his bold fingers could caress the soft, curly hair between her thighs before surging inside.

She gasped against his mouth and then moved in the same mind-altering rhythm as his stroking hand. When his pacing increased, she abandoned the sweet, addictive taste of his lips to thrash weakly among the pillows.

Damien's restraint broke at witnessing her wild response, and he wanted to take it a step further. He again repositioned so that each of her legs was draped over both of his shoulders, and then his mouth replaced his hand.

Angel cried out, and her hands automatically tried to push him away.

But Damien would not be deterred. The taste of her was intoxicating as he plunged his tongue in deeper. Soon her hands stopped pushing and started caressing the sides of his face. Her cries diminished to low whimpers, and then escalated again when her legs trembled around his ears.

She screamed out her release and tried to inch away from his greedy mouth, but he remained locked into position until another orgasm pitched her over the edge.

Damien climbed back above her with a cocksure grin, completely unprepared for when her hands drifted to his erection and she took him into her hot mouth.

He almost came instantly. Gritting his teeth, he closed his eyes and battled within himself for control. But as her skillful mouth continued to glide over him, he wasn't too sure he would win the fight. Cheating, he pushed her away and denied himself release.

Angel laughed when he forced her back against the pillows.

"You think that's funny?" he asked. He took his erection in hand and slid on the condom, placing his shaft at her entrance. No further.

She didn't answer, but smiled up at him.

Damien smiled back. "What's the matter? Cat got your tongue?"

In response, she squirmed against him in a silent offer.

But he wanted her to ask for it—beg for it.

Their gazes locked in private combat.

To maintain his edge, he took great care in rubbing his chest against her nipples and pressed the head of his arousal along her entryway.

She strained against him, once again feeling that throbbing ache in the center of her feminine core. As he refrained, the ache radiated outward until her head seemed to pound in the same insistent rhythm.

"Damien," she panted in sweet desperation.

"Hmm?" he asked, leaning in for a kiss. His shaft pressed a mere centimeter into her warmth.

"I need you," she whispered.

"You need me to do what?" He slipped in another centimeter.

Her breathing echoed loud and hard in her

ears. No one could stand such torture. Another threat of tears returned, and this time one slipped from the fan of her lashes and rolled down the side of her face. "Please, make love to me."

"My pleasure." Gently, he slid in until he was surrounded and caressed by her warm, slick passage. Damn, she felt good. He rocked against her, swearing that each time he sank into her it felt better than the last.

Angel moved against him while her fingers playfully stroked the broad span of his back, but her lips broke contact when his hips quickened and his thrust grew rough.

Damien's fingers flowed through her hair as he pulled her head back, and sealed their mouths together. He became mindless to everything but her.

Their bodies rocked together in a wild marathon, and after a long while, they grew moist with sweat.

Angel took the top position. Her exuberant bounce against him drew a stream of guttural moans and desperate calls for the Almighty from Damien.

His hands tightened around her waist, and he knew he was ready to climax. With great speed and agility, he reclaimed the dominant position and reached between their joined bodies to stroke the nub between her velvety folds. She chanted his name in the throes of her orgasm and only then did he allow himself to surrender to his own.

His head rested against the crook of her neck as he groaned low in his throat. It took a moment before his heart stopped slamming against his ribcage, another moment before his breathing returned to normal.

When she stirred, he was ready again. "You're going to be the death of me," he moaned.

"C'mon, Mr. Duracell. Recharge." She rewarded him with the laugh he loved so much. And he concluded that Nigel was right. All Damien needed in life was laughter and strawberries.

CHAPTER
24

With a Cheshire cat smile, Broche continued to watch the townhouse Black had entered.

After spending so much time trying to get into the head of his nemesis, Broche wasn't sure he was any closer to understanding the man than when he started.

He had staked out Black's estate again last night and followed Damien to the small townhouse this morning. It was one thing to read and see pictures of Black's possessions; it was another to see them in person. The house reminded him of the yacht, the yacht reminded him of the flock of expensive racecars. Broche wanted these things for himself.

It was just after eight A.M. when Black and his stunning beauty emerged from the townhouse.

Broche put away his box of Krispy Kreme donuts and started his car.

Black walked his mysterious woman to one of the cars in the driveway and then pulled her up against him for a long kiss.

Broche's jealousy deepened.

When the kiss ended, he was subjected to watching a few more loving pecks and open flirtations before the woman eased into her Camry and Black jumped into the sleek Italian car parked next to hers.

After the vehicles pulled out and headed toward the main street, Broche opted to follow Black's lady.

Angel's eyes darted again to her rearview mirror, immediately picking up the white Honda tailing her. "Damn it, Sean," she mumbled under her breath. This meant he knew about Damien. She cursed again and suspected it was just a matter of time before World War III started.

This was the last straw. She mumbled a few more expletives and reached for the cell phone in her purse.

After calling the restaurant, his home, and even his cell phone, Angel was unable to locate her brother. "Damn it." Her eyes jerked back to her rearview mirror and the car tailing her.

She arrived at work and rushed to gather her things to get inside.

The Honda parked a few spaces away, and to her surprise the man stepped out of the car. It wasn't Mutt or Jeff. In fact, the balding white man didn't look like anyone who would be employed by Sean—but he certainly looked familiar.

Turning, she headed toward her building. Her mind whirled trying to place the man's face.

She hurried her footsteps.

So did the man behind her.

When Damien returned home, Jerome was waiting for him in his study along with boxes of new equipment.

"I just love technology," Jerome cooed as he demonstrated a pair of nightshades that gave the ability to see invisible alarm beams.

"Do we know which room the merchandise is going to be held in?" Damien asked, scanning the floor plans again.

"I've narrowed it down to two possibilities." Jerome took his marker and circled two different areas. "Lucky for us the rooms are close together."

"What about the security guards?"

Jerome continued to point. "The red marks are the security posts." He reached into his back pocket and withdrew a folded slip of paper. "I got this from Amber. These are the times they perform their routine checks."

"Every twenty minutes a different guard secures the area?"

Jerome nodded.

Shaking his head, Damien whistled low. "That's going to be a tight squeeze."

"Except," Jerome held up a finger, "At nine P.M., they perform a shift change."

"That's a strange hour."

"Hey, don't look a gift horse in the mouth."

Damien shared a thin smile. "Okay, how much time does that buy us?"

"An additional fifteen minutes."

"That's a little better." Damien nodded and glanced over the blueprints again. "Not much—but better."

"I'm glad you approve." Jerome took the plans and rolled them up. "I'll be parked three blocks up. I found a nice spot that won't draw attention."

"Three blocks?" Damien's gaze shot up. "I have to travel three blocks to the getaway car? Isn't that a different zip code?"

"Hey, it's a heavily populated area with frequent police patrols. But if you travel through the back alleyways like I showed you, the trip might seem like two blocks."

"Gee, thanks."

Jerome shrugged. "Don't mention it." He began packing his bags. "I heard Rock came by to see you yesterday."

"What are you two—pen pals?"

"We talk via emails. He told me that you offered him a job," he said, laughing.

Damien joined in. "It was the least I could do for an old friend."

"Don't ever let it be said that you don't have balls."

"That was pretty gutsy of me," Damien said, shaking his head. "But hey, we're all old friends, right?"

"Yeah, just don't push that friendship crap with him too far."

Damien's brows rose in mild curiosity. "Is this your advice or his warning?"

"Both."

Releasing a long, tired breath, Damien nodded and lowered himself into his chair as his brain switched gears to Sean and his gambling problem. "I had an interesting conversation with Angel this morning," he said, leaning back to look at Jerome.

"Oh? She didn't happen to give you the security codes at her museum, did she?"

Damien's jaw twitched in annoyance. "I told you, I'm not using her."

Jerome rolled his eyes. "You and your strange ethics," he muttered.

"What's that supposed to mean?" Damien asked, defensively.

"It means between her brother and you, the

woman is getting screwed nine ways to Sunday. If you're not going to use her, then you need to leave her alone."

"There's no way she'll ever find out."

"Okay." Jerome held up his hands. "I know you're an expert at keeping things on the down low, but women have a funny way of finding things out. Trust me."

Angry, Angel stormed into her office and called every number she knew for Sean and finally reached him at the restaurant. "You have some nerve," she thundered the minute her brother came onto the line.

"Angel, I'm so glad you called."

"You have exactly ten minutes to call your dogs off before I go to the police and file a complaint. I'm tried of having your guard dogs follow me wherever I go. I'm a grown woman now, not some damn child."

"What are you talking about?"

"You know exactly what I'm talking about." She jabbed a fist into her hip and paced her office. "The old white guy you have tailing me. Get rid of him."

"Angel, I swear. I don't have any idea what you're talking about."

"Ten minutes, Sean. Or I'll call the police." She slammed the phone down and seethed under her breath with rage.

She barely had a chance to regroup when the

phone rang again, but like a professional actress, she answered in her best professional voice. "Angel Lafonte."

"Hello, Angel."

She smiled, for there was no mistaking Damien's rich, smooth baritone. "Hello, sweetheart."

"Ooh, sweetheart. I must be making progress if I've been assigned a pet name."

"Which is more than I can say."

"Actually, I was thinking about calling you hellcat."

"What?" She laughed.

"All one has to do is look at the scratches on my back to understand."

Embarrassment blazed up Angel's face as a wide grin spread across her lips. "Please, don't tell anyone that."

"My lips are sealed." His soft chuckle sent a low wattage of electricity crackling through her system.

"I want to see you tonight," he said.

"Mmm," she moaned. "I want to see you, too."

"My place, your place, or the Ritz?"

She was about to pick one when another line on the phone rang. "Hold just a minute." She placed Damien on hold and answered the other line. "Angel Lafonte."

"Hello, Angel. Tevin Merrick. I hope I didn't catch you at a bad time."

Her heart dropped. "Hello, Mr. Merrick."

"Tevin. Please call me Tevin."

His deep chuckle vibrated in her ears. "What can I do for you . . . Tevin?"

There was a slight pause before he answered, "I called to see when was a good time to pick you up this evening."

She frowned. "There must be some misunderstanding. Mr. Merrick. I can't go out with you. Didn't my brother tell you?"

"He called me. Said something about you two having some kind of disagreement." The man's tone deepened. "But he also stressed how much he wanted to pay back the five million he owed me."

Angel choked. "Five . . . million?"

"He didn't tell you?"

Her head pounded. "Mr. Merrick. I have to go."

"Ms. Lafonte—"

"I-I can't talk now." She slammed the phone down and then stared at it with incredulous eyes. "Five million dollars?"

She took deep breaths to stop the room from spinning around her, and when her heartbeat finally returned to normal, she snatched up her purse and bolted from her office. "I have a few errands to run," she informed Russell, her part-time intern. "I'll be back by lunch."

Angel was more than halfway to Lafonte's before she remembered that she'd left Damien on hold. However, she just made a mental note to apologize later. When she stormed into Lafonte's, she bypassed Lea at the hostess stand and made her way to her brother's office.

She bolted inside, causing Sean and some curly-haired waitress to jump from one of the corners.

"Angel?" Sean said, straightening his shirt and seemingly unaware that more than half of it was unbuttoned. "I'm glad to see you."

"I'm sure that's about to change." She glared at the woman behind him. "Do you mind giving us a moment alone?"

"Uh, sure." The woman quickly wiggled her feet back into her pumps and then rushed out of the room.

When the door closed, Angel leveled her gaze back on her brother. "You owe Merrick *five million* dollars?"

Sean's plastic smile melted. "He called you."

"Damn right he did. He called wanting to know about our date."

"Angel, you've got to do this for me. Otherwise he's going to kill me. I don't have his money."

"Sell the restaurant."

"I can't do that. It's all I have."

"So you rather sell me, is that it?"

"No. I-it's more complicated than that. I owe the banks more than the businesses are worth. I'm mortgaged up to my eyeballs. I don't even know how I'm going to make payroll next week."

"How on earth did you get in this position?"

He stared at her. His discomfort at having to discuss such matters with her was evident in his body language.

Angel shook her head, a little crushed by how old he appeared—much older than his thirty-three years. He had done a lot for her, much more than she would ever be able to repay. "Someone like Merrick doesn't wipe out a five-million-dollar debt just for a date, Sean. What else does he want?"

Sean didn't answer; in fact his eyes dropped to the floor.

"You disgust me." She turned and jerked open her office door and bolted through. She willed her tears not to fall. This was a historic moment between her and her brother. It was the first time Sean had placed her on an auction block.

Things would never be the same between them again.

During the drive back to the museum, she lost the battle with her tears and gave in to a good cry before she reached for her cell phone and called her best friend. "Tonya, I need a favor."

CHAPTER
25

RUBENS HEIST ROCKS ART WORLD

Captain Johnson cursed a blue streak and smashed the Thursday morning paper down on his desk as he entered his office. "I don't believe this crap."

He picked up the phone and yelled at the voice on the other end. "Find out who's the lead detective on the Shafrazzi robbery." And just as abruptly, he slammed the phone down.

Johnson dropped into his chair and jerked opened his desk drawer to rummage for his bottle of antacids. He popped the last two cherry-flavored pills, tossed the empty bottle into the wastebasket, and then grabbed the paper again.

Peter Paul Rubens's *The Massacre of the Innocents*, which has an estimated worth of
seventy-five million dollars, was stolen
Wednesday night despite tight security at the
Shafrazzi Art Galley.

A quick rap sounded at his door. He looked
up to see one of his detectives gracing his door.

"Captain, there is someone here to see you."

"Not now—"

"Captain." Broche, in his disheveled glory,
rushed inside. "Have you seen this morning's
paper?"

Johnson exhaled. "Yeah, I saw it."

"So what do you make of it." Broche made
himself at home as he settled into the chair
across from Johnson. "You have any leads yet?"

Johnson glared at him. "I've only been in the
office for a few minutes."

"Well, I have an idea who might be involved."

"I just bet you do. Mind if I ask where *you*
were last night?"

Broche's grin widened as he boldly met
Johnson's angry glare. "Right here. Booked for
trespassing . . . again."

"You weren't."

"I was. Made bail about an hour ago. Seems
Black had a reason to get me out of the way last
night. I never said that the man wasn't smart."

"Or he simply doesn't like you nosing
around his property."

Johnson jerked open his drawer again and this time he took two Excedrin dry.

"Why won't you take a closer look at the man?"

Johnson stood up and straightened his jacket, but loosened his tie for more oxygen. "Sure, let's take a trip over there right now. I bet he's just dying to confess."

"Are you telling me that you're not going to pursue a lead?"

"What lead? All we have is your accusations. And need I remind you that for years you've been unable to prove Black has done anything wrong?"

Broche's jaw set in a stubborn line.

Johnson jerked away from him. "Now get out of here. I have work to do." His line phone beeped before a voice filled the office.

"Captain?"

Johnson snatched up the phone. "Yeah." He listened and then grabbed a pen and paper. "Lieutenant Parks. Is he still down there?" He nodded. "All right. I'm on my way." He hung up.

"Are you going to the gallery?" Broche asked.

"I fail to see how any of that is any of your business. Frankly, I'm considering filing charges against you myself for harassment. In fact, the next time I see you in my office, I might do just that."

Johnson gave him a final hard glare and rushed out of his office.

* * *

"Good morning, sunshine," Tonya sang as she entered Angel's apartment.

"I'm glad somebody thinks so," Angel mumbled.

"I brought croissants."

Angel's gaze swept along the streets before she closed the door.

"Is something wrong?"

Angel waved off her concern. "Just seeing if anyone is watching."

"Sean?"

"I don't think so. It's probably a luxury he can't afford any longer."

Tonya frowned as she looked over at her friend. "Damn, girl. You look like you've been run over by a Mack truck.

"I feel like it, too." She massaged the side of her neck as she led the way to the kitchen.

"Don't worry. I can't stay long. I have a ten o'clock flight to New York—private jet."

"Oh? Ms. Big Shot."

"Business not pleasure. By the way, this is yours." She held up an envelope. "Cashier's check."

Angel took the envelope. "Thanks. I can't tell you how much this means to me.

"Hey, we're friends, right? I rub your back, you rub mine."

"I did it to help Sean. Though I don't know why."

"I'm trying to understand it myself." Tonya

opened the baker's box while Angel meandered to the cabinets.

"I hope you don't mind paper plates. I still haven't had time to unpack the dishes."

"No problem." Tonya glanced around. "But you might want to do something soon about all these boxes. Someone could hurt themselves around here."

"You don't have to tell me. I've tripped twice this morning alone. My ankle is killing me." She handed her friend a plate. "By the way, do you know any good private investigators?"

"Why—what's up?"

Angel slumped onto a stool at the breakfast bar and weighed how much she wanted to tell her friend. "There was this guy tailing me a few days ago. I can get a picture of him from the museum's security cameras, but I want to know who he is."

Tonya's features soured. "Are you sure he doesn't work for your brother?"

"Anything is possible but Sean is denying it." Angel selected a croissant.

"Do you believe him?"

She shook her head. "I'm not sure, but better safe than sorry. He might work for that creep Merrick. Can you see what you can come up with?"

"Sure. I don't see why not. Get me the picture and I'll see what I can do."

* * *

Captain Johnson arrived at the Shafrazzi Art Gallery in just under ten minutes, and just as he suspected, the entire block was filled with news vans and reporters. Who could blame them? Atlanta had never experienced a robbery of this magnitude.

Johnson parked his car and then maneuvered his way through a throng of people to get to the gallery's front door.

"I was surprised to hear you were coming down here." Lieutenant Parks, a tall, robust white man, scratched the back of his low buzz cut. "Whoever broke in knew what they were doing."

"Do we have any fingerprints?"

"Hell, this is a gallery. We have a whole mess of those. That's not going to help us."

"What time was the painting stolen?" Broche butted in.

Johnson turned and glared at the Frenchman.

"Captain, this man says that he's with you," an officer said, pointing at Broche.

"This isn't your office," Broche chimed good-naturedly.

"Has anyone ever told you that you're a pain in the ass?"

"My ex-wife."

Parks cleared his throat and regained Johnson's attention. "The theft was discovered last night," Parks answered, oblivious to the tension between Broche and Johnson. He led them to the wall where only an empty frame hung.

Parks glanced at Johnson. "Most of us think this was an inside job. The cameras didn't catch a thing. We're still working on that right now. But I bet some high-tech geek is somewhere laughing his pants off over that one."

"Why an inside job?" Broche asked, ignoring Johnson.

"We believe the thieves or thief broke through the construction site for the new library which is attached to the gallery. They apparently forced their way onto the site, then climbed over the rooftop until they reached the gallery and broke through the glass ceiling. Whoever it was used one the ladders from the construction site as well, because we found it and some rope up there. So we figured they used it to lower into the gallery and snatch the painting."

"What about the alarm system?"

"That's just it. It's off for the moment due to the construction. The new director, Craig Mitchell, said a new system was to be installed after the renovation. Only someone working on the inside would have known that. The security guards are the only people who had the time and the opportunity. Everyone on duty that night is still down at the precinct for questioning. Something on this scale, we're not letting them go until they start singing or rolling over on their own mothers."

Johnson cut his eyes to Broche, but he was too busy looking around.

"The roof is classic Black," he announced suddenly and then met Johnson's glare.

"Who's Black?" Parks asked.

"You don't want to know," Johnson huffed, tossing a warning to Broche not to say another word.

CHAPTER
26

The moment Captain Johnson returned to the precinct, every cop he passed made a point to tell him that Police Chief Chester Woods was searching for him.

"The day just keeps getting better," Johnson mumbled. He wasn't in the mood for an old-fashioned butt chewing, but his hope for escape dashed when Woods's brass bullhorn voice attacked him from behind.

"Johnson, my office now."

Johnson's broad shoulders deflated as he turned to face the chief.

Woods, who stood more than a foot shorter than him and wore a year-round tan, impaled him with a pointed gaze.

"Yes, sir," Johnson said.

Woods's eyes swept to Broche. "And bring

our favorite Frenchman with you," he added with enough sarcasm to choke a horse. He grunted and stalked away without waiting for either of them to respond.

Broche and Johnson's weary gazes shifted toward each other.

Quite frankly, Johnson was sick of dealing with the cocksure man and was positive Broche felt the same about him.

Seconds later, they sat tense in Woods's office, appearing as though they were career-long partners.

"Gentlemen," Woods said as he leaned back in his chair, "we have a situation." He bridged his hands and bounced the balls of his fingertips together. "Actually, it's more like a mess. Either one of you have any ideas about how I should go about cleaning it up?"

Johnson had learned long ago to recognize Woods's rhetorical questions and remained quiet.

Broche followed his lead.

"Let's start with you," Woods said pointedly at Broche. "Do you make a habit of breaking the law where you come from?"

Broche looked at Johnson, no doubt hoping for some type of sign to how he should answer. When the room remained quiet, he finally croaked out a "No."

"Glad you took the time to think about it, but two arrests in the past month say otherwise." Woods paused, and then picked up a folder from his desk. "I contacted your former superior in Paris. To my surprise, he has nothing but good things to say about you."

Broche smiled.

"*Except*, he did mention your obsession with Damien Black. Is this true?"

Broche's smile faded. "It's not an obsession."

Johnson palmed his head, but managed not to groan through this torture.

One side of Woods's thin lips quirked and became a caricature of a smile. "And what would you call it?"

"A determination to see justice," Broche said, lifting his chin.

Woods's brows cocked skeptically. "Is that right?" He glanced to Johnson. "Are you riding shotgun with Pierre here?"

"No, sir," Johnson answered, straightening himself in his chair.

"Then do you want to tell me why when I spoke with Lieutenant Parks a few minutes ago, he said that you allowed this man access onto a crime scene?"

"Lieutenant Broche—"

"Ex-lieutenant, if I'm not mistaken," Woods corrected.

"Yes, sir." Johnson shifted in his chair. "Mr. Broche sort of misrepresented himself when he came onto the crime scene. I didn't bring him."

Woods glare returned to the Frenchman. "Is that correct?"

"Well—"

"Yes or no," Woods prompted.

"Yes."

Woods's gaze shifted to Johnson. "So why hasn't he been arrested?"

"Quite frankly, I don't think arresting him does any good."

"Look, Chief," Broche cut in. "I know who robbed the Shafrazzi Gallery. I've been trying to warn Captain Johnson about this for weeks now."

"Are you telling me he told about this robbery before it happened?"

Johnson bit back his irritation. "No. Broche was arrested for trespassing on Mr. Damien Black's estate. His reasoning is because he believes Black is an international thief."

"Damien Black?" Woods asked. "The one you're obsessed over?"

"I'm not—"

"Can it." Woods came around the front of his desk and leaned against the middle, but he kept his gaze centered on Broche. "I want you out of my city within forty-eight hours."

Broche fell silent.

"Do I make myself clear, Jacques?"

Broche's angry features hardened. "The name is Louis Broche—not Pierre, Frenchie, or Jacques." Broche pulled at his collar, his face a blazing shade of red.

At least the man had balls, Johnson thought. Big ones.

Unimpressed, Woods crossed his arms. "I'm still waiting."

Broche balled his hands. "Look, there's no point of thinking that someone else pulled this job. Monsieur Black should be your only suspect."

"You really are a broken record." Woods frowned.

"Has Captain Johnson even shared with you what I'd discovered about Black's past? Do you know who the man really is?"

Woods's gaze cut to Johnson. "What's he talking about?"

Johnson opened his mouth, but Broche cut him off.

"Black's real last name is Blackwell. His father was a famous art thief, James Blackwell."

There was a long silence before Woods asked Johnson. "Is this true?"

"It doesn't mean anything," Johnson said.

The changes in Woods's features were dramatic. "James Blackwell," he repeated. "I remember that case. Whatever happened to him?"

Johnson shrugged. "He served a few years until he hooked up with the right lawyer with the right appeal. Once he was released he disappeared until his obituary showed up in some Italian paper some years back."

"Humph." Woods's forehead creased as he mulled over the situation. "You have to admit, Johnson, this is a very compelling bit of information."

Broche smiled. "I thought the same thing."

Johnson remained quiet.

Finally, Woods nodded in decision. "We have to start somewhere. Maybe it wouldn't hurt if we checked him out a bit more. Maybe even some of the people he knows."

"Actually," Broche spoke up again. "I know just the woman we need to see."

According to Angel's calendar, the following week was filled with press releases and interviews for her grand event. Being she was somewhat of a private person, public appearances had always been hard for her, but a necessary evil.

By two o'clock her stomach's growl for nourishment forced her to try and sneak ten minutes to eat her packed lunch at her desk, but before she could take a bite the phone rang again.

Groaning she snatched it up. "Angel Lafonte."

"Hello, Angel."

She smiled at the sound of Damien's smooth voice.

"Hey, good-looking," she cooed. "Whatcha doing?"

"Nothing much. I'm just sitting here missing

you. I was thinking that maybe we could go to Oscar's tonight for dinner."

"Mmm," she moaned. "That sounds good." Her gaze fell to the number eight on her calendar, and a small sigh whistled through her teeth. "But I can't. Not tonight."

"Oh?"

His disappointment dripped into her ears. "I've already made plans."

"With your brother?"

"How about tomorrow night?"

"Tomorrow night sounds great. I look forward to it. Shall I pick you up?"

A light rap at the door jarred her from her private world with Damien.

Russell, her college intern, poked inside and whispered, "Some cops are here to see you."

An instant frown anchored her lips. She opened her mouth to tell Russell to have them wait a minute, but suddenly two men appeared behind him. Shock rushed through her as her gaze bounced between her visitors.

"Angel?" Damien inquired.

"Just a sec," she whispered into the phone.

The men walked around the intern and planted themselves in the center of her office.

Russell shrugged apologetically, and then mouthed the word "Sorry."

Though displeased, she nodded with understanding and watched as the young man slinked out of the office.

"I'm sorry, but I'm going to have to call you back," she told Damien in her best professional voice.

"You can't talk right now?" The previous huskiness to his tone also lifted.

"That's right. I'll have to call you back later." She quickly hung up the phone and looked at the two men with trepidation and confusion. "What can I do for you gentlemen?"

The tall, broad-shouldered, black man then stepped forward and flashed his badge. "Sorry to have interrupted you, Ms. Lafonte. I'm Captain Roderick Johnson." He swept a hand toward his partner. "This is Mr. Broche."

Her confusion remained rooted in place as she stared at them. "Captain? I didn't know captains made field trips."

"I guess you could say that this is a special occasion."

Broche moved forward. "We came to ask you a few questions about Damien Black."

After a long pause, she crossed her arms and decided to play along. "What about him?"

"Have you seen the paper this morning?" Broche asked, removing the bundle beneath his arm and placing the paper on her desk beside her sandwich.

She didn't look at it. "Yes."

Broche and Johnson glanced at each other.

"Look, Ms. Lafonte," Johnson took over, "There's no real easy way to ask these questions, so we'll just get to the point. What's your relationship with Damien Black?"

Her jaw hardened at the invasion of her privacy. "I fail to see what business it is of yours."

"Ma'am, we're doing our jobs."

"Is that right?" She leaned back in her chair and crossed her legs and arms. "And what exactly *is* your job?" Her gaze leveled with Broche's and then with Johnson. "To pry in my personal life or try to get me to *betray* a friend?"

Johnson froze under her stare.

Broche laughed. "You looked like more than just friends yesterday."

"And you looked more like a Peeping Tom than a cop. Or should I say ex-cop?"

Broche's brows gathered.

"I do my homework."

"If you two are finished, maybe we can move on," Johnson said and waited for their gazes to fall away from each other.

Johnson drew in a breath. "We were talking to Russell outside and he told us about a charity ball the Shafrazzi Art Galley hosted three weeks ago. Did you attend it?"

"If you talked with Russell, then you know that I did."

"Did Black go with you?" he asked.

It was a direct question she didn't know how to sidestep.

"Ma'am, this would be a lot easier on you if you just cooperate with us. We're not saying that he's guilty of anything."

"But you're suspicious of him?"

"With good reason," Broche cut in.

Johnson turned toward the Frenchman. "Will you let me handle this?"

"You guys are way off base. Damien Black is not a thief," she assured them.

Broche shrugged. "His father was one."

Angel's gaze jerked back to him. "What?"

"Have you ever heard of Le Fantôme?"

"Of course I have. A lot of people in this business have." She waited for Broche to continue and then slowly caught on.

"You think that Damien Black is Le Fantôme? Are you insane?"

Broche clamped his mouth shut, but Johnson threw him an angry glare.

To Angel, Johnson said, "None of Mr. Broche's accusations has been proven. How long have you known Black?"

She hesitated and wondered at what game he was playing at, but at dark plea in his eyes she answered, "Not long."

"Were you with him last night?"

She hesitated. "Why?"

He huffed out a breath. "Maybe we're totally off base and maybe we're not, but you do have a lot at stake."

Angel frowned, not sure where he was going.

"There's quite a few expensive art pieces here at the museum, and aren't you having a big exhibit next month?"

Her breath caught in her throat.

Johnson continued. "About how much do you think the collection is worth?"

Uneasiness crept up the ladder of her spine. Of course she knew how much; she'd been on the phone with insurance companies all morning.

"A guess," he encouraged.

"Over a hundred million."

Playing the devil's advocate, Broche whistled low and made tsking sounds. "That's a lot of money."

Angel shifted in her chair.

Johnson continued. "I have another question."

"Just one more?" she asked, irritated.

"Maybe two." He smiled. "Where did you meet Mr. Black?"

Angel didn't answer.

"Any chance that your meeting was . . . prearranged?"

The two men had finally maxed out her patience. "What is it that you want from me?"

"I think Black is going to hit this museum next," Broche blurted out. "It makes sense. A beautiful new art director meets up with a handsome art thief. Is it romance or is it business? What do you think?"

She swallowed her retort, but her body trembled with rage. "I think it's time you left, gentlemen."

"Just stay alert," Johnson said in a softer voice. "If you learn anything or suspect anything I want you to call me." He reached inside his jacket pocket and withdrew a card. "Call me day or night."

"Spy on him?" She laughed at the incredible idea. "You want me to spy on him?"

To her surprise, Johnson kept his eyes leveled on hers. "It's not like you don't have a vested interest." He shrugged. "Who knows? He might be innocent." And then his brows rose. "And he might not. Are you willing to risk the exhibit to find out that you were wrong?"

CHAPTER
27

The rest of the day passed in a blur. No matter how hard Angel tried, she couldn't concentrate during her scheduled meetings and business calls; she couldn't get Captain Johnson's voice and Broche's hard glare out of her head.

Why would they choose her to spy on Damien? What made them think that she would?

She didn't like Broche, and Johnson confused her. One minute he sounded like he didn't believe Damien was guilty of anything, and in the next instant he sounded determined to put Damien behind bars.

During rush hour traffic, Angel watched the sky swell and darken with unshed rain and found it ironic how it mirrored her mood.

For a month, she had done little more than

think about Damien. She kept catching herself daydreaming about the way he kissed her, touched her, and made love to her. However, nothing compared to the way he made her feel.

"Do you believe in love at first sight?" he had asked her.

She hadn't until she'd met him.

Before Damien, she'd never believed she could find such happiness and contentment again. He was more than just tall, dark, and handsome. He was mysterious, adventuresome, and downright easy to be with. There was something else between them—something special.

Love. She grinned. Had she truly fallen in love in such a short time?

She pushed out an exhausted breath as her car rolled a few inches through the interstate gridlock. Like her brother, she never trusted the police—with good reason.

Why didn't she tell those cops to go to hell?

She should have.

Her cell phone's loud shrill startled her. Dread seeped into her bones when she read Sean's name from the caller ID. "Where are you, Sean?"

"Are you still mad at me?" he asked.

Angel frowned against the receiver. Her brother sounded strange. "I'll get over it," she said, though she wanted to shout a resonating yes into the phone.

"Look, Angel. I don't know how, but I swear

I'll make this up to you. In a few weeks I'll be back on my feet."

"What's happening in a few weeks?" Her shoulders slumped with worry at his hesitation. "Sean?"

"About Merrick—"

"Sean," she started, drawing a deep breath. "You need to see someone about your gambling problem." The silence was deafening. "Are you still there?"

"Yeah, I'm still here," he said.

"I'm saying this out of love. I'm not looking down at you, but you have a problem, and I want to help you address it."

"Angel, it's not as bad as you think."

"What—you're going to deny you have a problem?" A car horn blared from behind her, and Angel eased off the brake pedal to creep up another few feet. "Sean, just look at what you're on the brink of losing."

"I have it under control."

"Do you?" She shook her head when he didn't respond. "Look, we should have this conversation later. Face-to-face." Again he didn't respond, but she knew he still held the line. "I'll come to the restaurant tonight so we can talk and I can give you something."

He released another long, steady exhalation. "I don't know about tonight—"

"Hello?" She frowned when she realized the call had been dumped. "I'll just swing by later."

Pressing the end button on her cell phone, she braced herself for her next challenge: talking to Damien.

"Today in local news, the Atlanta Police Department are still baffled over the heist of Rubens's *The Massacre of the Innocents* from the Shafrazzi Art Gallery last night. Art Director Craig Mitchell held a press conference just moments ago announcing a ten-million-dollar reward—"

Damien switched off the television and swung his gaze over to Jerome. "Well, I guess that's that."

"You don't want to watch the rest of it?"

"I don't see a point to it, do you?" He winced and sucked in a deep breath as he removed his swollen foot from a tub of iced water.

From beside him in the den, Jerome whistled low and shook his head. "Now that looks painful. I told you not to make that jump."

"Are you going to gloat or cheer me up?"

"Don't see why I can't do both," he said, dropping onto the leather sofa beside him. "I know you take good care of yourself and all, but our bodies aren't what they used to be. You can't keep pulling the same stunts."

"I'm only thirty-six."

"Which is a far cry from sixteen."

Damien's lips curved upward. "I still pulled it off, didn't I?"

Jerome's disposition soured. "Just barely." He chugged from his bottled beer.

Nigel suddenly appeared at the den's archway. "Ms. Lafonte is here to see you."

Surprise tingled through Damien's body. "Show her in." He pushed himself up from the sofa, careful to shift his weight to his good foot.

A few seconds later, Angel breezed into the room wearing a powder blue business suit that was as smart as it was sexy.

The pain in Damien's foot diminished at the mere sight of her. "Well, hello. What a pleasant surprise."

"Hi. I, uh, hope I'm not interrupting anything," she said, looking from him to Jerome.

"Of course not." He, too, glanced at Jerome. "My friend here was just leaving."

Jerome nodded with a big smile but didn't move.

Damien swatted him on the back. "That means you."

"Huh?" Jerome jerked his gaze to Damien, and then winced in embarrassment. "Oh, yeah. That's me. I was just leaving." He picked up his basketball and gulped down the rest of his beer. "I'll hook up with you later, D." To Angel, he winked. "It was nice seeing you again."

"It was good seeing you, too," she said, smiling.

Jerome nodded and still didn't move.

Damien cleared his throat.

"Oh, yeah. Right. Bye," Jerome said and rushed from the room.

Angel laughed. "He's something else."

"No argument here." Damien reached over to the side of the sofa for his lion head cane. As he started toward her, her eyes widened.

"What happened to your foot?"

"Basketball. More accurately, my lame attempt at a slam dunk."

Now her brows lifted in disbelief as she helped narrow the gap between them. "I didn't know you played."

He shrugged. "There's a lot you don't know about me."

Though he was teasing, Damien caught a strange glint in her eyes a second before she looked away. "Is there something wrong?"

Her lips curled but they didn't quite resemble a smile. She hedged a bit and appeared unsure. Only bad news came with a look like that, and Damien braced himself.

"Come on, you can tell me."

She shook her head. "Look, I can't stay long. I guess I just came over to apologize for not being able to call you back."

Damien blinked at the obvious lie. "No need to apologize. I know you're a busy woman." He smiled but didn't feel it.

"Yeah, it's been a little crazy." She forced out an exhalation and appeared thoughtful for a long moment before struggling for a beginning again. "I know we haven't known each other very long, but I want you to know"—she met his gaze again—"you can trust me. With anything."

Her delicate features held a level of intensity and conviction that touched him, but he was also puzzled by the declaration.

"That's always good to know," he said softly.

She nodded, but looked disappointed in his answer. "Well, I guess I better get going." She glanced at her watch. "Dinner tomorrow?"

He nodded as well. "Early. Seven o'clock. I'm planning a surprise."

"I'll be ready." She turned and walked away.

He watched her for a moment. "You know," he said, stopping her at the archway. "That trust runs both ways."

Angel faced him again with her brows suspended in mild curiosity.

Damien shrugged again. "If you ever want to talk about anything. I'm here."

A new smile fluttered to her lips, and this one appeared genuine. "I'll remember that."

Angel's mind swirled with reprimands of should'ves and could'ves as she backtracked through the city's busy highway. No doubt Damien now considered her a complete nutcase. "I just came over to apologize for not being able to call you back," she quoted herself and rolled her eyes skyward.

A while later, traffic dissipated, and her mad dash to Lafonte's was uninterrupted by flashing blue lights. Once at the restaurant, she was surprised to see such a large dinner crowd.

"Good evening, Angel." The same curly-haired blond she'd seen with her brother the other day greeted her at the hostess stand. "Will you be dining here this evening?"

Angel forced an amicable smile. "No, I just need to speak to Sean."

"Sean?"

Angel scooted out of the way of a large crowd being led to their table. "I'm sure he's busy, but it'll only take a few minutes."

"But Sean's not working tonight."

She frowned. "He's not?"

"No. I believe he flew up to Vegas."

Angel flinched as if she'd been sucker punched. "What?"

Lea waltzed up to the hostess stand. "What's the holdup here?" she asked in low voice pinched with irritation.

"She's looking for Sean," the waitress responded with a shrug. "Isn't he in Vegas?"

Lea elbowed her and hissed under her breath, "Don't you know how to keep your mouth shut, Carrie?"

Angel swallowed her rage and cleared her throat. "When did he leave? I just talked to him not too long ago."

Lea shooed Carrie away and then smiled politely at Angel. "He said that he would be back Monday."

"Monday?"

Lea glanced behind Angel. "Hello, sir. Welcome to Lafonte's. Will you be dining with us this evening?"

"Yes," a male voice said. "I made reservations for two under Cummings."

Lea's finger strolled down the list of names in the reservation book.

Angel refused to be ignored. "Did Sean leave a number where he could be reached?"

"Have you tried his cell phone?" She marked through the diner's name and turned to grab two menus. "Of course, he might be up in the air by now."

"I don't believe this." Angel jerked away, struggling to contain her rage. "Where in the hell did he get the money to pay for the trip?"

"Ah, a question I ask myself often."

Angel stopped and looked over at a smiling Tevin Merrick.

"I came to speak with your brother but I'd rather talk to you instead." His smile widened as he approached her. "Won't you join me for dinner?"

CHAPTER
28

It was close to midnight, and Damien couldn't get Angel's strange behavior out of his mind. Though he hadn't known her long, he knew her well enough to know there was something she was trying to say. For a moment, he thought she had come over to end their relationship. Who knew—maybe Sean had found out about them.

He frowned and shook his head. If that was the case, Sean would be at his house by now threatening to wage a war. It had to be something else. But what?

The phone rang and startled him.

"Hello."

"I know it was you," a man's voice slurred onto the line.

Damien frowned. "Who is this?"

"You pulled another job." The man shared a

pathetic laugh. "I have to admit I'd thought better of you. So how much did that job pay?"

Damien finally recognized the voice and the familiar sound of slot machines. "Sean?"

"Ah, so you do remember me. That's good to know." Sean sighed. "How much did the Shafrazzi job pay you? Surely the one painting didn't bring you as much as I was offering for the Degas collection."

"What makes you think *I* pulled the job?"

Sean's laugh sounded odd. "Call it a hunch."

Damien laughed.

"I'm glad I amuse you." Sean sniffed. "I need this job, Black. My back is against a wall and I'm running out of time."

The line fell silent.

"Are you still there, Black?"

"Yeah, I'm here."

"I need you to do this job. Fifty-fifty. Right down the middle. What do you say?"

The desperation in Sean's tone surprised Damien.

"Sean—"

"No, no, no. Think about it." Sean sighed again. "I'll be back in town on Monday. Come by my office at noon. We'll discuss it then. Okay?"

Damien hesitated.

"Please. All I'm asking is that you think about it."

"All right."

"Good," Sean said, his relief evident in his voice. "See you Monday."

Damien hung up and stared at the phone. Sean's desperation bothered him. Mainly because he'd always been wary of desperate people. Leaning back, he remembered what Jerome had told him about Sean and his rumored gambling problem. Was that what this was all about? Had Sean's gambling backed him into a corner he couldn't get out of? At least it fit the puzzle because only a desperate man would steal from his family.

Damien stood and decided to go for a walk. With the use of his cane, he walked along the curvy cobblestone pathway through the garden. His restless thoughts returned to Angel and the job at the Atlanta High Museum.

The weight of his thoughts grew heavier. His father always said it was best to quit while ahead—especially in this business.

He smiled and thought of the time when his father was released from prison. It was hard for Damien to leave the boys' home, but Jerome, Peter, and even Rock found a way to remain tight—despite their differences.

Damien had never met a cooler person than his old man. He'd taught Damien about art, business, and even economics. Like supply and demand. Today art theft was a five-billion-dollar-a-year industry that mostly involved a bunch of rich people or private collectors, as they liked to be called, trying to outdo one another.

For a long time, Damien had no quarrels if someone wanted to pay him eight or nine figures for a painting. It wasn't like stealing food from someone's mouth. It was more like pampering some rich idiot.

Being the best was important to him. That was what his father had always preached. So he decided to go into the family business, and he brought along his second family. And for a time, they *were* the best. Only Rock kept his nose clean.

He did retire for a while and everyone went their separate ways. Jerome went on a marrying spree, Pete decided to go it alone but was caught, the Rock also married and couldn't stop blaming Damien for Pete's death, and then Damien lost his father.

He drew in a deep breath. Maybe it was time to settle down.

Angel's image surfaced from his memory, and he imagined her with children. He smiled and liked the thought of a tribe of kids bearing Angel's beautiful features.

"I don't believe this," he mumbled under his breath. "I've fallen in love with a woman I hardly know."

A twig snapped behind him, and Damien jerked around sharply. "Who's there?"

Jerome held up his hands as he suddenly materialized from out of the shadows. "Don't shoot."

"What the hell are you doing here?" Damien winced against the throb of his ankle. "Don't you have a life or something?"

"Not since my last divorce." He grinned. "Besides, I figured you might want to know what Broche has been up to."

Damien groaned as he rolled his eyes toward the heavens. "Let me guess. He's been spouting to the authorities that I'm the one responsible for the Shafrazzi heist?"

Jerome nodded.

"Well"—Damien shrugged—"Broche is nothing if not predictable."

"You didn't predict the rest."

Damien stilled, not liking his friend's expression and definitely not liking what he'd begun to suspect.

Jerome drew in a deep breath. "Broche talked to Angel."

Angel was little more than a zombie by the time she returned home. Dinner with Merrick hadn't been planned, but she couldn't stop her mild curiosity about just what was going on between him and her brother. Had Sean told her the truth about the money? If so, how was it that he could afford these trips to Vegas?

To be fair, it wasn't such a bad evening. There were no fighting off octopus arms or having to squeegee off slobbering lips. Then again, she was in a safe environment with the Lafonte's employees watching their every move.

The brief dinner ended with Merrick confirming her brother's story. And as she suspected, Sean's debt wouldn't be wiped out with her just agreeing to a date, but with her agreeing to become Merrick's mistress.

There were no words to describe the pain that revelation caused. Sean had a problem, a sickness, a disease, she kept telling herself. Though she believed the words, the pain refused to go away.

She pulled into her driveway and was startled when another car pulled up behind her.

Frowning, she got out her car the same time Merrick stepped out of his black Mercedes. He had followed her and she hadn't realized it.

"What are you doing here?" she asked.

A broad smile stretched across the man's features. "I just wanted to make sure that you made it home."

His answer as well as his presence freaked her out.

"That wasn't necessary."

"I thought that it was the gentlemanly thing to do after a date."

She stiffened as he approached her. "It wasn't exactly a date," she said.

"Then maybe the next time we go out, you'll consider it a date."

Next time? She didn't know what to say, and for the moment she didn't know what to do. If he attacked, two years of self-defense training gave her the confidence that she could handle herself.

"Well," he said with a smile too wide and broad to be trusted, "I had a lovely time."

She flinched when he reached for her hand and then watched warily as he brought it to his lips.

"Until next time," he said.

She didn't respond.

His disappointment smoothed out his laugh lines, and the result made him dark and foreboding, but in the next second, he was Mr. Charming again. "Who knows? Maybe next time you'll invite me in for a nightcap."

"Yeah, who knows?"

"Good night," he said and then headed back to his car.

Angel walked slowly to her front door. She slid her key into the lock, but waited patiently until she saw Merrick pull out of her drive.

They gave a final wave, him from his car and her standing inside the doorway. Only after she closed the door and locked it did she allow herself to slump in relief. "Thank goodness that's over with," she muttered under her breath.

Once again she maneuvered around the

boxes in the foyer and climbed the stairs to her room. But when she walked in and switched on the light, she emitted a gasp.

From across the room, Damien, cloaked in black, stared back at her. "Hello, Angel."

CHAPTER

29

"How did you get in?" Angel asked as she placed her hand across her racing heart. "What are you doing here?"

Damien's dark expression didn't change. "I came by to see you." He slowly moved away from the open window.

She took another step back. "But why did you break in?"

His lips transformed into a bemused grin. "I don't have a key." He stopped in the center of the room and continued to study her. "Don't be frightened. I would never harm you."

For some reason she believed him and relaxed. "This is a little unconventional, don't you think?"

His brows cocked. "You know I like to do things differently."

"I didn't see your car."

"I took a few precautions as necessary. I had to make sure I wasn't followed."

Tension returned to her body. "Who would want to follow you?"

"A little pain-in-the-ass Frenchman named Broche." His eyes locked on her. "Perhaps you know him?"

She lifted her chin while she contemplated her answer. "I've met him." To her surprise, his smile grew wider.

"I suppose he told you some wild stories about me?"

"I was thinking more along the lines of 'colorful' or maybe even 'interesting.'" She crossed her arms and stared at him. "Did you come here to tell me that none of it's true?"

"As a matter of fact, I did." Damien crossed his arms as well. "But while I was waiting for you and praying that you didn't ask that creep to come in, I decided you deserved the truth."

"The truth," she repeated. At his slow nod, she wondered if she was prepared for this. "What makes you think I can handle the truth?"

"Maybe it was something you said today. Your comment about being able to trust you." He moved toward her again, their gazes merged as one. "This was what you were referring to, wasn't it? You wanted to know if I'm a thief?"

She sucked in her breath. "Are you?"

He held her gaze. "Yes."

Angel's breath thinned in her lungs. The room spun beneath her.

"You're Le Fantôme—the art thief?"

He took another step toward her. "Ex-art thief. If it's of any consequence. I'm retired."

"Retired?" She laughed. "Is that why you still linger around museums?"

He frowned and looked at a loss for words.

Angel moved to a chair. She needed to sit down. "Broche said that you were dating me because you're planning to rob my museum. Is that true, too?" She looked at him.

"No." Damien gripped his cane and moved toward her. "I would never do that."

He lifted a hand to her cheek and caressed it with such tenderness, she regretted having to question him.

"I was drawn to you the moment you walked through the museum's doors soaked with rain."

Tears burned and obstructed Angel's vision. "I don't believe this."

"I know this is a lot to spring on you. But I figured if Broche has talked to you, then I owe you the truth."

Her gaze fell.

"I don't want to lose you," he said.

Her body trembled, and Damien stared down at her. She looked as if she was laughing and crying at the same time.

"If you only knew," she said.

Their eyes met again.

"There's so much I haven't shared with you." Her eyes searched his face. "There's a lot you don't know about me, my brother, the people we hang around."

"Actually . . . I do know Sean."

Her body stiffened. "Please tell me that you don't work for him."

"No. Although when I first learned who you were, I almost backed off." His hand returned to her cheek again. "But I couldn't. I'm aware of the kind of people your brother associates with, and believe me, I'm in no hurry to cross paths with any of them."

Angel's heart squeezed, and she couldn't stop her natural instincts to defend Sean. "I love my brother," she admitted. "Right or wrong. For good or bad."

"How do you think he would take us dating?"

"Badly," she answered. "Then again, judging by his behavior lately, I don't know. Right now, I'm afraid he's gotten himself into something that he can't get out of."

Damien frowned. "Are you mixed up in it?"

"Sort of." She stood and set her purse down on one of the many boxes. "However, getting a straight answer out of Sean can sometimes be an impossible task."

"Who was the man who brought you home?" he asked. "I didn't recognize him."

She rolled her eyes and stepped out of her

shoes. "Tevin Merrick. He's a friend of Sean's. One I hope I never have to see again."

"A friend of Sean's?" he questioned with a frown. "The great protector allowed you to go out with one of his friends?"

Angel puzzled over his reaction, but then smiled at the possibility of him being jealous. "I promise you, it's nothing serious."

Damien drew her into his arms. "Good."

Angel's body warmed to his possessiveness and even loved reading a certain level of need in his eyes. When was the last time a man had made her feel needed?

He closed the distance between them, leaned in, and lightly brushed his lips against hers.

This wasn't the time for her to lose herself. There were still questions to be asked and problems to be resolved, but who could think with such lips masterfully intoxicating her every thought?

She wanted to hold back, she should hold back, but her body had a mind of its own. Melting against him, she molded perfectly against the contours of his body. Were their bodies somehow made for each other?

Mindlessly, her arms slid up his chest and then looped around his neck to draw him even closer. Maybe if she held him tighter, the rest of the world would melt away. At least it was worth a try.

She barely remembered him undressing her,

but when he attempted to pick her up, she nearly found herself back on the floor. "Your foot," she gasped.

He laughed and held on to her to steady himself. "I guess I got a little carried away."

"Here, I'll help." She draped one of his arms around her shoulder. "Lean against me."

Damien did as she instructed, limped over to the bed, and sat down. "I bet I lost some serious romantic points on that smooth move."

"Don't worry. You have more than enough points to cover it."

"I haven't lost you?" Uncertainty crept into his voice.

Laughing, Angel settled her hands on her hips, seemingly unaware of the provocative pose she struck dressed in only her black panties and bra.

He groaned, reaching for her like a starved man set before a banquet. She hadn't rejected him as he'd feared. He didn't know what he would've done if she had.

Damien pulled her toward him and rested his head against her flat stomach. It was as if he lay in a field of fresh strawberries—a place he could live forever.

Soft, featherlike strokes brushed against the back of his head, and he languished in her tenderness.

Leaning his head back, he looked up at her

and was entranced by her desire-filled eyes.

Slowly, her head lowered until their lips were but a whisper away. He watched as her eyes searched his face.

With a groan, he captured her lips and pulled her down as he leaned back onto the bed. To-night she tasted like wine and peppermint, an interesting but heady combination.

Damien moaned at the feel of her fingers as they skimmed along the center of his chest, un-doing one button at a time. Soon after, she peeled back his shirt, ran her smooth hands across his chest, and then pulled at his trousers.

Never one to play submissive for long, he rolled her onto her back and claimed the domi-nant position. Just seeing her full breasts pressed against the lacy material of her bra made his erection throb.

He removed the bra and lowered his mouth to feast on her round mounds. His hands, how-ever, slipped inside her panties, and she opened to his probing fingers. She was warm, slick, and ready for him, but he refused to rush the moment.

She writhed against him, thrusting to match his hand's rhythm. He drew pleasure from lis-tening to her husky moans as they climbed up and down the musical scale.

He sucked a taut nipple between his teeth, and she gasped aloud and sank her nails into his back. He groaned but didn't alter his pacing. When her hips bounced up from the mattress, he knew she was seconds away from her first climax.

"Damien," she moaned, pulsing around his fingers and clawing at his shoulders.

He smiled, enjoying the way she trembled beneath him while trying to push away his probing fingers.

"I'm not through with you," he said.

Angel squirmed and begged for a moment to catch her breath.

Smiling, he finally relented and pulled his hand away. She only had the few seconds it took for him to remove his clothing and slide on protection before he returned.

The storm inside Angel renewed its force as Damien helped her remove her panties and positioned himself between her legs. His soft lips rained kisses up the column of her neck, along her jawline, and once again settled on her lips.

She could taste him forever and never grow tired. And at the brush of his erection against her thigh, she drew in a breath of anticipation.

"Angel," he whispered. "Look at me."

Her eyes fluttered open and focused on his handsome face. At that moment, she realized that he belonged to her and she to him. This dark, mysterious man was created just for her.

Damien entered her in one slow, deep thrust. Her body arched and adjusted to his size, but their eyes never severed contact. Synchronized, they moved together. Tears swelled as the luxurious feel of him consumed her. They had passed the realm of just having sex and ventured into the world of making love.

Angel had never experienced anything more beautiful.

No matter how deep or hard Damien thrust, he wanted more. He took all she gave and in return he poured all he had into her. And he prayed that it was enough.

The minutes mounted and their bodies grew damp with sweat, but neither wanted to end their trek to the finish line. But someone had to win the race.

Angel's body was the first to submit to a burgeoning climax. The walls of her slick passage tightened and her toned legs clamped around Damien's hips. And there went every ounce of his control.

Slipping his hands beneath her, he angled their bodies for each long, powerful stroke. His eyes squeezed shut and his teeth ground together.

A high-pitched gasp hitched in the back of Angel's throat, and then another and another as each orgasmic wave crashed within her.

Lost and desperate to reach the pinnacle, Damien's hips quickened to a manic pace, and he was caught up in the throes of an earth-shattering orgasm.

At long last he collapsed against her and

murmured her name repeatedly in the scented strands of her hair. He gathered her close and grew content with just holding her.

Angel snuggled closer, not sure of what to say or if she should say anything. He'd confided a lot of information to her tonight, and she very little. Now the hour was late and she didn't want to put forth the necessary brainpower to analyze all she'd learned.

Tomorrow, she promised, she would process everything and decide what she should do, what she should say, and how much she should confess.

CHAPTER
30

As the morning sun brightened with each tick of the clock, Damien watched Angel while she slept. Though he didn't think it was possible, his feelings for her had grown stronger than the day before.

He smiled and brushed a kiss against the center of her forehead, the tip of her nose, and then finally the soft petals of her lips.

She moaned, smiled, and snuggled closer.

How could he not want to do this every morning for the rest of his life? At thirty-six, Damien had found his reason for living.

There was no way he would do the museum heist. It was as Jerome had predicted—ethically impossible. Plus Damien now believed he had a reason to walk away from his dangerous and risky career forever.

At long last, Angel's lashes fluttered and then lifted to reveal her beautiful eyes.

"Good morning." She sighed, her breath still tainted with peppermint.

"It is now," he said, inching closer so she could feel his morning arousal.

"Oh," she cooed, her eyes sparkling.

Damien laughed and allowed her to push him onto his back, grab a packet from the nightstand, and roll a new condom on him. He stared up at her naked body as she straddled him.

"How long have you been waiting for me?" she asked, sliding him into her.

"All my life, sweetheart. All my life."

Sean didn't sleep all weekend. At least he broke even during his last trip to Vegas, which meant the whole thing was a waste of time. His endless calls to Angel's cell resulted in him just reaching her voice mail, while calls to her house gave him a fast busy signal. Where was she? Why had he agreed to fire Martin and James?

Pushing Lea's loving mouth away from his lap, he ended her attempt to take his mind off of things. He stood up from the couch and zipped his pants.

"Where are you going?" Lea asked, astonished.

"I have to do something. Go over there and check on her. Something."

"She's fine. Even if she is with Merrick, he's

not going to hurt her," she reasoned. "You've sent me out with him before. He's a complete gentleman when it comes to women."

His anxiety refused to budge. "Then why hasn't she called me?"

Lea stood up, wearing nothing but a garter belt, hose, and high heels. "Honey, I don't know. Maybe she got in late and she'll call you this morning."

At that moment the phone rang.

Sean rushed and snatched the hand unit off the receiver. "Where in the hell have you been?" he thundered prematurely.

"I didn't know you were looking for me," Merrick's deep baritone poured through the line.

Sean's heart tightened to the point of chest pains. "I was expecting someone else."

"I see." Merrick paused, and then continued. "I called to confirm the meeting at twelve. We are still on, aren't we?"

The meeting was the last thing on Sean's mind. What he wanted was to interrogate the slimy bastard on his sister's whereabouts. "Yeah, uh, the meeting is still on."

"Good. Then I'll see you at Lafonte's at noon."

Sean was about to lose his opportunity to question the man, but damn if he could get the words out of his mouth. "All right," he said. "I'll see you then."

The call ended with a soft click. Sean placed the cordless back into the cradle and balled his hands at his side. When had he turned into this sniveling coward? He was a stronger man than this. At least once upon a time he had been.

"Well?" Lea asked timidly from behind him.

He closed his eyes and sighed. "Put on your clothes. We have to get down to the restaurant."

The weekend was too short. Early Monday morning, while Angel took her shower, Damien decided to see what he could muster up in the kitchen. Granted, his cooking skills weren't the best in the world, but surely he could manage something as simple as breakfast.

In the refrigerator, he found turkey bacon, canned biscuits, and enough ingredients to make omelets. "Okay, this shouldn't be too bad," he said with a boast of confidence.

Inching along with his cane, he removed some papers and folders from the countertop and accidentally dropped them. Kneeling, he picked them and stacked them on the kitchen table, when his eyes snagged on a cashier's check.

"Where on earth did she get this kind of money?" he wondered, thunderstruck.

"Damien, where are you?" Angel's voice floated down the stairs.

"In here," he called out and quickly finished putting her things away.

She walked into the kitchen, wearing a white plush robe and a bright smile. "There you are. I thought you left me."

"Nah. I figured I'd help get some nourishment into your system before you start your day." He took her into his arms and gave her a quick kiss.

"That's awfully sweet of you." She glanced around. "I'd better help you find the skillets or you'll be in here all morning."

He chuckled. "That thought did cross my mind."

A half an hour later, the couple sat silently across from each other at the breakfast bar. Their frequent glances at each other were sweet on one hand and awkward on another. They had a lot to discuss and iron out, but the task seemed long and arduous.

Angel took another bite of her omelet and continued to wonder how to start the conversation. In the end, she decided to dive in and pray that the waters weren't too shallow.

"About your . . . job," she started, glancing across at him.

Damien's gaze jumped to hers, while his fork stopped in midair.

". . . and my job." She stalled and tried to unscramble the words in her head.

"Look, I know what you're going to say," Damien jumped in. Uncertainty managed to seep into his gaze. "I'm retired. I don't want you to ever think I'm using you in any way."

Her shoulders slumped in relief, but it wasn't exactly what she wanted to discuss. She labored over her speech while she finished breakfast.

"You know Broche wasn't the only person who came to see me yesterday."

Damien frowned. "Oh?"

"Yeah, a police captain accompanied him."

"Oh." Damien's gaze fell to his breakfast as a small grin massaged the corners of his lips. "Don't worry. Broche has pulled this stunt just about everywhere I go."

"Damien—"

The phone rang and Angel groaned at the interruption.

"That reminds me," he said. "Somehow we knocked the phone off the hook last night."

"That doesn't surprise me." She winked.

"You better answer that." Damien stood. "I'll clear the table."

She pushed up from her chair. "Damn, is there anything you don't do?"

"Yeah, windows."

Laughing, Angel rushed over to answer the wall unit. "Hello."

"Where in the hell have you been?" Sean's voice roared through the phone line. "Do you have any idea of how worried I've been?"

Angel's morning high crashed without warning. "Well, what do you know? It's my pimp calling."

"Very funny," he said, his tone hard with anger.

She sighed and glanced over her shoulder to find Damien watching her. She flashed him a smile in an attempt to ease his concern.

"That's it? You were tired? How come your phone was busy all night? Did Merrick spend the night? What the hell happened between you two? The whole staff told me about you two having dinner."

"Whoa, hold on a sec." Angel turned her back to Damien. "If I remember correctly, I was doing you a favor."

"Damn it, Angel. Don't tell me you've already slept with him. I swear to God I'll kill him."

"Spare me the dramatics," she hissed into the line, and then quickly tried to rein in her emotions. "I can't talk about this now. I'll come by later and we can talk then."

"Why can't you talk now? Is Merrick still over there?"

"What difference does that make? You wanted the man to write off your tab, right?"

Silence filled the line.

Angel drew in a calming breath, but could feel her frustrated tears burn the backs of her eyes. It was too hard trying to save her brother from his destructive ways. She took another glance at Damien. Hell, she had her own set of problems to fix.

"Look, I'll be there later. Okay?"

At her brother's long hesitation, she assumed he was going to turn her down.

"I'm sorry, Angel," he croaked. "I've messed up."

The raw emotion in his words finally caused a few tears to spill over her lashes. "Don't worry about it," she whispered. "We'll work it out."

Hanging up, she wiped away her tears and gathered herself before facing Damien. "I gotta get going. I have a lot to do today."

"Are you all right?" Damien asked, moving toward her.

"Yeah," she said, sidestepping his attempt to embrace her. She needed to think, and she couldn't do that in his arms. "We're still on for dinner tonight?"

He studied her and then nodded. "Sure. Seven o'clock?"

"Sounds great." Angel turned to lead him toward the front door.

"I think I better go out the back," he said, and then shrugged. "You never know who might be watching."

She nodded.

At the back door, she realized her behavior was coming off a little cold, but she couldn't help it. She needed time to think.

"See you at seven," she confirmed.

Damien smiled and leaned down for a kiss.

She stood still and struggled not to melt into him. They would never get out of the house if she did that.

When the kiss ended, she saw the haunting disappointment lingering in his eyes.

"Have a good day."

"You, too." She smiled and then closed the door behind him.

Broche saw the writing on the wall. He had worn out his welcome in the Atlanta Police Department. As usual, he was unable to convince anyone of Black's guilt in the Shafrazzi Gallery heist. After he'd gotten a little carried away in the interview with Ms. Lafonte, Captain Johnson refused to allow him to play tag during their investigation.

It was the same no matter where he went. Black either had an angel on his shoulder or a deal with the devil. Broche was inclined to believe the latter, and he also believed that Black would get away with this last robbery just as he had on countless of other jobs.

As he stared up at Black's estate, Broche's skin crawled with jealousy and envy. How much longer could he continue to play this cat-and-mouse game? How many more years would he invest in chasing a ghost?

He turned his attention to the passenger seat and leaned down to remove the metal box beneath it. Opening the box, he stared inside at the illegal Glock he'd purchased and wondered just how far he was willing to take this.

Damien arrived at Lafonte's an hour ahead of his scheduled appointment. He'd driven around the city for the past two hours and decided he had to talk to Sean now instead of later.

"Black, you're early." Sean jumped to his feet, his surprise evident in his expression.

"Sorry to impose," Damien apologized. He gripped the lion head cane and moved farther into the room.

Sean rushed over to the door and closed it. "No problem, no problem." He swept a hand out to a vacant chair. "Please have a seat."

"Actually, I think I'll remain standing," Damien said with a tight smile. There was something different about this Sean from the one he'd met with a month ago. His eyes were red, edgy—almost as if he hadn't slept since Damien had last seen him.

Confusion crept into Sean's features, but he managed a brave front. "I have to tell you that your money isn't here yet. My, uh, buyer won't be here until twelve."

Damien drew a deep breath and delivered the bad news. "I'm not taking the job."

Sean's smile melted away. "But why?"

"I mean I can't do it."

"B-but I agreed to the percentage." Sean's

eyes steadily grew wider. "That collection is worth millions."

"I know." Damien exhaled, wishing he could tell the man more. "I wish I could do this for you, but I can't."

Sean blinked and looked as if he was slowly coming out of his shock. "Is this your way of trying to squeeze me for more money?"

Damien laughed. "No, it's nothing like that. Trust me."

"Trust you?" Sean echoed. "You're backing out on a deal of a lifetime, jamming me between a rock and a hard place, and you want me to trust you?"

Damien shook his head. The man had a way with guilt. "You know, there's something I can't figure," he said, scratching his head. "Doing a little research I, uh, discovered who the new art director was . . ."

"Is that what this is about? You found out that my sister works there?"

"Doesn't that bother you—or is she in on it, too?"

"Who, Angel?" he laughed. "Hardly. My sister doesn't have a dishonest bone in her body."

"So why are you doing this?"

"What are you, a therapist now?" Sean dropped into his seat. "Let's just say that I have my reasons. Besides, Angel will never know."

"But still—"

"But still what?" Sean thundered and tossed up his hand. "All you need to know is that I need this job done."

There was that air of desperation again. Sean was in over his head.

"I have to go," Damien said suddenly. He was convinced if he hung around much longer, Sean would make him change his mind. "I'm sorry. I wish I could help you."

Sean stood and followed him. "Black, I need you."

Damien shook his head as he walked through the restaurant. "Find someone else."

"You're the best."

Outside, Damien handed his ticket to the valet and then turned toward Sean. "Thanks for the compliment, but there are others."

"It's not like they're listed in the phone book," Sean hissed.

Damien smirked. "I don't know. Have you checked lately?"

"Very funny," Sean said.

When his silver Lamborghini rolled into view, Damien slid on his Oakley shades and took a deep breath. "I'm sorry, man, but good luck to you."

A strange look came over Sean as he looked from Damien to the car and back again. "Is this your car?"

"Yeah, she's a beauty, isn't she?" He hobbled

around to the driver's side, but Sean was suddenly at his heels. Before Damien knew what was happening, the unmistakable feel of a gun pressed into the center of his back.

CHAPTER
31

Damien moved away from his car. "What do you think you're doing?" he asked.

"I'll ask the questions," Sean hissed. "Go back into the restaurant."

Damien hesitated, and then felt the gun grind into his flesh.

"Don't think I won't shoot you right here."

Clueless as to what prompted the man's sudden anger, Damien played it cool and did as he was told.

Entering the restaurant, Sean stayed close to Damien so the casual observer couldn't see his weapon.

Neither man spoke the rest of the way to Sean's office. Once there, Sean again had to threaten to pull the trigger to get Damien to enter.

Numerous plans of escape clogged Damien's mind, but he was unable to settle on any one of them. In the end, he decided to play it by ear, waiting for a window of opportunity to open.

Sean closed the door behind them. "You think you're smart, don't you?"

Damien's brow furrowed as he stopped in the center of the room. He didn't need to be a genius to spot a loaded question. "What do you mean?"

"How long have you been screwing my sister? Can't be too long, she just moved here a month ago."

The first trickle of alarm coursed through Damien.

Slowly Sean walked a wide path in order to face Damien. "Maybe you two knew each other before she moved to Atlanta?" He cocked his head to the side. "Hmm?"

Damien stared and remained mute.

"That car," Sean said. "Angel drove the same car home from work a couple of weeks ago. She said a *friend* loaned it to her. You must be that friend."

Damien's jaw clenched as his eyes fell from Sean's accusing glare.

"Are you going to answer me, or am I going to have to bust a cap in your ass?"

"Don't do something you might regret," Damien said, coolly. "You're already in over your head on a lot of things."

Sean's gaze hardened as he lifted the gun higher. "How about I make you regret the day you met me?"

"Playing the noble brother is a bit old, don't you think?" Damien asked with a chuckle. "Especially since you're in the habit of sending her out as *entertainment* for your friends."

"What?" Sean barked. The gun trembled in his hand and then lowered slightly. "Is that what she told you? That I used her?"

"She didn't have to. I know how men like you and this guy operate. Let me guess, you owe him money?"

Sean's angry mask cracked and allowed ridges of doubt to crease his forehead. "I would never do anything to harm my sister."

Damien laughed. "You're planning to steal a multimillion-dollar art collection from under her nose and you sent her out with some loan shark to pay off your gambling debts. This is just my opinion, but I don't think you're going to win any brother-of-the-year awards anytime soon."

"What? You think allowing her to date a thief is any better?"

"A retired thief."

"No." Sean shook his head. "Not until after you pull this last job."

Sighing with regret, Damien slid his hands into his pockets and met the man's stare. "I can't do that to Angel."

The gun came back up. "Why the hell not?" Sean thundered.

Damien simply shrugged. "Because I'm in love with her."

Broche's curiosity peaked at an all-time high while he watched Damien and some guy rush back and forth through Lafonte's. For a brief, startling moment, he even thought he'd seen a gun being pressed against Damien's back as they returned inside the restaurant.

Standing from his isolated table with warm baked bread and a half glass of sweet tea, Broche slyly followed the two men toward the back. No one stopped him, and as he pressed his ear against the door, he realized he'd finally hit the jackpot.

Damien watched Sean's hand tighten on the gun and he was sure that at any second a bullet would explode into his chest.

"You're a bold son-of-a-bitch, you know that?" Sean sneered. His lips curled into a snarl.

"Hardly a reason to shoot me."

"I don't need a reason."

A sharp knock sounded at the door, and Damien flinched as though the gun had finally discharged.

Sean glanced at his watch, and an additional line of worry creased his brow. "Merrick," he said, and then looked up at the closed door.

Damien tensed at the name and instantly recalled the large man who'd walked Angel to her door the other night. "Merrick is your buyer?" Damien inquired.

"Merrick is always looking for ways to launder money from his . . . businesses."

"Take dirty money and invest in stolen art—"

"In order to resell to private collectors for clean money. Simple supply and demand."

The next knock sounded more like a pound.

Sean lowered the gun and cast a look of warning in Damien's direction. "Don't screw this up for me." Toward the door he said, "Come in."

The steel knob twisted and the door glided open.

The first man who waltzed through the door took Damien by surprise. "Broche."

Broche's hard gaze landed on Damien while utter loathing etched every line of his face.

The next man impressed Damien by his sheer size. No doubt the man's past had interlaced with the great game of football at some time or another.

"Merrick," Sean said, frowning. "What's going on?"

"Get in there," Merrick instructed Broche before meeting Sean's inquisitive stare. "I found this guy listening to your conversation outside the door. "You might want to consider lowering your voices in here. Do you know this clown?"

"Never seen him before in my life," Sean admitted. "Black?"

Damien assumed by Broche's demeanor that Merrick had a gun pressed against his back and struggled over how he should answer. Admitting that Broche was an ex-cop would definitely sign the Frenchman's death certificate, but saying no probably would warrant the same results.

"He's with me," he finally answered. "He was probably wondering what was taking me so long."

Broche blinked in surprise, and then a calming look of gratitude covered his face.

Dark, hawklike eyes landed on Damien, seconds before a wolfish grin took up residence on Merrick's thick lips. "Ah, finally I get to meet Sean's little secret." He crossed the room while putting away his weapon. In his hand, he carried a large briefcase.

"Actually," Damien said with more calm than he felt. "There's been a misunderstanding."

From the corner of his eyes, he saw Sean jerk. "Black . . ."

Ignoring the note of warning, Damien continued. "I'm—we're not taking the job." He grabbed Broche by the arm and eased past Merrick to stop at the door. He could feel the bulky guy's gaze follow him with confusion.

"Hold on a minute." Broche planted his feet and jerked his arm from Damien's grip. "I don't see why we can't take the job." His cold, blue eyes centered on Damien.

He should have let them kill the greedy Frenchman.

"Yeah, why don't you listen to your partner," Sean quickly jumped in.

"Because he has no say in this," Damien seethed.

"Aren't you two partners?" Merrick asked. His hand slid to his weapon.

"Oui. We are." Broche smiled. "We've already agreed to split *our* take fifty-fifty. Isn't that right, Black?"

Everyone fell silent waiting for Damien's answer.

"It isn't because I pulled a gun on your little buddy, is it?" Merrick asked. "It was just a misunderstanding."

Damien took a final glance at a seething Sean and saw in his eyes that he regretted not pulling the trigger when he had the chance.

"No hard feelings," Damien said, "But I told you why I can't do this." He turned for the door and prayed he wouldn't get a bullet in his back. However, his prayers fell on deaf ears as Broche yelled, "Black, *prendre garde!*"

In the next second, there was a bang, and pain suddenly ruled his world.

Angel shook hands with a staff writer for the *Atlanta Journal-Constitution* and bid him goodbye at her office door. She was flattered the newspaper's art division wanted to do an article about the Degas collection arriving soon.

Returning to her desk, she took her phone off "do not disturb" and wasn't surprised when it started ringing.

"Angel Lafonte."

"Guess who's back." Tonya's teasing voice came onto the line.

"Wow. That was fast. That was hardly enough time for me to miss you."

"Well, my client bailed out on me. Seems he's having a little problem with the IRS. He even had the nerve to ask for his down payment back."

"The nerve of some people. What did you tell him?"

"Told him that I don't do refunds."

"Damn right." Angel laughed.

"Great. Hey, do you have time for a late lunch? I have to talk to you. I need some advice on something before I see my brother."

"Please don't tell me more bad news about Sean. I don't think I can handle it."

"No, actually, it's about Damien."

"Black?" Tonya's voice hitched a few octaves. "You're still seeing him?"

Angel slid back in her chair and played with the phone cord. "I'm more than just seeing him. I think I'm falling for the guy." Saying the words brought an instant smile to her face.

"You've got to be kidding me."

Angel smiled at the shock in her friend's tone. "Come on. Be happy for me."

"Deep down, I'm sure I am. But—"

"No buts," she insisted, closing her eyes. "I don't want to think about what Sean might do. Even though these days he's more interested in selling me to the highest bidder."

"What?"

"Long story." She sighed. "Which is why we need to meet for lunch."

"Yeah, yeah. Get back to the part where you think you're in love."

Angel shrugged. "There's not much else to tell. I never thought it could happen again. Though it's scary to trust this feeling, I love him and I want to be with him."

"Come on. A man like Black must have women falling all over him everywhere he goes."

The thought had crossed Angel's mind. "Why don't you like him?" she finally asked. "You've been trying to steer me away from him since I told you about him."

"I like him," Tonya said almost defensively. "I just . . ."

Angel frowned at the long pause. "Do you know him . . . professionally?"

Another line rang on Angel's phone.

Her gaze jerked to the flashing red light.

"Tonya, wait a sec. I have to take this." She pressed the hold button and quickly answered the other line.

"Oh, thank God you're there," a woman's hysterical voice blared over the line. "Angel, you need to get down here right now."

Angel's heart leaped to her throat. "Who is this?"

"Lea from the restaurant," she rushed on, her voice trembling. "Honey, you need to get down here. Sean has been shot."

CHAPTER

32

Angel dropped the phone back into the cradle. Her mind whirled, wondering what Sean had gotten into now. Who hadn't he paid? Who had he pissed off?

Up and out of her chair almost in the same motion, she gathered her purse and hurried out of the office. A startled Russell glanced up from his computer as she gushed out instructions for him to cancel the rest of her meetings and was past him in a flash.

His "Yes, ma'am," barely reached her ears as she zigzagged around people in her path. By the time she reached her car, her heart had accelerated to a pace that brought her in peril of hyperventilating.

"Why doesn't he ever listen to me? Why does

he keep doing this?" The questions flowed like a waterfall and showed no signs of letting up.

The twenty-minute drive to Lafonte's was reduced to ten, and Angel sighed with relief when the chic restaurant finally materialized. Not bothering to slow down, she jumped a curb, jetted up to the valet, and then slammed her foot down on the brake and stopped behind a line of police cars.

Lea greeted her outside. The woman's hysterics only fed into Angel's fear.

"What's going on? Where is my brother?"

"In his office. They're waiting for the paramedics. He's lost a lot of blood." Lea clutched Angel's arm as she kept pace with her.

"Please, let me through," Angel pleaded as she navigated through a throng of waiting patrons with curious expressions.

"There must have been six or seven shots fired," Lea said. "The whole restaurant cleared out in seconds." She grabbed Angel's arm and lowered her voice. "But I saw Tevin Merrick sneak out."

When she heard the name, Angel's stomach lurched while a swarm of questions buzzed her brain. Did the fight have something to do with their having dinner the other night?

Reaching the back of the restaurant, she fought her way, telling anyone who would listen her relationship to the victim. However, she was unprepared to see another body lying in close proximity to Sean.

She gasped at Broche's frozen expression. *What in the hell was he doing here?*

"A-Angel," Sean croaked.

Alarmed, Angel flew to her brother's side. The possibility of losing the only family she had left filled her with terror.

She reached for him and forced a calm into her voice. "Sean?"

When he didn't move, her hands seized his arm and shook him.

He winced as an irritable grunt resonated from his chest.

"Be careful," Lea warned next to her.

Worry crinkled the corners of Angel's eyes. "Sean, speak to me. Are you all right?"

He coughed, and more blood spattered against his once white shirt. "I'm going to be all right," he promised. "It just hurts. That's all."

Angel started to speak, but when her brother erupted with a long spasm of coughs, she looked to Lea. "Does anybody know what happened?"

"I have no clue. It happened at the beginning of lunch. I didn't see anything."

The paramedics rushed into the room and immediately hurried over to Sean. Angel and Lea were quickly pushed aside.

"What are you doing in here?" a voice thundered behind the women.

Angel turned and had another surprise. "Captain Johnson."

"You two are contaminating a crime scene."

"Sorry, but my brother—"

"Is going to be transported to the hospital."

Sean groaned as he was lifted on a gurney.

"You're more than welcome to go with him," Johnson added. "But I need you out of this room."

"What was Broche doing here?" she asked.

"That's a question I'd like to know myself. Soon as your brother is feeling a little better, I intend to ask him."

She studied him, her mind clogged with questions. But none was appropriate at the moment. Lea clutched her arm.

"They're taking him away. We better go."

She nodded and allowed herself to be tugged away, but at the door a cane with a gold lion head caught her eye. "Damien?"

Captain Johnson waited until Angel left with the paramedics before he, too, made his way out of Lafonte's. He was happy and lucky that no one asked him why he was there. Which was a good thing because didn't know what his answer would be.

Climbing into his Mercury Sable, he started up the engine and drove away.

"What took you so long?" A weak voice floated up to him.

"Your girlfriend showed up."

Damien smiled as he lay flat on the backseat, but another jolt of pain erased it.

"Thanks for coming to get me, Rock. I'll never forget it."

"Yeah, yeah. Do you want to tell me what happened to Broche?"

Damien hesitated. "He died saving my life." He shook his head, still unable to believe it himself. "I think because I didn't rat him out about being a cop. I don't know."

"Then who shot you?"

"Probably that bastard Sean. He's not too happy that I'm dating his sister."

Rock frowned. "He tried to kill you because you're dating his sister?"

Damien would have laughed if he hadn't been so certain that it would've killed him. "I can't say that I wasn't warned about him. I guess I should've listened."

"You think?" Rock shook his head and drove in silence for a while.

"How was Sean Lafonte when you saw him?"

"Like you: weak. But I think he'll live. I really should get you to a doctor, too."

"Just take me home. This is nothing that Nigel can't fix."

"Are you going to tell me that the man is a doctor, too?"

Damien managed a chuckle. "I wouldn't be surprised." The car fell silent as Damien tried to limit his movements. "What about Angel? How was she?"

"Devastated, but strong. She seems like a remarkable woman."

Smiling, Damien closed his eyes. "Yeah, she is."

During the ride in the ambulance to the hospital, Sean's pulse weakened while he faded in and out of consciousness. He'd taken two hits, one in the chest and another in his upper right thigh.

Once they reached the emergency room, he was rushed into surgery, and Angel was left alone with a sobbing Lea.

Two officers arrived later and questioned her, but she didn't know anything. Her mind flashed to the gold lion head cane lying on the office floor, and she tried her best to come up with a good excuse for it being there.

However, she made no comments about it to the police. And she wouldn't. Damien had nothing to do with this fiasco.

The surgery was over in two hours, but felt like two days. When the doctor informed her that Sean had pulled through and was being transferred to recovery, a wave of relief swept through her like nothing she'd ever experienced.

When she and Lea were finally able to see Sean, Angel's eyes swelled with fresh tears.

"Here are my favorite girls," Sean croaked the moment they walked into the room.

Both women rushed to opposite sides of his bed to smile down at him.

"How are you feeling?" Angel asked. "Is there anything we can do for you?" She took his hand and gave it a gentle squeeze.

"Your being here is enough."

Her vision blurred. Suddenly their past grievances seemed small and unimportant.

"Baby, what happened in there?" Lea asked, taking his other hand.

Sean swallowed before his gaze shifted to Angel.

Fear clutched Angel.

"Black," he whispered. "Damien Black tried to kill me."

CHAPTER

33

The Edgar Degas collection turned out to be a big hit at the Atlanta High Museum. Angel was proud that everything had gone off without a hitch. Which was why it probably surprised everyone when she turned in her resignation.

At her apartment, Tonya watched as she packed her things. "You know, I don't think I'll ever understand you. You move more times than anyone I've ever known."

Angel kept grabbing clothes from her closet. "It was a mistake to move back here. I'm not happy."

"Happiness is where you find it."

"And what is that supposed to mean?"

"Damned if I know." Tonya laughed, but quieted when the joke failed to amuse her friend. "Look, why don't you call him? He must have left you a hundred messages in the past few weeks."

"I'm not interested in talking to him."

"You still believe Sean's cockamamie story about Black shooting him?"

Angel returned to her closet.

"I wouldn't believe a thing that man said if I was you. When was the last time he told you the truth about anything?"

"Can we please just change the subject? Since when did you start liking Black anyway?"

"Since you told me that you were falling for the guy. Just because I haven't found true love, it doesn't mean I can't root for my best friend."

Angel plopped another armload of clothes onto the bed. "I know Damien was there. I saw his cane lying on the floor."

"But why would he shoot Sean? That's what you have to ask yourself. And if he did do it, maybe there's a good reason. Sean has a wonderful way of pissing people off."

"Sean said—"

"Angel. Listen to yourself. You know your brother better than anybody." Tonya stood from the bed and held her friend's gaze.

"Look, there a few things you don't know about Damien."

"Like what?"

"Like he's a . . ." She searched for the words. "We're both . . ."

Tonya shook her head. "I know you want to

be loyal to your brother but ... Sean hasn't earned your loyalty. Did you give Sean the cashier's check yet?"

"Yeah, I gave it to him last week when he came out of the hospital. I told him I borrowed it from you."

"Uh-huh. That must explain why I saw him in Las Vegas this past weekend."

Angel stiffened. "What?"

"Come on. A leopard can't change its spots, and you can't change your brother."

Angel's body deflated in defeat. "I'm afraid of what Damien's going to say. What if he really did try to kill Sean?"

"Personally, I'd like to buy him a drink."

Angel laughed and the tension evaporated. She really did want to see Damien again. She needed to hear his side of the story, but she was afraid. "I don't know, Tonya. I don't know."

It was a beautiful summery day. Jerome joined Damien while he sat outside by the pool. For a long while both just watched the wind ripple the water.

"So I hear you're heading out?" Jerome finally asked.

"Yeah." Damien didn't bother to look at him. "Time for me to move on."

"You know, I'm going to miss Broche hanging around." Jerome shrugged. "He sort of grew on me."

Damien smiled. "I know what you mean."

"I take it she hasn't called yet?"

Damien didn't answer.

"You know, Sean probably told her—"

"It doesn't matter. I would've thought that she would have come to hear my side of things. Give me the benefit of the doubt. Instead she chose to walk away."

"Did you tell her what you did for a living?"

"What I *used* to do."

"Come on, D. We were seriously thinking about coming out of retirement. And you didn't tell her until Broche approached her."

"I was a thief not a murderer. Besides, you don't go around broadcasting that sort of thing." He sighed. "I just thought . . ."

"What?"

"I thought that she understood me." He shrugged. "I thought we shared a kindred spirit."

"Well, I'll be damned," Jerome said in awe. "You're in love." He laughed. "I don't believe it."

"No. I'm heartbroken."

"Excuse me, sir," Nigel interrupted. "There is a Ms. Marshall here to see you."

"Marshall?" Damien frowned as he recognized the name, but was mystified about why the woman was there. "Tell her I'll be right in."

Nigel nodded and left to carry out his instructions.

"Marshall," Damien mumbled, and the name echoed hauntingly in his head.

"Surely it's not our Marshall," Jerome said.

"Stay here." Damien frowned. He had only met the woman once, but had worked for her on numerous occasions. What he liked most about her was that she was professional, direct, and fair. Whatever job she had lined up for him would no doubt be lucrative, but he would have to decline.

Waltzing back into the house, he went to greet his guest in the study. Opening the door, he immediately launched into an apology. "Sorry to . . ."

The beautiful redhead he remembered was now blond, and when she turned her tall and slender frame toward him, he was stunned speechless.

Tonya Caine-Marshall lifted her martini glass to him in salute. "Surprise."

He blinked and broke his hypnotic trance. "Surprise? Try shock." He stared at her. "I don't know what to say."

"I can see that." She crossed her arms with great satisfaction. "Though I can't tell you how much it hurts to know you've forgotten our first meeting."

"You looked different. Your eyes were brown."

"The wonderful world of contacts." She

chuckled and walked over to him. "I hate to rush our game of catch-up, but I came to ask you something."

"So you are still in the business?" he asked cautiously.

"As long as the money is good, I don't see a reason to quit. Besides"—she winked—"my clientele might not like it."

"I'm sure they appreciate your dedication." Damien gestured for her to take a seat.

She nodded and eased onto the nearby leather sofa. "I came to ask you a question."

He sat in the adjoining chair. "And what is that?"

"Did you shoot Sean?" Her sharp emerald gaze impaled him as she took a sip of her martini.

It was hardly what he expected, so he asked her to repeat the question.

"You heard me correctly," she said. "Sean said that you were the one who shot him. I personally don't believe him so I came to hear for myself. After all, my best friend's happiness is at stake."

"Speaking of your best friend, does she know what you do for a living?"

Tonya's eyes lowered to stare at the clear liquid in her glass. "What difference does that make?"

"I'm just trying to figure out who stands to have the worst influence on her: her brother, her best friend, or the man who loves her."

Her gaze returned for another attack. "You love her?"

"More than life," he answered truthfully.

Doubt lingered in her expression. "I know for a fact that you're a man who never lacks for companionship."

"You haven't been around much these last few weeks have you?"

Their staring war raged on for a while, before the corners of Tonya's lip sprang upward. "You two would make a good couple."

Finally Damien smiled as well. "Too bad Angel doesn't think so."

"Did you shoot Sean?"

"Unfortunately no."

"Damn." Tonya drained the rest of her drink and stood up.

Damien smiled. "So are you still acting as her big protector?"

"Everyone wants to protect Angel. Don't you feel the need to?"

His smile grew wider as he nodded. "I guess I do."

Tonya met his eyes. "Go talk to her. You two belong together."

"Ah, Angel," Merrick said, when Angel opened her front door. "Imagine my surprise when I got your call."

"What are you doing here? I said would meet you tomorrow."

"Yes, I know. You wanted to meet at your brother's restaurant. But I hate crowds, don't you?" He stepped through the door. "Looks like you're packing."

"Look, Merrick—"

"Tevin. I insist." He glanced around. "Besides, the last time I was at your brother's restaurant, he tried to turn it into the Alamo by shooting up the place."

"What? Did Sean start the shooting?"

Merrick's golden gaze fell hard on her stunned expression. "You didn't know?"

Angel's chest hurt with every breath she took. "He said that Damien tried to kill him."

"Black. I don't think the man even had a weapon."

She could almost hear Tonya say "I told you so." "Look, I prefer we do this tomorrow," she said.

"Why put off tomorrow what we can do tonight?" Merrick's smile broadened.

She opened the door. "I don't think so."

Merrick closed it. "I didn't drive over here for nothing."

Angel swallowed, but remained calm. "I wanted to meet so I can pay my brother's debt."

"You mean the six million?"

"Six?"

"Interest."

Angel held her ground, determined to show no fear. "Yes. The whole thing."

His smiled vanished. "Where would you get that kind of money?"

"That's none of your business. What's important is, this ends your business with my brother." Despite her outward calm, Angel could feel the tension thicken.

Merrick laughed and clapped as though applauding a performance. "Looks to me that not only are you the beauty in the family, you're also the brains."

Angel's skin crawled. "This ends it."

He shrugged. "It's a nice gesture, but how long do you think it will be before your brother comes to me for another loan? A week—two weeks?" Merrick flashed her a plastic smile. "Business is business." He inched closer. "Then again, my other offer with your brother still stands. If you agree to be my little . . . playmate, I could overlook a few things."

Angel took a step back. "What are you talking about?"

He gasped in mock surprise. "You mean he didn't tell you? Your wonderful brother was planning to steal the Degas collection."

"Damien worked for my brother?" She stared at him, not because she didn't believe what he was saying, but because she needed a moment to gather her thoughts. "Once I pay you, I want you to leave Sean alone. And as for being your personal playmate, not if you were the last man on earth." She opened the door again. "Now please leave."

"I'm the one who decides the terms of this deal or any other deal, Ms. Lafonte." His hand snaked behind her and grabbed a fistful of her hair. "And I've already decided that I want you." He kicked the door closed.

Angel's hands flailed out and landed a good whack across his face. He seized one hand, but she delivered a punch to his groin.

He hardly flinched.

All her effort proved futile. He was too large, too strong.

She opened her mouth to scream, and his other hand choked off that attempt.

"I'll show you how you can pay off your brother's debt," he hissed before he brought his mouth down against hers.

Angel was unable to move away from the man's slobbery kiss because she was praying for air. She could feel her shirt being tugged up, even feel his dry hands scale up her body, but there was nothing she could do about it.

In the next instant, they fell to the floor with him on top. She did her best to scramble away, but he followed every inch up the hallway.

From the corner of her eyes, she saw the door explode open and in the next second, Merrick was off her.

She gulped down air, and the sudden supply

of oxygen made her dizzy and caused her chest to hurt.

Damien threw a punch into Merrick's side in hopes of doing damage internally. His other punches seemed to bounce and just piss his opponent off.

"What are you, a thief or a bodyguard?" Merrick sneered a second before he landed a punch across Damien's jaw that sent him reeling and crammed his head with stars.

Damien shook off the punch in time to see Merrick hurtling toward him. Quickly he rolled to his side and allowed the large man to smash into the wall.

Merrick's loud howl was the first sign that he might be human after all.

From the corner of Damien's eyes, he saw the man reach into his jacket, and he knew what was next. He tried to get to his feet so he could get out of the way of a bullet, but it was too late as the unmistakable sound of gunfire filled the room.

Angel and Damien froze.

After a few heartbeats, Angel pried her eyes open and was stunned speechless to see her brother standing in the doorway. A cool splash of relief hit as the mere sight of him overwhelmed her.

But just as quickly, fear crawled along her neck when she remembered he'd fired several shots.

"Damien . . ." She jerked up to scan for him.

Drawing in large gulps of air, Damien turned toward the sound of Angel's voice. Their gazes locked, and he felt a surge of relief to see that she was okay. And then belatedly his eyes shifted to Sean's ominous stance at the door and the gun that was pointed at him.

At the thump behind him, Damien turned to see that the gun from Merrick's hand had fallen onto the floor.

Merrick, however, stared disbelievingly at the widening spread of blood across his chest. Trembling, he glanced up as the look of death touched his eyes. "I should have killed you when I had the chance," he hissed at Sean.

Slowly Merrick slid to the floor, leaving a bright smear of blood against the wall.

Everyone's eyes remained glued on Merrick's final acts of life and even awhile longer after he'd drawn his last breath.

"Sean," Angel said, soft and solemn.

Damien slowly twisted back toward the door and the still armed man.

"Don't shoot him," she urged. She eased toward him in slow motion. "If he hadn't shown up when he did, God knows what Merrick would have done to me," she said.

Damien's gaze traveled from the weapon and up toward the strange look in the man's eyes. He remained still; ready to accept whatever fate tossed his way.

"Sean," Angel said, reaching him. "I love him."

Sean blinked as though his trance had been broken, and then turned to look at his sister. "You don't even know who or what he is."

"I know what he does for a living, Sean. I know that you hired him to steal the Degas collection from the museum."

Now Damien's eyes shifted to her in surprise. "I never took that job, Angel. I told your brother that I couldn't."

She glanced at Damien and smiled. "I believe you."

Sean appeared at a loss for words.

Angel faced her brother again. "You lied to me, Sean. Damien didn't shoot you at the restaurant. You tried to kill him. Didn't you?"

"Angel—"

"I want the truth."

Sean's eyes glistened with tears. "I needed the money."

"But we're *family*." She sniffed. "Business is business, but you don't do this to family."

Sean's gaze lowered.

"What did you do with the money I gave you to pay Merrick off?"

"I have other debts, Angel."

"You have some in Vegas, too? Is that why Tonya saw you there this weekend?"

When he didn't answer, she shook her head. "You have a problem," she said through gritted teeth. "One you can't control. That man tried to rape me." She pointed at Merrick. "All because you offered me up like a poker chip."

"It wasn't like that." Sean lowered his gun, but remained in denial. "I never meant for you to get hurt."

"The only person that hurt me was you. I'm not going to let you continue to do this to me. If you can't get help, then I can't continue to be around you anymore."

"But Angel—"

She turned and walked over to Damien. "And I owe you the biggest apology of my life. I should have never walked away from you. Can you ever forgive me?"

Damien smiled. "Already done." He leaned forward and kissed her tenderly. "Did you mean it when you said you loved me?"

"Absolutely." Tears glistened in her eyes. "I love you with every beat of my heart."

He drew in a deep breath and felt his heart explode. "Good, because I'm crazy in love with you. And I'm never letting you go."

Sirens sounded in the distance, but as Angel and Damien's lips connected the world melted away.

CHAPTER
34

Entwined in the silk sheets on Damien's large mahogany bed, Angel snuggled against Damien after another round of lovemaking. "Are you sure you still want to marry me? After all, we've only known each other for few months."

Damien leaned up on his elbows and stared down at the beautiful face that was illuminated by candlelight. "Having second thoughts?"

Angel smiled up at him. "Not in this lifetime."

It was the answer he wanted to hear. He leaned down and brushed his lips against hers. As he inhaled her signature fragrance, he gave thanks to the powers that be for delivering him his personal angel.

"Damien, there's something I have to tell you. Something that might be a shock to you."

He frowned at her serious expression. "What is it?"

"Well, it's about the Shafrazzi heist."

"Look, I've told your brother that I didn't steal that Rubens's painting."

"I know you didn't." She paused and took a deep breath. "I stole it."

Damien sat up. "You what?"

Angel clutched the sheet to her breasts as she sat up, too. "Now before you get upset. Let me explain. I had a very good reason to steal it. Well, sort of."

Damien just stared at her. "When? How?" Then his features twisted. "Tonya has something to do with this, doesn't she?"

"No . . . yes. Well, sort of." She sighed. "I first started working with Tonya in France. I met her through Gary. She had a couple of jobs, they convinced me that it would be an adventure, so I tried it. I made good money and lived a good life." She shrugged. "It's funny. The few jobs I pulled, the police attributed them to the great Le Fantôme."

"You rode on my coattail?"

"I took it as a compliment. Everyone knew that Le Fantôme was the best. Then when Gary was killed, I lost all interest in the work." She glanced up at Damien's intense stare. "So I wanted a new start. I wanted a new life. I found a good charity and donated all the money I made. When I told Tonya I wanted to quit, she was disappointed, but supportive. She helped me get a legitimate job in art."

"As art director at the Atlanta High Museum?"

Angel nodded. "I knew it would be difficult living back in Atlanta with Sean, but I was desperate for a new start and I thought I could handle him." She lowered her gaze and drew another deep breath. "When Sean told me how much money he owed Merrick. I figured I could come out of retirement for one last job. I couldn't very well steal from my own museum—that would be unethical."

Damien shook his head before a low rumble of laughter resonated from him. "You're a thief?"

"I'm retired," she stressed, lifting her chin. "There's a difference."

His laughter deepened as his arms swept around her and pulled her close. "I knew we were kindred spirits. I just knew it."

"You're not mad?"

"Mad? I'm ecstatic." He kissed her and relished her sweet mouth all the more. "So when do you want to do this?" he asked, hoping he'd hidden his anxiety. "When do you want to get married?"

"You still want to marry me?"

He laughed. "More than anything."

Her eyes locked with his. "Tomorrow wouldn't be fast enough."

Their lips met again, this time a little longer, a little deeper.

Before Damien knew it, his blood stirred and burned for her. He was content to believe that he would never tire of making love to her, and as a result spend the rest of his days in bed. "When is your last day at the museum?"

"Next Friday." She chuckled, nibbling on his ear.

"Good, I want us to travel the world," he said. "I want to experience everything with you."

"I can't tell you how happy you make me." Her hands slid between their bodies until she found his swollen flesh. "It looks like you're ready for another round, Duracell."

"I thought you'd never notice." He shifted to take the top position, and her legs nudged open with the gentlest of urging.

"I love you, Angel Lafonte. I'm positive it happened the moment I laid eyes on you."

"I love you, too, Damien Black. My soul mate, my kindred spirit, my copper top battery."

He smiled, and then swallowed her laughter in a deep searing kiss. In no time at all their bodies came together with a basic primal need. Each gave their all and in return took very little.

Damien was now complete. He had found what he never knew he was in search of: true love.

Epilogue

Maui
Two weeks later . . .

Angel had always harbored the dream of getting married in Hawaii, and it was just like Damien to try and make all her dreams come true. She couldn't have hoped for better weather, better friends, or a better man to share the rest of her life.

She was especially touched when, for the second time in her life, she saw tears in her brother's eyes as he walked her down the aisle. Each day, he struggled with his addiction, but he was determined to redeem himself in his sister's eyes. She would always be his Angel perched on a pedestal . . . even though she was no angel.

Damien was the happiest man on earth. As he stared into the beautiful eyes of his future wife, he envisioned a life with children, laughter, and strawberries.

Their vows were elegant, beautiful, and true. And when the preacher announced them as man and wife, a hundred-plus of their closest family and friends shouted with joy.

The wedding and reception was held on his yacht *La Femme Noir*, where Lea caught the bouquet and Sean caught the garter.

"That should make an interesting union," Damien whispered to his wife.

"As long as the wedding isn't in Vegas, I'll be happy," she said, shaking her head.

Damien swept her into his arms and began swaying with the music.

"Hey, man," Rock said, interrupting their dance. "Congratulations." He opened his arms and hugged them both. "It's about time you settled down. Maybe now you'll knock out all this foolishness?"

Damien and Angel joined in on his laughter.

"You don't have to worry about us. You're looking at two retirees."

"Yeah?" he asked with hope brimming in his eyes.

"Yeah," Damien agreed.

Rock looked at Angel.

"Yeah, sure," she chimed in.

"Great," he exclaimed. His smile suddenly

monopolized his face. He swatted Damien across the back, gave him the thumbs-up signal, and went in search of his wife.

Angel and Damien returned to each other's arms smiling.

"I'm glad we made him happy," she said.

Jerome tapped Damien's shoulder. "Hey, you're not going to hog her all for yourself, are you? That's what the wedding night is for."

Angel laughed at the joke and at the sour look on her husband's face.

"Besides, I'm celebrating, too. I'm finally off probation. So I deserve to dance with a beautiful woman."

"Fine. Just one dance," Damien warned, and then winked at his wife. "Clock him one if he gets out of hand."

She winked back. "You got it."

Damien moved away, but was cut off by Tonya. "May I have this dance?"

"Most certainly." Taking her by the hand, he led her to the center of the dance floor. "So are you having a good time?" he asked.

"Wonderful time. Who knew a wedding could be put together so fast?"

"Ah, you can do anything you put your mind to." At her overly dramatic laugh, Damien suspected something was up. "What's on your mind?"

She opened her mouth, and then quickly closed it.

His eyes narrowed. "Out with it."

"Well," she hedged. "I was just wondering what you and Angel were going to do next?"

"What do you mean?"

Tonya gave up the pretense and got down to the point. "I have a job you two might be interested in. But," she went on. "That friend of yours—"

"Rock?"

"Yeah, him. He might be a problem."

Damien couldn't help but laugh. "Well, he has this thing about our working in his city. Said something about it reflecting badly on him."

"Uh-huh."

He frowned at her. "Angel and I are retired, remember?"

"I think this job just might change your mind."

"What job?" Angel and Jerome asked, joining them.

Tonya's eyes sparkled mischievously. "Well, I'm glad you asked . . ."